Falling Like
Snowflakes

FALLING LIKE SNOWFLAKES

A SUMMER HARBOR NOVEL

Denise Hunter

THOMAS NELSON
Since 1798

Published in Nashville, Tennessee, by Thomas Nelson. Thomas Nelson is a
registered trademark of HarperCollins Christian Publishing, Inc.

Thomas Nelson, Inc., titles may be purchased in bulk for educational,
business, fund-raising, or sales promotional use. For information, please
e-mail SpecialMarkets@ThomasNelson.com.

Unless otherwise noted, Scripture quotations are taken from THE
NEW KING JAMES VERSION. © 1982 by Thomas Nelson, Inc. Used by
permission. All rights reserved.

Publisher's Note: This novel is a work of fiction. Names, characters, places,
and incidents are either products of the author's imagination or used
fictitiously. All characters are fictional, and any similarity to people living
or dead is purely coincidental.

Library of Congress Cataloging-in-Publication Data

Hunter, Denise, 1968-
 Falling like snowflakes / Denise Hunter.
 pages ; cm. -- (Summer Harbor ; 1)
 ISBN 978-0-7180-2371-3 (softcover)
 1. Single women--Fiction. 2. Man-woman relationships--Fiction. 3.
Christmas stories. I. Title.
 PS3608.U5925F35 2015
 813'.6--dc23
 2015011117

Printed in the United States of America

17 18 19 20 21 22 LSC 6 5 4 3 2 1

AUTHOR NOTE

Dear Reader,

Welcome to my brand-new Summer Harbor series! I'm so excited to introduce you to the Callahan brothers. I didn't have to go far for inspiration. As the mother of three sons, I sometimes joke that I suffer from testosterone poisoning. But I've secretly enjoyed our male-dominated household. I've had a front-row seat to the camaraderie, comedy, and competition that goes on when three male siblings interact. It's fascinating and entertaining, even more so as they become grown men! I hope you enjoy getting to know the Callahan brothers.

Before starting this series I had never been to Maine. Since my author friend and critique partner Colleen Coble was also setting a series there, we decided to take our research trip together. We had a blast. The rugged coastline, the quiet harbors, and the hearty communities—it was the perfect place for our characters to fall in love! As we brainstormed, we decided to set our fictional towns close by each other and share a couple of characters. So if you're a reader of Colleen's, you might recognize a few places and faces as you read *Falling Like*

Snowflakes. We hope that brings a smile to your face. If you're not acquainted with Colleen's work and decide you can't get enough of Down East Maine, check out her Sunset Cove series!

In the meantime, grab your favorite drink, settle back in your chair, and come along on a journey to a wonderful place called Summer Harbor.

Blessings!
Denise

CHAPTER 1

It was amazing, the depth of courage a mother could find when the life of her child was on the line. Eden Martelli frowned at the map on the console beside her. She was somewhere northeast of Bar Harbor, following the coastline on Route 1. She'd made a wrong turn somewhere—it was starting to become a way of life.

She focused on the highway that stretched ahead, the weight of fatigue pushing on her shoulders. How many hours since her last catnap? It would be heaven to stretch out on a hotel bed for a few hours.

Micah slept against the passenger door, his lovey, Boo Bear, clutched in his arms. He had his days and nights mixed up. She wished he could see the pretty harbors and the colorful lobster buoys that dotted the water.

She checked her rearview mirror. The green minivan had been behind them since Ellsworth, a young woman driver with two kids in the back.

The engine made a loud clunking sound, and Eden frowned at the gauges. She had half a tank of gas, and the motor wasn't running hot. The Buick was twenty-three years old, just two years younger than she was.

She'd picked it up for a grand in Jacksonville, Florida. It wasn't much, but then, it only had to get them to Loon Lake, Maine.

She'd risked a phone call to Karen on a burner phone that she'd since trashed. The woman had been surprised to hear from her. They hadn't spoken since Karen and her daughter had moved to Sacramento during Eden's senior year. Karen had been like a mother to her. Her property up in Loon Lake was sitting empty, she'd said. She was thinking of selling it. *"Of course you can stay there awhile. No, I won't mention it to anyone."*

So they had someplace to go. A place no one knew about. And they were almost there. She'd get them new identities, new lives.

She'd pawned her wedding set when they passed through Atlanta. God knew, they hadn't given her what it was worth, but it was enough to buy them time while she got WhiteBox Designs back up and running. She'd had to abandon her clients, but she'd do whatever was necessary to win them back.

A loud clattering sounded, making Eden's heart seize. The noise continued for several moments before blue smoke began billowing from beneath the hood.

No. No, no, no! Leave it to you to buy a lemon, Eden. You're hopeless.

She eased off the accelerator but the clattering continued, and the smell of burning oil reached her nose. She put on her flashers, and a moment later the minivan passed.

There was nothing around but hills and trees. She'd

gone through a town awhile back, but if she'd passed a service station, she hadn't noticed. Her mind had been elsewhere for miles, making plans.

So much for that, she thought, watching blue smoke drift past. She spotted a green sign ahead and squinted through the smoke.

Summer Harbor 5 miles, it read.

The sign pointed right, and seeing little choice, Eden took the turn. She hoped the town was big enough to have a garage. She only had fifteen hundred dollars after the purchase of the car, and she was counting on that for her new start.

Her heart clamored inside her chest. *This can't be happening.* They were so close. The clattering continued, so she kept a slow pace, hoping she wasn't ruining the engine. It began to snow, big, wet flakes splashing onto her windshield, further hampering her vision.

What was she going to do?

First things first, Eden. Find a garage. Get an estimate.

Maybe it was something simple like a loose hose or wire. Or something cheap. Maybe a friendly mechanic would take one look at her hollow eyes and her quiet son and have mercy on them.

The two-lane road was hilly and curvy, and the five miles seemed to take forever. Finally, she passed a sign. Welcome to Summer Harbor, Inc. 1895. Houses popped up on the left and right as the road wound along the coast.

The road dipped and leveled as they entered the town proper. Summer Harbor looked like a Christmas postcard with quaint little shops and old-fashioned lamps, all of it glimmering under a fresh layer of snow. She caught a glimpse of the rocky coastline as she rounded a curve, keeping her eyes peeled for a service station.

On a different day, a different time, she might enjoy a visit here. Preferably during the summer when she imagined the wharf bustled with lobster boats and tourists. Though the town had a certain charm even now, primed for a festive Christmas season.

There! She spied a gas station with a tiny garage, tucked down a lane. She turned into the parking lot and shut off the engine. The sudden silence was profound.

She hated to awaken Micah. He hadn't slept soundly since they'd fled. She touched his shoulder, and he startled awake. His body stiffened as reality settled once again on his little shoulders, and his eyes widened in that frightened-doe look she was starting to hate. No child of five should have to endure the things he had.

"Hey, kiddo. We're having a little car trouble. Let's get out and stretch our legs, okay?" She pulled their jackets from her book bag and helped Micah slip into his.

As she headed toward the garage, she pulled her cap low over her newly cut hair, checking over her shoulder as they hustled toward the door. She pulled up Micah's hood and gathered him close.

There was only one guy in the building. He was sitting behind the register with his feet propped on the counter, working his iPhone with practiced fingers. He looked no older than a teenager with his boyish face, though he was making a valiant attempt at a beard.

He looked up, his pale cheeks flushing as his eyes

cut to hers. He lowered his feet and sat up straight. "Hi there. How can I help you?"

She gave her best friendly smile. "I'm having some car trouble, and I'm in a bit of a hurry. Any chance someone could check it out?"

"Sorry. Our mechanic's off today. He'll be in Monday, though."

Her heart thumped to the floor of her chest cavity. "Is there another garage I can try? I'm really hoping to get back on the road."

He shrugged. "I'm afraid we're it."

She bit her lip. She should've stayed on the main road. *Way to go, Eden. Another one of your stupid decisions.*

"Well, hey, I can't fix your car or nothing, but I know a little about engines. I could take a peek."

She gave him a grateful look. "Really? Would you? I'd appreciate that so much. Maybe it's just a loose hose or something, and I can be on my way."

He followed her out to the car, Micah hugging close to her side. She explained the *thunk* and the clattering sound. The smell of burned oil still hung in the air, and a bit of smoke escaped as he lifted the hood.

She bit her lip as she watched him look around. After a few minutes he started the car, listening for a moment before shutting it off and getting back out. "I think you've thrown a rod."

"What does that mean?"

He gave her a regretful look. "It's not good. You'll need to have the engine rebuilt."

"Rebuilt! How much does that run?"

"I'm not really authorized to—"

"Just a best guess. Please. I won't hold you to it."

He sighed, his cheeks flushing. "Normally somewhere between a grand and fifteen hundred."

All the air left her lungs.

"It really depends on the engine, and I'm not qualified to give an estimate. Sorry it's not better news. Wish I could help you."

"Can I drive it like this? If I take it slow?"

"How far?"

"Four, maybe five hours?"

He shook his head. "Driving it'll only cause more damage. And if the rod tears through the side of the engine block, you could have a serious fire on your hands."

Eden sighed. She couldn't risk that. She'd have to wait till Monday for an official estimate, which meant spending two nights here.

"Looks like you'll be stuck here through the storm."

"What storm?"

"Six to eight inches, they're saying. First of the season." *Fuhst.* His Mainer accent peeking through. "Snow's supposed to go all night and all day tomorrow. There's a hotel just down the street, left on Main. Good café close by, too, Frumpy Joe's, if you're hungry. The Roadhouse is a bit of a walk, but it has great chowder." He smiled at Micah. "You like snow? We got some nice hills around here for sledding. The inn might have a sled you can borrow."

Micah buried his face into Eden's side.

"Can I leave the car here? And I can get an estimate Monday?"

"Sure, no problem. Let me get your name and number."

"Oh . . . I'll just stop back by. Thanks again for your help."

CHAPTER 2

Beau Callahan grabbed the stack of mail off the sofa and dumped it on the kitchen table. Newspapers to the trash. He grabbed Riley's Red Sox sweatshirt and tossed it over the recliner. Five minutes later, he'd barely made a dent in the mess. How'd the place get to be such a dump?

The door opened and Zac entered, bringing a gust of cold wind and the tangy smell of buffalo wings. Snowflakes dusted his brother's dark, longish hair. Zac was the middle son, a year younger than Beau, but he towered over Beau's six-foot height. He could grow a beard quicker than anyone Beau knew, and he was sporting one now.

"Sorry I'm late." Zac set down the bag and shed his coat.

"Thanks for bringing the food," Beau said.

"Where's Riley?"

"Paige had a work crisis. He took her back into town for me."

He'd hoped Paige could make their family meeting. Maybe she wasn't family, but she was close. She'd been Riley's best friend for years, and now she and Beau were an item. It had been awkward at first, dating his brother's best friend, but things seemed to have settled to a new normal.

He grabbed a few cans of Coke from the fridge and carried them into the living room, where he set them on the bare coffee table. What Aunt Trudy didn't know wouldn't hurt her.

Zac scanned the room. "Dude. What happened in here?"

"You do know Aunt Trudy's in the hospital, right? And that Riley and I are getting ready to open the Christmas tree farm?"

"I know, I know. We'll get it figured out. That's why I called the meeting. You need help."

"I can handle it just fine."

"You're always taking care of us. Moving back home when Dad died, quitting your job for the farm. Let us help you for a change."

"I don't mind." The acres of evergreens had been in the family since his great-grandparents had bought the tree farm years ago.

Beau returned to the kitchen for a stack of paper plates and a roll of paper towels. In truth all the worries of the farm sometimes made him long for his days as deputy sheriff. There was something to be said for steady, interesting work. Not that he didn't enjoy running the farm. There were just a lot of pressures that went along with it.

In the living room he settled on the couch and turned on the TV to ESPN where they were previewing tomorrow's Patriots game.

Zac was unpacking the Styrofoam boxes. His face was a blank slate, but that didn't fool Beau. A month ago, a week before their wedding, Zac's fiancée had left town, without so much as a note. Zac hadn't heard from her since and he was completely wrecked. Aunt Trudy always said the Callahan men loved once and loved deeply. For Zac's sake he hoped that wasn't true.

"How you doing?" Beau asked. "I haven't seen much of you lately."

He scowled. "I'm fine. Wish people would stop asking me that."

Zac had thrown himself into his restaurant since Lucy's departure. Beau had gone days without seeing him. They were all busy. He wasn't sure any of them had time for the crisis at hand.

The front door opened, and Riley strode in. He was the shortest of the three brothers, not quite six foot, but he'd gotten their dad's broad shoulders and beefy arms. He shared the house with Beau and Aunt Trudy and helped on the farm during the winter. During the warm months he worked as a lobsterman.

"Hey, guys." Riley turned his nose up in the air. "That smells like heaven." He set his hand on Zac's shoulder, squinting in pity. "How you doing, man? Holding up okay?"

Zac gave Beau a *See what I mean?* look.

Beau tossed the roll of paper towels to Riley. "He's getting tired of that question."

"Well, it's not every day your fiancée—"

He cut off at Zac's glare. "Okay, okay . . . ," Riley said. "How 'bout those Patriots?"

They dug into the wings, watching the preview of Sunday's game. Outside the picture window, sheets of snow obscured the view of the acres of trees. A fine white powder was beginning to stick to the ground.

"Roads getting slick yet?" Beau asked.

Riley nodded as he chewed.

"I hope Paige doesn't stay too late." Paige ran Perfect Paws Pet Shelter. She dropped everything when an animal was in need.

"How's Aunt Trudy today?" Riley asked.

Beau wiped his hands and muted the TV as a commercial came on. "Looks like she's going to be laid up awhile."

Aunt Trudy was the Callahan brothers' surrogate mom. She'd fallen on the ice yesterday in the Knitting Nook parking lot and fractured her leg. Now she sported a cast and an ugly outlook on life.

"That's why I called a meeting," Zac said. "You're going to need to put in a lot of hours. I know we're all busy, but we need to figure out something."

"I hired a few teenagers," Beau said.

"But you'll still need people who can manage things when you're not there."

"When's Aunt Trudy coming home?" Riley asked.

Their aunt worked part-time at the visitor center, but they depended on her to keep the house running, and on her spunkiness to keep things interesting. She hadn't let them down yet.

Beau shifted. "The doctor's hoping she'll be able to recover in a rehab center."

Riley gave a puff of laughter. "Bet she loved that idea."

"Yeah, it didn't go so well. But she'll need twenty-four-hour care, and we sure can't do it with the season almost here."

"How long will she be in the rehab center?" Zac asked.

"If insurance approves it, several weeks. Her leg needs a lot of therapy."

"There goes Thanksgiving," Riley said.

Beau shot him a look. "Did you really just say that?"

"What about the visitor center?" Zac asked.

Beau shrugged. "They'll probably just shut it down till she's back on her feet. It's the slow season anyway."

"I can put in some hours early in the day and on Mondays," Zac said. "I know evenings and weekends are busiest, but that's peak hours for the restaurant too."

Beau had a feeling staying busy was a priority for Zac right now.

"That's all right. That'll give me time to keep up with the business end and visit Aunt Trudy."

"I'll work as much as you need me," Riley said.

"You're still going to need more help."

Zac was right. Beau needed to staff the gift shop, needed people to handle the tree shaker and assist customers with loading. And he needed enough employees to work shifts.

"I have a couple interviews this afternoon. And I was hoping Paige could help out," Beau said. "Might be good for her to be on the farm, get a feel for the business."

"Paige has her own business to worry about," Riley said, his voice gruff.

Zac gave Riley a strange look, then popped open his Coke and addressed Beau. "You two getting serious?"

"Heading that way. Heck, she's practically part of the family anyway." Beau had an instant gut check. They'd gotten off to a pretty good start, but things had been kind of . . . off between them lately. They were just busy, that was all.

Riley stood, wiping his hands. "I have to go."

"What?" Beau said. "You just got here. We're having a meeting."

Riley shrugged into his coat. "Forgot I promised old Mrs. Grady I'd look at her hot water heater. Sounds like you got it all figured out anyway."

Wind tunneled through the room on Riley's exit. The door clicked shut behind him, and a moment later his truck started, the engine revving low.

"What's his problem?" Beau asked, frowning as his truck receded down the drive.

"Probably just tired." Zac reached for another wing. "Don't worry, he'll be fine."

CHAPTER 3

Eden hoisted the book bag higher on her shoulder. The wind picked up, blasting her with frigid air. Cold seeped through her thin jacket, chilling her to the bone. She knew Micah was no better off. They weren't prepared for Maine's brutal winter. Weren't prepared for any of this.

Her empty stomach twisted hard. There was nothing she could do about her car for the moment, but she could do something about their hungry stomachs. Spying a diner up the sidewalk, Eden headed toward it.

The sign on the glass window read Frumpy Joe's Café.

"Brrr! It's cold out there," she said to Micah as they entered the restaurant. The smell of grilled burgers wafted over, and she inhaled deeply. "Doesn't that smell good?"

The restaurant bustled with the lunch crowd. Servers ran about in green aprons, filling coffee mugs and balancing trays. All the booths were full, but there were a few open seats at the counter.

Through the kitchen pass-through, a man in his fifties called out orders as he flipped burgers and dropped fries. A gray ponytail hung from his white paper hat, and a pair of wire-rimmed glasses perched crookedly on his nose. Eden wondered if he was Frumpy Joe.

Micah's eyes darted around as he clung to her leg and to Boo Bear with equal fervor. At a server's nod, Eden pulled Micah to the empty stools closest to the door, casting another look around the place.

A young family of three, a gray-haired business-man squinting at the *Harbor Tides*, two middle-aged women laughing loudly. A scruffy-looking man stared back from a couple stools down. He leaned forward, his beady eyes sweeping over her.

She looked away as a shiver passed through her. *He's nobody, Eden. Just a random creepy guy.* Her grip tightened on the menu.

They ordered, then used the restroom while they waited for their food to arrive. Eden's mind was awhirl with plans. She'd check them in to the cheapest motel Summer Harbor offered, and over the next two days they'd both catch up on their sleep. It wasn't ideal, but she'd been so careful. Surely it was safe to lie low a couple days in this off-the-beaten-path town.

Her eyes aligned with the scruffy guy's, and she hastily looked away. She'd be glad to finish up here and get away from him. She'd had enough creepy guys for one lifetime.

Awhile later, Eden took the last bite of her burger and pushed back the plate. Micah's thin legs dangled from the stool, his Superman tennis shoes not even reaching the bar. He'd need a sturdy pair of boots. They both would.

"Anything else I can getcha?" Lines fanned from the server's kind eyes as she smiled. Her red hair was as fake as Eden's new blond locks.

"No, thanks." Eden pulled her cap low, kept her eyes down. *Don't engage. Be invisible.*

The server ripped the bill from the tab and laid it on the bar. As the woman headed back across the diner, Eden scanned the room. She'd thought they were safe before. She'd let her guard down, and look what had happened. She was beginning to think safety—freedom—was an illusion.

Just keep going.

They were so close.

Micah dragged a thick french fry through ketchup and slid it into his mouth. He'd almost put away his entire meal and a glass of chocolate milk. It was good to see him eating heartily.

Suddenly he grabbed her shirt, his hand twisting frantically. His eyes widened on hers, his breathing coming fast and hard.

She set her hand on his. "What is it? What is it, baby?"

He whimpered, his intelligent eyes working hard to communicate something.

Had he seen someone? Her heart in her throat, Eden scanned the restaurant again. No one was looking their way.

Micah clutched his hands to his chest as if holding something. His brown eyes filled with tears.

"Boo Bear," Eden said as understanding dawned.

Micah nodded.

"I'm sure he's here somewhere." She grabbed the

backpack from the floor and unzipped it, rifling through it. Not there.

"You brought him in, remember? You had him in your arms. We'll find him." She looked under the stools, and then she remembered. "The bathroom. I'll bet you left him in the bathroom."

She stepped off the stool, tugging Micah along, and slipped around the corner to the ladies' room, five feet away. She pushed through the door and opened the empty stall Micah had used.

Propped up on the toilet paper dispenser was the small blue bear in his little straw hat.

Sighing heavily, she turned. "Look who I found."

Micah took Boo Bear and hugged him close. His blue fur had long ago turned nappy, his straw hat was frayed, and the vest was missing a button. But that bear had seen her boy through so much.

She stooped down and wiped away Micah's tears. His cheeks were baby soft, and his dark lashes were wet and spiky. His fawn-colored eyes were a mirror of her own, but the mop of black curls was all Antonio.

"See, he's safe and sound. Everything's going to be okay." *Everything, Micah. I promise.* She held him close and stood, lifting him in her arms. He was growing up, his slender frame getting heavy.

She shifted his weight as she exited the bathroom and returned to the stools, already looking forward to a nice, long nap. Micah squirmed down to finish his milk while she reached for the book bag.

The book bag. It was gone. She spun around, scanning the area. It was nowhere.

She scrambled back to the bathroom, Micah's hand in hers. She was sure she hadn't brought it in here, but where else could it be? She pushed open the stall door, growing frantic. Maybe the server thought they'd left. Maybe she'd stowed the pack behind the counter.

That was it. Of course.

She dashed back out, her wobbly legs not quite buying in to the idea.

"Excuse me," she called as the red-haired server passed behind the counter. "Did you see my book bag? I left it here on the floor."

"Sorry, honey, I haven't. Sure you brought it in?"

"Yes." The money. Eden's heart thumped against her ribs. All their money. She drew in a deep breath and ran a hand over her face.

"Excuse me?" a woman's voice called. "Are you looking for a gray backpack?"

Eden whirled to the booth. "Yes. Have you seen it?"

"I saw that man take it. The one who was sitting there." She pointed to the stool. "He took the bag and left, just a few minutes ago. I thought you were together."

Eden ran outside, Micah close behind. She looked up and down the street but saw no sign of him. A young lady was entering the shop next door.

"Excuse me," Eden called. "Did you see a man go by just now? Dark coat, longish hair, kind of scruffy?"

"Sure didn't. Is there anything I can help you with?"

Eden drew a breath, then two, her breath vaporizing on the exhales. "No. Thank you." Her racing heart fluttered in her chest.

Not long ago, a quick trip to the ATM would have

fixed it all. Heck, she could have bought anything she wanted with a friendly smile and the flash of her ID.

But everything was different now. They had no money. No ID. Nothing but the clothes on their backs and a broken-down Buick she could no longer afford to repair. Panic welled in her chest cavity, a weight settling low and hard.

How could you be so stupid, Eden?

The bells above the diner door jingled, and the server appeared, crossing her arms against the cold. "Any sign of him?"

Eden looked again, her eyes scanning the sidewalks. "No."

The woman put her arm around Eden's shoulders. "Come back inside out of the cold, honey. We'll call the police, and they'll get to the—"

"No!" Eden pulled away. "I mean . . . it's okay. It's no big deal."

"You want it back, don't you? Sooner we call the better, though. That guy's just getting farther away."

The police would want her name, her address, her phone number. All things she couldn't give. She couldn't trust anyone. Especially not them.

"It's okay. I'll handle it." Eden zipped up Micah's jacket, her fingers shaky and uncooperative.

"If you're sure. I don't mind making the call."

"Thank you, but we have to be on our way." Eden's eyes swung to the café's picture window. Her stomach dropped. The bill. She couldn't even pay for lunch. "Listen . . . all my money was in that pack . . . I'll pay you as soon as I can, and I'll be happy to—"

"Honey, trust me, Joe and I won't miss a few measly dollars. No worries." She opened the door, her eyes flickering down to Micah, then back to Eden. "I hope you get your bag back."

And with that she was gone.

Eden stared sightlessly down the street. They didn't have a dime to their name. Or a place to stay warm. The motel was an impossible dream now. Maybe they could go back to the garage and sleep in the car tonight. It would get awfully cold. Her insides quivered, and her lunch churned in her stomach.

She had to think.

She grabbed Micah's hand and headed toward the library on shaking legs. They could stay warm while she came up with a game plan.

When they reached the building, she found a quiet corner in the deserted kids' section. She found Micah a few picture books to occupy him while she sat in the child-sized chair next to him. "Look at the books while Mommy thinks, okay?"

They were maybe five hours from Loon Lake. But there were no buses running into the remote regions of Maine and no taxis to be had. Not that it mattered, since she had no means to pay their fare. That left hitchhiking, and she couldn't chance that with Micah even if there were cars going that direction—and she doubted there were. Especially with a storm moving in.

She'd sold the only thing of value she'd had left. She looked down at her designer jeans and cashmere sweater. They wouldn't bring much second-hand. And the car hadn't been worth much even when it was running.

They were going to have to stay here awhile. She didn't see any other way. She needed a temporary job and quick. It was almost Christmastime; surely one of these shops was hiring. If she explained that her ID had been stolen, maybe someone would have mercy on her. She had no idea what she'd do with Micah while she worked. Maybe there was a preschool that needed an assistant.

Just before Thanksgiving break?

They had no money for food. No place to stay tonight. And oh yeah. Someone wanted them dead.

Micah had set the books aside. He bounced Boo Bear on his lap, and she wondered what was going on inside his troubled mind. He looked at her then, and she saw worry in the depths of his brown eyes.

"Well . . . change of plans." She injected some enthusiasm into her voice. "Looks like we're staying here awhile. Might be nice to stay by the sea, huh?"

She waited for a response, hoping. He just blinked, but the questions in his eyes remained.

"I'll get a job, and we'll hang out in this pretty little town for a bit. How's that sound?"

She'd start with the diner. Then, if they weren't hiring, she'd check the shops along Main Street. Micah would have to tag along as she inquired. It wasn't ideal, but it couldn't be helped. At least she looked presentable in her nice jeans and gray sweater.

There was another critical detail she needed to tackle first. She shifted on the chair. "Remember the game we've been playing? The one where your name is Adam and mine is Andrea?"

Micah nodded, his eyes lighting.

"Yes, I know, you're winning. But only by one point. And only because I was caught off guard."

A ghost of a smile appeared on his lips.

"You're very good at this game. And I want to keep playing, but I'd like to start over."

He frowned, his brows drawing together.

She ruffled his hair and breathed a laugh. "Don't worry, you're still ahead by one point. But let's make it more challenging. We'll change our names again. But this time you can pick any name you want."

She looked at him expectantly. Someday she'd ask a question and he'd answer her. Not today, though. He only stared back with an inscrutable expression.

"How about SpongeBob?" she asked, her face serious.

Micah's brows tightened, his eyes confused.

"No? What about Pinocchio?"

His nose crinkled up as he stared back.

"Oh, that's right, he had a lying problem, didn't he? And a big nose. Nothing at all like yours." She tweaked his nose. "Well, there's always Ebenezer. Banana? Pooter?"

His eyes lit, and his lips curled up in the first smile she'd seen since they'd been on the run. He shook his head hard.

"Wow." She frowned at him seriously. "I didn't know you were going to be so picky. This might take some time." She thought of the kids' series he used to watch, with the smart, lovable hero who always found himself in a mess of trouble.

"Well, you've already passed on all the good ones, but I guess there's always something. Like, oh, I don't know . . . Jack?"

He nodded enthusiastically.

"You like that, huh? Well, okay. Jack it is, then. Jack Bennet," she said, borrowing the surname from her favorite Austen heroine. She ruffled his hair. "I think you make a good Jack. And you know what? I've always wanted to be named Kate, so that's mine." She tipped his chin up. "But it's still Mom to you, mister."

Her smile faded as she realized he hadn't called her anything at all for ten months.

Soon. My boy will come back to me soon.

"Okay, so let's go over the three rules just in case you forgot." She held up a finger. "One, you have to respond immediately whenever someone calls you Jack, or you lose a point. Two, you can't tell anyone your real name, or you lose a point. Three, this game is a secret, just between you and Mommy, and if you tell anyone else about it, you lose the *whole game*."

He nodded, smiling.

"You think you're going to beat me, don't you?"

His smile widened.

"Well, we'll just see about that, Mister Jack."

CHAPTER 4

Eden pulled Micah closer to the shoulder of the road as a truck rumbled past. At least the trees were shielding them from the wind. She'd never felt such a brutal cold. And while she missed nothing else about home, she'd give the hair on her head for a warm, sunny day. Her tennis shoes had long ago begun leaking, the slush soaking through her socks until her feet felt like cold blocks of ice.

She'd checked Micah's at their last rest, and his were dry. He'd been a real trouper today. She'd hit every place in town looking for work, but not a single job was available.

At least they'd found some free food. The tiny library was celebrating a new addition with an open house. It had been poorly attended because of the weather, but she and Micah had gotten their fill. She'd stuffed two Christmas cookies into her pocket for tonight. She wasn't proud of it, but there it was. Micah had to be getting hungry again, but she was hanging onto the snack as long as she could.

A car passed, bearing to the other side to avoid them. The sun was going down, and there was only one option left. Three different shopkeepers had told her the Christmas tree farm was hiring. It would be perfect, but it was also a couple miles outside of town, so she'd saved it for last. She'd tried calling but had gotten voicemail.

Micah pulled his hand from hers, and she stopped while he removed his shoe.

"What's wrong, Jack?" She had to get used to calling him that. Had to get *him* used to answering to the new name. She'd used it often today. "Are your feet wet?"

He shook his head, holding on to her as he emptied a pebble from the shoe.

"Well, how'd that get in there?" She felt his sock again, just to be sure, then looked around at the darkening woods as he put his shoe back on.

She wondered if she'd hidden their trail well enough, or if even now Langley was closing in on them. Her last moments at the safe house two days ago resurfaced, her blood pumping at the memory. Her body grew cold from the inside out, and she suppressed a shiver.

Oh, Walter. I'm so sorry.

Micah took her hand.

She flinched, shelving the memory far away from her vulnerable son.

"Ready now?"

Ten minutes later, up a hill and around a curve, a sign appeared.

"Callahan Christmas Tree Farm," she said. "Well, there it is, Mister Jack. Let's go see about a job." The sign was old and rustic with bright red letters and bulb lights that were not yet lit. She wondered if anyone would even be in the office this late on a Saturday.

They turned into the drive, their feet crunching on the fresh snow. Pine trees in various sizes lined the lane, rolling with the snow-covered hills as far as the eye could see.

Soon they came to an unplowed parking lot. A large red barn was closed up tight. Unlit strands of bulbs were strung over an area where the cut trees, she presumed, would soon be displayed.

"Looks like they're closed. We'll just try the house. The lady in the store said it's at the end of the lane."

Please, God. I know it seems like I've done a lot of asking lately, but I need this job.

Even if she got it, it was no help for their immediate needs. It would be at least a week before she was paid. How would they eat? Where would they stay?

Walk by faith, Eden.

Every now and then Karen's voice would sound in Eden's head as if she were still right here with her. Those simple days seemed so far away, so long ago, almost another dimension. Karen would be so disheartened by the choices Eden had made.

And look where they've gotten you, Einstein.

Micah stopped, pointing to their left. A drive cut back to a small, wooden outbuilding with a pipe coming from the roof. The short lane was unplowed and unmarred by tracks or footprints.

"I don't think that's it, Jack."

They continued up the long, winding drive, and as

they crested a hill, a house came into view in the valley below. It was a two-story farmhouse with a wide, inviting front porch. Eden breathed a soft sigh at the golden light shining through the window.

She glanced at her watch, the cheap one she'd bought after selling her Cartier. It was almost suppertime. Oh well. At least someone was home.

Several minutes later, they clomped up the porch steps. She pulled Micah into her side, rubbing his arms for warmth.

She tried to wiggle her stiff toes. "Doing okay, Jack?"

He nodded. His cheeks were red, his nose running.

She reached out to press the bell with her gloved finger, and the door opened suddenly. She stepped back, pulling Micah closer.

A man came to an abrupt halt on the threshold. His dark brows lifted as their gazes connected. He was tall, and standing in the doorway boosted him by a couple of inches. His hair was black and longish.

His eyes dropped down to Micah, then returned to hers. "Hi there."

"Hi." Her heart thumped violently against her ribs. "I was just—getting ready to ring your doorbell."

The porch light placed shadows on the sharp angles of his jaw and highlighted the rest of his handsome face with a golden glow. His eyes were the deepest shade of brown she'd ever seen. Maybe that's why she couldn't seem to look away. That and the fact that he looked like Keanu Reeves.

"Can I help you? I was just on my way out."

His gaze drifted over her face, making her conscious

of her appearance for the first time in months. She resisted the urge to tuck the loose hair back under her cap. Wished the new shade of blond didn't make her look washed out.

"Charlotte from Frumpy Joe's suggested I come out. I'm looking for a job, and she said you're hiring for the tree farm."

The corners of his lips fell, and the light in his eyes dimmed. "Oh. I'm sorry, I don't think—"

"I'm a hard worker," she said quickly. "I learn fast, and I can start as soon as you need me." Like yesterday. Her words were rushed, probably desperate, but the look on his face was making dread sink its cold fingers into her flesh. "I only need something temporary, so this is perfect. And I'm strong. Stronger than I look."

She backed up as he stepped outside, pulling the door closed, but not before a delicious smell wafted out. Her stomach gave a hard growl.

"I wish I could help, but the positions aren't open anymore. I filled them today actually."

"Oh." The word exhaled on a puff of vapor. No job. No money. No food. No place to stay.

"Why don't you leave me your information? If one of my new hires doesn't work out, I'll give you a call. Some of them are teens—you know how that goes."

No. She really didn't.

"They're only part-time jobs anyway. I'm sure you're overqualified."

"You'd be surprised." She gave a wry laugh, hoping he wouldn't guess at the traumatic blow he'd just delivered.

He glanced at his watch. "I have to go. I'm running late." He looked over to the side of the house where an old red pickup truck and a Ford Explorer sat side by side. "Did you walk from town?"

"Yeah," she said, injecting enthusiasm into her voice, like the brisk walk had made her day. "Very scenic. Very . . . woodsy. It's beautiful here."

He hiked a brow, glancing again at Micah.

She pulled off her glove to write down her information and realized she didn't have anything to write with. Or on. "You have a pen?"

"I can just put it in my phone." He pulled it out and extended his hand. "I'm Beau, by the way. Beau Callahan."

"Kate." If she hung on to his hand for a tad too long, it was only because it was deliciously warm. "This is Jack."

"Hey, Jack."

Beau raised his phone and looked at her, waiting.

Oh. What was she thinking? She didn't have a phone number. Or even an address. Her face went warm.

She shifted under his direct gaze. "Um. You know what? How about if you just call the café if anything comes available. Frumpy Joe's?" She'd check back every day. Possibly every hour. "Leave a message with Charlotte."

"Sure. You related to the Duprees?"

"Um, no."

He pocketed his phone, then pulled out his keys, tilting his head. "You need a ride back into town? I'm headed that way now."

He seemed friendly enough, but so had Antonio. And Langley. She'd long since stopped trusting other people. Not to mention her own judgment.

She grabbed Micah's hand, heading toward the steps. "No, thank you. We'll be just fine."

The space between his brows furrowed. "It's going to be dark soon. I hate that you came out here for nothing."

"No worries."

Five minutes later Eden was seriously questioning her decision. She was shivering hard, her teeth rattling. Micah had begun whimpering, and they hadn't even made it out of the driveway. How were they going to make it back to her car?

"I know, kiddo. I'm cold too."

And hungry, though she didn't mention that in case he hadn't noticed his own empty stomach. Beau was right. The sun had sunk below the hills, and darkness was closing in fast. It was a long walk back to town. The café had closed at six. She doubted anything in this dinky town stayed open past that. She'd seen a little church, but it had been shut up tight, and the town was too small for a homeless shelter.

Lord. Eden Martelli, wishing for a homeless shelter. How had that even happened?

Micah whimpered again, and she bent over to pick him up. "Need a break, Jack?"

He tucked his face into her neck, his cold cheeks contrasting with his warm breath. By the time she reached the top of the hill, her arms and back ached, her lungs burned, and she could no longer feel her toes.

She stopped, panting. She bent over to set Micah back on his feet, but he clung to her neck, whimpering. Poor baby.

You can't even take care of your son. What kind of mother are you?

She pushed the voice away, squatted beside Micah, drawing him into a hug. Might as well warm him up while she thought.

She looked around the darkening landscape, as if a deserted cabin might magically appear. Making it back to town was out of the question. She had to get Micah out of the cold. They'd passed a few houses on the way up, but she knew better than to trust a stranger.

Up ahead, the lane heading to the small outbuilding caught her eye. The building wasn't much, and it was probably locked. But she'd break a window if she had to. She'd pay Beau Callahan back somehow.

CHAPTER 5

Beau hung up the phone as he backed out of Paige's driveway. Their evening had been cut short by the phone call. Not that it had been going well before that.

Paige had been out of sorts tonight because of the canine emergency she'd dealt with. Beau had made the mistake of mentioning his need for her help at the farm. She'd made it clear she was too busy with her own work to pitch in.

Things had only gotten better with the phone call he'd just received from Aunt Trudy.

He put his truck in drive and accelerated as he speed-dialed Zac.

His brother answered on the fourth ring.

"Got some bad news," Beau said. In the background, Roadhouse chatter and TV noise carried through the line. "You have a minute?"

"Sure, what's up?"

"Aunt Trudy just called. Her insurance won't pay for the rehab center."

"What does that mean?"

"It means if we can't fork out the thousands of dollars it's going to cost, she's coming home tomorrow."

"What about her therapy?"

"It'll be outpatient twice a week. Insurance will cover it, but she has to have someone to take care of her, someone to get her to therapy."

"I can help."

"She needs someone there all the time, Zac." Beau sighed. This wasn't happening. Not now, just before Christmas. The timing couldn't be worse.

"Riley could—"

"I need him on the farm. He's the only experienced help I have."

"I don't suppose Paige has extra time."

That was a big fat no. "We're going to have to hire someone. And we're going to have to move Aunt Trudy down to the main level. And keep her off that leg. And out of the kitchen."

"Lord, she's going to drive us crazy."

His thoughts exactly.

"Did you say tomorrow?"

"That's what I said. Know anyone looking for a caretaker position?" Beau thought of the woman who'd appeared on his porch late this afternoon. Maybe if she had good references . . .

She had short blond hair, honey-brown eyes, and the face of an angel. A guarded and desperate angel.

"Let me give it some thought," Zac said. "I'll call you before church."

"Sounds good."

Beau hung up, and a few minutes later he pulled into his driveway, his mind on the logistics of rearranging the house. There was a formal dining room in the back of the house that went unused. A bathroom nearby. He'd move Aunt Trudy's bed down there. But where would he put the dining room furniture?

The outbuilding. There was a bunch of junk stored there. The generator, old boxes of literature, broken-down equipment his dad had never thrown out. He'd have to make room. Aunt Trudy'd have a fit if he scuffed up her furniture. He'd better get that done tonight.

He swung into the lane that led to the outbuilding. It was unplowed, but there were only a few inches of snow so far.

He frowned as his headlights swept over footprints. Must belong to the woman and her kid. But no, there was only one set of prints. It was hard to gauge their size as they were partially filled with fresh snow.

His headlights swept over the building, illuminating a broken pane beside the door.

"Ah, heck no."

He shoved the truck into park and stepped out, thinking of the expensive generator he couldn't afford to replace.

Summer Harbor was pretty safe, but as the former deputy sheriff, he'd been privy to every single incident. Not to mention the recent murder in nearby Folly Shoals. Had a way of making a man cautious.

. . .

Eden sprang upright at the sound. An engine hummed nearby, getting louder, closer. Her heart raced, her breaths becoming shallow and reedy. Lights swept across the broken window, then away, leaving the shack in darkness again.

The owner was already home. A truck had rumbled down the drive over an hour ago. It was late. Too late for anyone to be out here working in this dank shed. Dread trickled into her bloodstream, spreading fast and thoroughly.

It was Langley. Every instinct she had was screaming loud and clear. He'd found them. She could almost smell him, the acrid odor of cigarettes and the sweet scent of the cloves he sucked on.

"Micah, wake up!"

She felt for her son, lifting him to his feet. Her arms shook, her fingers trembled. The sound of her heartbeat thrashed in her ears.

The back door. They could escape that way. But they wouldn't make it far. Micah would slow them down. She had to stay and fight. Give him time to get away. It was his only hope.

She pulled him to the back door, tripping over something on the wood floor. Micah whimpered.

"Someone's here. You have to run." She grabbed his shoulders, her fingers biting into the padded jacket, as she pierced his eyes with hers. "Do you understand? Run out into the woods, that way. Keep going. Don't stop, no matter what. Stay off the road. Go to the first house you find and ask for help."

She unlocked the back door and pulled, panicking when it refused to budge. *Come on!* Finally it squeaked open. The hum of the engine continued outside, and shadows spilled across the back of the building.

She pushed Micah forward. "Run, Micah!" she whispered. "Don't stop!" She watched him go, her eyes following his small frame until the shadows swallowed him up.

Please, God.

The doorknob rattled behind her. She spun and stared into the darkness. She'd locked it, but that wouldn't matter with the broken window beside it. She felt around for something. Anything. Then she remembered an old rusty shovel in the corner.

The door opened as she darted for the shovel. Footsteps sounded behind her.

Please! She fumbled in the darkness, knocking things over. They clattered at her feet.

Her hands closed over the solid wood handle just as arms came around her. They shackled her arms to her sides. She kicked, connecting with a shin. She tried for his instep, missing, and his grip tightened painfully.

"Stop it!" he said. "Let go of it!"

She tried to angle the shovel, jabbing it back toward his legs. A *thud* sounded as it connected.

He gave a grunt, but his tight grip held. "I said, let go!"

She had to keep fighting. Every second gave Micah more time to escape. Remembering her training with Walter, she leaned forward and threw her head back as hard as she could.

He grunted at the impact.

Pain exploded in the back of her head. She twisted and writhed, adrenaline giving her strength. But there was no escaping his iron grip.

He lifted her from her feet. She kicked and squirmed as he forced her forward, and then she was flat against the wall, the raw wood cutting into her cheek.

"That's enough! Be still or I'm calling the sheriff!"

His words more than anything else stilled her body. Her breath came in deep huffs. Something on the wall dug into her ribs. Her lungs fought for room to expand.

One of his arms fell away slowly, as if he didn't quite trust her. He leaned closer as he reached for something. She felt his breath on her ear, the sandpaper of his jaw against hers. A click sounded, and the dim bulb flickered on. Heart in her throat, Eden closed her eyes and prayed.

· · ·

Beau clutched the jacket, holding tight as the light kicked on. Some punk kid probably, by his size. The guy's ball cap had gone askew in the skirmish. He was scrappy, Beau would give him that.

The kid's hands still grasped the shovel, and Beau pried his fingers away. "Let go!"

The shovel clunked to the ground.

"All right, punk, what do you think—" He whipped the kid around, and his words died on his lips. Wide, honey-brown eyes looked up at him from under the crooked brim of the baseball hat.

Familiar brown eyes. Female brown eyes.

He stepped back, hands up to his sides. "Whoa! It's you. I . . . Crap, are you all right?"

"I'm sorry!" Her eyes were wide and panicked. "I'll leave right now."

He surveyed her face as she cowered against the wall. Remembering his manacled grip on her arms, he winced. *Way to rough her up, Callahan.*

"Wait." Beau scanned the room. "Where's your boy?"

She flew through the back door, running toward the grove of Frasier firs. He had a feeling she'd find her kid and keep going.

"Jack!" she called "Jack, stop! It's okay."

Beau followed, opening the flashlight app on his phone. The wind was frigid, blowing right through his coat and stinging his cheeks. A terrible night to be out.

Why had they been in his shed? Maybe she'd been planning to steal from him. Or maybe she had no place to go. Was that even possible? Someone like her, with delicate blond hair and the face of an angel?

Up ahead, the light cut through the woods, revealing mother and son. She squatted by her boy, holding him, murmuring things he couldn't hear. She ran her hands over his wet face. The kid's jeans were wet to the knees from the snow.

The boy jerked away, his face panicked. He made gestures his mom seemed to understand immediately.

"Boo Bear. Don't worry, we'll go back for him." She stood and addressed Beau, her voice trembling. "He left his bear back at the shed. I have to get it."

"Of course." Beau followed them, questions churning though his mind. When they entered the outbuilding, he gave voice to the most prominent one.

"What were you doing in here?" His throbbing nose made his tone sharper than he intended.

The boy picked up the bear from the floor and returned to his mom's side, plastering himself to her leg.

She wrapped an arm around him. "I'm sorry. I'm sorry about the window. I'll pay for it, I promise, just as soon as I can. We were just bunking down is all. We didn't mean any harm."

He ran both hands over his face and sighed hard. "I can't let you stay here."

"Just for tonight? Please . . . We won't take anything. We won't cause any trouble—"

"That's not what I mean. It's twenty-five degrees and falling. There's no heat in here, no running water . . . Is there someone I can call for you?"

"No. No, we're on our own. We'll be fine. I just—we need a place. Just for tonight. This is fine. More than fine."

He wasn't sure what her normal standard of living was, but this shed was not fine. Not even during their mild summer months, much less in the dead of winter.

He scraped his fingers up the back of his neck, clutching the hair at his nape. "I have an extra bedroom right now. My aunt isn't home and—"

"No. No, thank you. It's very—generous."

He saw retreat in her eyes an instant before her body followed.

"We should just move on. We'll be—"

"Where are you fixing to go? It's almost midnight. Everything's closed down. You know someone in town?"

"No, but—"

"I assume a hotel isn't an option."

She shook her head. Twin pink patches bloomed on her cheeks. "We had money, but it was stolen this afternoon."

He frowned. "Did you report it?"

"No." She looked down, long eyelashes covering her pretty eyes. "It wasn't much."

He wondered if she was lying or just embarrassed. "You should still report it. I can call—"

"No, thanks. I can handle it." She reached for the door handle.

"Wait. You can't go back out there. Listen, my girl-friend has a spare room. I'm sure she wouldn't mind putting you up for the night." This was true—if she didn't kill him first for waking her.

She wavered on the threshold. "I don't think so."

It was the closest thing he'd gotten to a yes. "Come on, where else you going to go?" He looked down at the kid, hugging his ratty blue bear and shivering. He appealed to the mother in her. "He needs someplace warm to bed down. A good breakfast in the morning. Though with Paige, that'll probably consist of a bowl of Lucky Charms."

The kid's eyes lit as they turned up to his mom. She didn't miss it either. Beau wondered what they'd had to eat today. No wonder she'd been so desperate for that job.

"Are you sure she won't mind?"

He held up his phone. "I'll call her right now." He lifted his eyebrows, waiting until Eden gave a nod, then punched a button and moved toward the front door for privacy. "Don't go anywhere."

She stared back, as cautious as a wounded animal.

"Promise?" he asked.

She nodded. It was the best he was going to get.

CHAPTER 6

"I think we should see if Kate wants the position," Paige said the next morning. They were having an emergency meeting at Wicked Good Brew before church. "She needs a job and has no place to stay. It's the perfect solution."

Beau squeezed Paige's shoulder. With Aunt Trudy due home in hours, something had to be done and quick.

"What do we even know about her?" Riley asked. "She turns up out of the blue, with nothing but the clothes on her back, breaks into the shed . . . How do we know she won't drug Aunt Trudy and make off with all our stuff?"

"She's got a kid, Riley," Paige said. "What do you want to do, turn them out on the street?"

"She may not even want the position."

Beau emptied his cup. "She won't turn it down."

"Riley's got a point," Zac said. "We need to check her references at least."

"A background check wouldn't hurt." Riley looked Beau's way. "I'm sure you can get that done."

Yeah, that wasn't going to happen by two o'clock. "So are we all in agreement?"

Paige and Zac nodded.

Riley gave a shrug and half nod. "This is going to cost us."

"You can factor the room at my house into her pay if you want. It's just sitting empty, and God knows I could use more estrogen around here."

Beau gave Paige a grateful smile. "All right then. I'll swing by your place and talk to her. I might be late to church."

. . .

Eden woke with a start. She lay still until her surroundings made sense. Beau Callahan's girlfriend. The morning sunlight streamed in through the sheer blue curtains, washing over Micah's face. He was beside her on the bed, one knee popped out to the side, Boo Bear smashed between his chest and the mattress.

It was Sunday. She longed to walk down to the chapel she'd seen in town and sit in the pews among the congregation.

Memories of last night surfaced. Beau's image popped to mind. He was an interesting man. As a website designer, her forte was designing a site to suit the company's personality. She rarely missed. As she got to know people, she tended to identify them in terms of the colors she might use if she were designing their personal website.

She barely knew Beau, but she already saw him as

blue. Loyal, reliable, protective. His confidence might inspire the use of white as an accent color and perhaps a dash of yellow to complement what she suspected was a strong bent toward independence.

The doorbell rang and Eden jumped, clutching the sheet in her hands.

Bad guys don't ring the doorbell, stupid.

Besides, she'd been so careful to cover their tracks. They'd changed taxis twice before they'd bought the car, and they'd altered their appearance each time, just as Marshals Walter and Brown had instructed. Langley wouldn't find them here.

Please, God.

The doorbell rang again, and she realized Paige had probably already left for church. She eased from the bed, quickly but quietly, hoping she wouldn't wake Micah.

She padded barefoot down the hallway, conscious of the borrowed yoga pants and skimpy tank. Paige's gray tabby cat, Dasher, jumped off the sofa and followed her to the door.

A quick peek through the peephole revealed a familiar face. She pulled the door open, crossing her arms against the cold air.

"Good morning," she said.

Beau looked even better in the morning light. He was freshly shaved, and there were two small nicks low on his jaw, as if he might've rushed.

"Can I come in?"

She stepped aside, catching a spicy, masculine scent as he passed, then closed the door.

He rubbed his hands together as Dasher swished around his legs. "You look well rested."

"I woke up like two seconds ago." She tucked her short hair behind her ears, trying to smooth it, then gave up, knowing it was futile. He didn't care what she looked like. He had a girlfriend. He only felt sorry for her. She didn't have to be psychic to see the pity in his eyes.

She moved away from the door, wondering why he'd come. "Can I get you some coffee?" She grimaced. "I should probably know where the coffee's kept before I offer."

He had a nice smile. The crease to the left of his mouth was almost, but not quite, a dimple. "No worries, I just had a cup. But the coffee's to the left of the sink if you need a caffeine fix."

"After a warm shower, I think."

He picked up Dasher, who immediately began purring. "So, you never said what brought you to town. You may have noticed it's not exactly tourist season." He gave a crooked grin.

He was trying to make a joke of it, but she knew a probing question when she heard one. "We're just passing through. My car broke down."

He picked up a ceramic nativity, looked it over, then set it back down. "Where you from?"

"Down south. All over, really. I like to travel."

Maybe Paige had asked him to come and make sure she didn't make off with the computer or something. She'd been so kind—they both had. "I'll leave Paige a note thanking her. I'm grateful for her hospitality. And

I *am* going to pay you back for the window just as soon as I—"

He waved her off. "I'm not worried about that. I was actually coming to tell you that—"

Her eyes darted to his face at the abrupt quiet. His lips had flattened.

She followed his gaze to a cluster of fresh bruises on her biceps—the remnants of their tussle in the shed.

"Aw, jeez . . ." He reached out, his fingertips brushing her skin, soft as a whisper. "Did I do that?"

Gooseflesh pebbled in the wake of his touch, at the rasp of his voice. She shrugged off his hand, self-conscious of his appraisal and her reaction to it.

"Please, it's nothing. I've had worse from wrestling around with Mi—Jack."

Her words didn't erase the pained look on his face. It was even worse than pity.

"I am so sorry."

She crossed her arms, effectively hiding the bruises. "I was just grateful for a warm place to sleep. Paige was so kind, and she heats up a mean bowl of soup."

"She shared her Campbell's. She must like you."

Maybe she did, but Eden wasn't about to take advantage of her kindness. "Well . . ." She took a step toward the hallway. "I'll just wake up Jack, and we'll be out of here in a few minutes. You can tell Paige—"

"Actually . . ." He took a step in her direction. "I was just talking with her and my brothers. We think we might have a job for you."

Was she supposed to believe a job had come up between last night and this morning? She might be penniless and homeless, but she was no fool. She scratched her neck as heat rose into her face, hating that she couldn't afford to turn it down.

She lifted her chin, trying for a smile. "Oh yeah?"

"Our aunt Trudy's about to be released from the hospital. She fractured her leg. She lives at the farm with me and my brother Riley, and she'll need help, plus a ride into town a couple times a week for therapy. I'm busy with the tree farm—we open day after Thanksgiving. Riley works with me, and Zac—that's our other brother—he runs the Roadhouse. It's a local hangout right outside of town on the coast."

"I stopped in there yesterday to ask about a job. I talked to one of the servers."

"He's not hiring right now."

"Yeah, I got that."

"So, anyway, the job . . . She'll need help getting around, but mostly she needs to stay put. We need someone to help out for five or six weeks, through Christmas, probably. Do the chores and whatnot—cooking, cleaning, basic household stuff—and shuttle Aunt Trudy to therapy."

It sounded like a legit job, but she sensed he was holding something back. Plus her qualifications were less than stellar. Though she'd fake her way into an accountant position at this point and be thankful for the opportunity.

"We kind of need someone soon—like in a few hours. I could get your references later. Sound like something you'd want to do?"

Her mind was processing the details. Namely her

lack of references, not to mention her lack of ID. Maybe they'd pay her under the table. She'd worry about that later.

"Of course. Thank you."

He named the figure they'd be paying. "Paige said she'd be happy to let the room out to you as part of your pay—if that's agreeable. You'd have to share with your son."

Her breath left her body. Agreeable didn't come close. A lump welled up in her throat, and she swallowed it back. "That's—that's wonderful. Really. I can't tell you how much this means."

"Hey . . ." He shrugged. "We need a caretaker, and you need a job. The timing couldn't have been more perfect."

Definitely blue. She blinked the sting of tears away and soaked in the warmth of his dark chocolate eyes as she realized the look she'd seen before wasn't pity at all. It was simply compassion.

CHAPTER 7

The woman, who looked to be on the doorstep of sixty, scowled up at Eden from the full-size bed in the makeshift bedroom. She had short silver hair, a narrow face, and startling blue eyes. Time had etched a network of crow's feet into their corners, but the twin commas between her sparse brows were the most pronounced lines on her face. Her leg, casted up past her knee, lay stiffly against the baby-blue sheets.

"Who's that?" Miss Trudy asked.

Beau gave Eden an apologetic smile. "Now, Aunt Trudy, that's no way to talk to our guest. She's going to be helping out around here, so you might want to play nice."

Miss Trudy's scowl deepened. "You hired me a babysitter?"

"Don't be silly," Beau said. "You haven't been a baby for ages. This is Kate—I just realized I don't know your last name."

"You hired a stranger to babysit me?"

Micah melded into Eden's side at the gruff tone of her voice.

"Bennet." Eden's face warmed under the woman's perusal. "Nice to meet you, Miss Trudy. This is my son, Jack."

"Should keep things lively around here while I'm working," Beau said.

"Perfect. Bed rest, pain, and a noisy boy around. Just what the doctor ordered."

Beau shot Eden a chagrined look. "Her bark's worse than her bite."

"And she's right here in the room. Respect your elders, Beau Callahan."

"Yes, ma'am." He looked down at Micah. "We have some old toys in the attic. I'll bring them down for you. How does that sound?"

Micah blinked up at him silently. Beau's eyes toggled up to Eden.

She rubbed Micah's tousled curls affectionately. "He hasn't been speaking lately."

"Oh, sorry," Beau said. "I thought he was just shy."

A moment later he led Eden and Micah from the room. Beau fetched the toys from the attic, and Micah settled in the living room with a coloring book and box of crayons.

Eden realized what Beau had been holding back from her yesterday morning. His aunt was going to be a challenge. Eden was beginning to wonder if she should have asked for hazard pay.

In the kitchen there was a sink full of dishes, and the floor needed to be swept. It was late afternoon, so her first chore would be supper. She sent up a silent prayer at the daunting task.

Beau gave a wry grin. "Sorry about that. She's usually not so cranky. Well, yeah, she actually is, but she's got a tender heart. You just have to dig awhile to find it."

His aunt's direct manner had brought the color indigo to Eden's mind immediately. "I'm sure we'll get along fine."

He handed her the release instructions from the hospital. "As you'll see, weight bearing is encouraged as tolerated, but she'll tolerate more than she should. You'll have to keep her from overdoing. She's got crutches. I'm not sure how she's faring with those."

"We'll be just fine. Mi—son broke his leg when he was three. If I can keep a three-year-old boy down, I can manage your aunt just fine."

"I heard that!" Miss Trudy's gruff voice carried through the wall. "I'm not a child, you know!"

Oops. Eden bit her lip.

Beau lowered his voice. "I should've warned you. She has, like, bionic hearing. I can't even tell you."

Eden laughed at the look on his face. The laugh sounded rusty even to her.

"If you can keep her out of the kitchen," Beau continued in his quiet voice, "it'll be a miracle. She's kind of a control freak, and this is definitely her territory."

"Keep her out of the kitchen. Got it. Anything else?"

"The place is a mess, and we're kind of low on groceries. Things have been a little hectic since she's been in the hospital. Whatever you can round up for supper will be fine."

"Got it."

He shuffled through a stack of papers on the kitchen desk and handed her one. It was a W-4. Her heart sank.

"This is for you to fill out when you get a chance."

"Anything else?"

"Where's my knitting basket?" Miss Trudy called. "And what's that odor in here? Smells like someone barfed up baby snot."

She met Beau's twinkling eyes and couldn't squash the smile forming on her lips. "I'll be right there, Miss Trudy!"

"Her knitting's probably in that bag we brought home from the hospital. I have to get in a couple hours at the farm. You can reach me on my cell." He jotted the number on a scrap of paper. "I'll leave Zac's and Riley's, too, but call me first. I have emergency money in the desk drawer." He pulled it out and showed her a couple twenties lying amid the pens and bills. "Let me know when you're going to the grocery, and I'll leave you money. You can use Trudy's Explorer—here are the keys. Riley and I get home around six. Sometimes Zac comes over to eat, but not usually. Of course, you and Jack are welcome to eat with us." He set a check on the table. "I thought I'd go ahead and pay you for this week, given the circumstances."

Eden's heart softened at his thoughtfulness. "I appreciate it."

"I guess I'll have to get up and get it myself!" Miss Trudy called.

Beau grinned at her. "That's my cue."

When Beau left, Eden rushed into the living room and found the knitting basket. There was a ribbed blue-gray piece lying on top made with tiny, intricate stitches. Eden took the basket to Miss Trudy, who picked up the needles and resumed her work without a word.

Micah had abandoned the crayons and was watching a cartoon. After getting the woman settled and the house straightened up, she focused on supper. She stared into the freezer, feeling overwhelmed. She'd been hoping for something simple, like a box with directions, but there were no convenience meals. There were chicken breasts and ground beef in the freezer. Where did she even start?

She'd wanted to learn to cook. When she'd married Antonio she'd imagined serving four-course dinners by candlelight each night. But he wouldn't hear of it. Wives in his world didn't perform such tasks. That's what the help was for. It had been all she could do to talk him out of a nanny when Micah was born.

When she asked Miss Trudy where she kept her recipe books, the woman gave a sharp laugh. "Real cooks don't use recipes."

Eden wished she'd asked Beau for permission to use his computer. She closed the freezer door. She was going to have to bring in the expert on this one. But when she reached the doorway to Miss Trudy's room, the woman's eyes were shut, and her chest was rising and falling in a peaceful rhythm. Eden didn't have the heart—or the nerve—to waken her.

She pulled the door quietly shut. Looked like she was on her own. Eden drew in a breath and blew it out. *Come on, Eden. You've survived a lot worse. How hard could one little meal be?*

. . .

"The biscuits will be ready in a minute," Kate said as they settled at the kitchen table.

Beau said grace, then passed the bowl to Riley who passed it to Zac. He was hungry, and the savory smell made his stomach rumble. He took a bite of the steaming goulash.

The contrasting temperatures and textures momentarily confused him. The sauce was hot, but something in the mixture—the meat?—was crunchy and frozen. The strange consistency temporarily diverted his attention from the taste—but not for long.

Some pungent spice dominated the flavor. He wasn't sure what it was, but he hoped to never have it in his mouth again.

Beside him, Riley coughed, bringing his napkin to his mouth.

Beau was pretty sure the goulash had found a new home. He felt a moment's jealousy as he forced down his own bite.

His gaze flickered to Kate, whose eyes were glued to her plate. Her boy was chewing, his brows pulled low.

"Merciful heavens, what's this supposed to be?"

"*Aunt Trudy*," Beau said.

"There's enough sage in here to cure a decade's worth of hot flashes."

Sage. So that's what it was.

Kate's cheeks flushed. "I'm so sorry. I didn't have a recipe—I didn't want to use your computer without asking."

"Have at it," Riley said, giving one final hack. "Please."

Fear flashed in her eyes. "I'll do better next time. I promise."

Beau gave Riley a dark look, then addressed Kate, who was looking ill. "It's okay. You can use the computer anytime. We'll just fill up on biscuits tonight."

"What's that smell?" Aunt Trudy said about the same time he became aware of a burning odor.

"The biscuits!" Kate jumped up from the table and rushed into the kitchen.

Riley's eyes met his over the table. "Wings from the Roadhouse, anyone?"

. . .

Beau carried his plate to the sink. "Can I help with dishes or anything?"

They'd finished their take-out meal, and his brothers were settling Aunt Trudy on the sofa in the living room.

"Please. It's the least I could do." Kate set the dishes in the sink and turned to face him, a contrite look on her face. "I am so sorry about supper. It won't happen again, I promise."

Her long blond bangs had fallen over her worried eyes, and his finger twitched to brush them back. He pocketed his hands. "Relax. You never said you were a gourmet chef."

"I don't have much experience in the kitchen, but I'm a fast learner. I'm sure I'll be fine once I have some recipes."

"I'm sure you will." He wondered how a mother like her had gotten this far without knowing some kitchen basics. Even he could throw together a few decent meals.

"Beau," Zac called from the living room. "Get in here."

He left Kate and Jack to the cleanup and entered the living room. The ESPN program had been muted, and everyone was eying Riley.

"What's going on?"

"Riley said he needs to talk to us," Zac said.

"You've met a woman, haven't you?" Aunt Trudy said.

Riley rolled his eyes. "No, Aunt Trudy."

She was always trying to marry them off. Strange, since she'd rebuffed any attempts at matchmaking since their uncle had passed fourteen years ago.

Riley's face was a serious mask. His eyebrows were pinched together and his jaw was set.

His countenance filled Beau with dread. He leaned forward, elbows planted on his knees. "What's up, bro?"

"It's a woman, I tell you. Is it that Millie Parker from Frumpy Joe's? She was flirting up a storm last time we were in."

Riley frowned at her. "If I had a woman, I'd bring her around now and then. I've made some plans I need to tell you about. I—" Riley stared at the sofa table between them. "I enlisted in the marines."

"What?" Zac said.

"Merciful heavens," Aunt Trudy muttered.

Beau's heart gave a hard thump that set off a series of quakes inside. "Why?"

"I always talked about doing it."

Beau frowned. "We *talk* about lots of things. We never thought you'd really follow through."

Riley's eyes darted up, flashing. "Well, I did."

"Without even running it by us?" Beau couldn't believe he'd made such a critical decision without hashing it out. It wasn't like him.

"I'm twenty-four. I don't need your permission."

"When do you leave?" Zac asked.

"Four weeks."

"Before Christmas?" Beau and Aunt Trudy said simultaneously.

Beau couldn't believe this. "Our first Christmas without Dad?"

"It's not like we have a real one anyway."

They hadn't really celebrated since their mom died on Christmas Eve twelve years ago. But still. "With the farm and everything we've got going on . . . that's when you decide to bail?"

"I'm not bailing. I'm joining the armed forces."

"If you say so."

"Stop making it sound cowardly. Most families are proud when a relative enlists."

A beat of silence only amplified the tension in the room.

Zac's eyes sharpened on Riley. A second later he set his hand on Beau's shoulder. "Come on, Beau. What's done is done."

"We've already lost Mom and Dad, and now you're going to go risk your life across the world somewhere. What if you come back in a body bag, huh? You think about that?"

Riley rolled his eyes. "I'm not going to die, Beau."

"You don't know that."

"Come on, guys," Zac said. "Let's just cool it. We'll talk about it tomorrow after it's had a chance to sink in."

Beau stood, pacing the room. "I can't believe you did this."

Riley sprang to his feet. "I can't believe you're reacting like this!"

"Does Paige know?"

"Why would I tell *her*?"

"Because she loves you, you numbskull!"

Riley huffed.

"I guess ten years of friendship means nothing to you. Did you think about anyone other than yourself when you did this?"

Riley stalked toward Beau. "Oh, you're one to talk."

"What's that supposed to mean?"

Riley glared at him. "Nothing! It means nothing."

"All right, you two!" Aunt Trudy said. "No fighting in the living room."

Zac stepped between them. "Calm down, Riley. Beau's taken care of us all his life. You know he has. He feels responsible for us."

"What about the farm?" Beau leaned around Zac. "Your life here? You just going to leave it all behind without a second thought?"

"What life? All I do is work. Aunt Trudy has you guys, Zac has the Roadhouse, you have Paige . . ."

"You have Paige too." Beau watched the emotions flicker over his brother's face before he turned away, palming the back of his neck.

Aunt Trudy pulled slowly to her feet, grabbing the crutches. "All right, I think I've had enough drama for tonight. I'm heading to bed." She fixed them with a look. "You two are behaving like you're twelve, and I'm in no shape to break up a scuffle."

Beau moved forward, his hands shaking with the news. "I'll help you."

Aunt Trudy swatted his hand away, giving him a sour look. "I can get myself to bed. You stay here and fix this."

Silence reigned for a full minute after she left. Riley's jaw was set, his lips pressed together. His arms were folded over his chest. Beau imagined his brother getting wounded, or worse, not coming back at all. He didn't know if he could take another loss like that. Losing their dad had been hard enough. He swallowed past the lump in his throat.

He grabbed his coat off the rack and shoved his arms into it. "I'll be out in the barn setting up wreaths."

"Need some help?" Zac asked.

"Nope."

He stepped out into the night, barely feeling the cold air as it skated across his face.

. . .

Micah scooted off to use the bathroom, and Eden stowed the broom in the closet. She'd heard the brothers' argument and Beau's abrupt departure. She hesitated to enter the living room. She was tempted to slip quietly out the back door.

But that seemed cowardly and unprofessional. It was her first night, and she hadn't exactly made a good impression with the goulash and burned biscuits. When she entered the living room, Zac and Riley were facing away from her, their shoulders rigid, ESPN muted in front of them.

"This is about Paige, isn't it?" Zac said as she crossed the threshold.

Eden stopped.

"I've always wanted to join up, you know that."

"But you never did." Zac looked at his brother. "I saw that look on your face the other night when Beau was talking about Paige in terms of forever."

"Well, what do you expect? That I'm just going to stick around here and watch my brother marry the woman I love?"

Holy cow. Eden inched back.

"It's been hard enough just watching them—"

The floor creaked under her foot.

Riley's head whipped around. His eyes rounded, then the muscles in his jaw twitched. He nailed her with a look.

Shoot. "I-I'm sorry. I was coming to say good night. I didn't mean—"

"How much did you hear?" Zac asked.

Eden winced.

Riley turned away. "Great. Just great."

"I won't say anything. This is none of my business." She grabbed her jacket off the rack. "Let's just pretend it never happened, okay?"

She heard the bathroom door close, then Micah

came through the kitchen door. She helped him into his coat.

"We'll see you tomorrow." She smiled at the brothers but only got one smile in return.

CHAPTER 8

What a horrible day. What kind of mother couldn't make one decent meal? She couldn't believe Beau hadn't fired her on the spot.

Eden put Micah to bed and took a long bath, trying to shake her bad mood. Afterward she found Paige in the dining room. Dasher wove between Eden's feet as she entered the room, and she bent down to run her fingers down the cat's arched back.

"Mind if I join you?" she asked.

"Sure." Paige looked up from her laptop. Her pretty blue eyes were bloodshot, and a crumpled tissue lay at her fingertips.

Eden had a feeling she'd heard Riley's news. She couldn't help but feel a little envious of the guy. He had so many people who cared about him.

Paige sniffled. "How was your first day? Did you survive Miss Trudy?"

Eden made a face. "She was the least of my worries. I ruined dinner. We ended up with wings from the Roadhouse for supper."

Paige breathed a laugh and dabbed at her eyes with a tissue. "The guys were probably thrilled. They love wings."

Paige was striking, with her straight blond hair and big blue eyes. She was petite with a trim, athletic build and curves in all the right places. And she was nice to boot. It wasn't hard to see what Beau—and Riley—saw in her.

"I take it you don't have much experience with a stove?"

Eden picked at the cuff of her borrowed pajama top. "Not much. I'm sure I'll get the hang of it, though."

"I don't think you ever said where you were from."

Eden tucked her hair behind her ears. "Down south."

"You don't have an accent," Paige said softly.

"You do, a little. I'd never heard the Mainer accent before."

"Beau said you had some things stolen, that you were just passing through."

She never should've sat down with Paige. "Basically everything. Plus my car broke down. We'll stick around long enough to get it fixed and get Miss Trudy back on her feet. I can't tell you how much I appreciate the job . . . and the place to stay. Beau and his family have been great."

Paige's eyes went to her phone, and her countenance fell.

"You okay?" Eden asked.

"I just got off the phone with Beau . . . Riley enlisted in the marines." Paige pushed her laptop closed.

Eden was glad the conversation had shifted to a safer topic. "I kind of overheard them talking. You've known them a long time?"

"Since Riley and I were fourteen." She smiled as if remembering those days. "He challenged me to a game of basketball after school one day, and I beat him."

Eden smiled. "Ouch."

"Yeah, I'm sure it smarted, but he took it pretty well. Of course it helps that he's beat me about a hundred times since. Once he shot up and grew all those muscles, it was a lost cause. I challenge him to pool now, where I still have a chance." Her smile fell, and her lips trembled. "He's my best buddy. I can't believe he's going into the military."

It must be hard for Riley, loving someone who had him firmly in the friend zone. Watching her fall for his big brother. No wonder he wanted to skip town.

"How'd you and Beau end up together?"

"He's four years older than Riley, so he wasn't really on my radar growing up. But I was around the family a lot when their dad passed away. And then one night we ran into each other at the Roadhouse and ended up talking until they closed. We never run out of things to talk about. He's a great guy. He's really upset tonight. Riley leaving so soon after his dad died . . . I don't know what he's thinking."

"It sounded like they were ready to come to blows earlier."

Page gave a wry grin. "This is what you need to know about the Callahan men. They're strong-willed, overprotective, and they think they know it all. They're also the town's most eligible bachelors—though I've got Beau tied up at the moment. There was weeping and wailing when we became exclusive, but Zac is back on the market now. He got jilted by his fiancée about a month ago. They might be a little rough around the edges, but what can you expect? After their mom died they were raised by their father with nary a decent female influence through their teenage years."

"What about their aunt?"

Paige smirked. "Have you met Miss Trudy?"

"Well, I hope things calm down tomorrow. I could've swum though all the tension in the air tonight."

"It'll blow over, you'll see. The Callahan brothers are passionate, but they don't hold grudges long."

. . .

It didn't blow over. The next day Riley missed supper and seemed to be avoiding the family in general.

Eden stifled yawn after yawn. Micah had had a nightmare the night before. She'd awakened to a scream and gathered his sweaty little body into her arms, trying to soothe him with words. He must have wakened Paige, because she'd asked about him that morning.

A call to the garage had brought bad news. It *was* a thrown rod, the mechanic said, and the engine would need to be rebuilt to the tune of a thousand dollars. Eden thought about it all afternoon before calling back and giving the go-ahead. A rebuilt engine would make the car last a long time. She warned him it would be awhile before she could pay for it.

She walked to town on Monday evening and cashed her check at the grocery store. Her next stop was the diner, where she paid her tab, and the next was the

Bargain Barn. The secondhand store was a treasure
trove. She found warm winter clothes for Micah, a pair
of jeans for herself, and a cheap purse. She splurged on
a bright red sweater, feeling a little nervous and a little
rebellious as she set it on the counter.

On the way back to Paige's house, they passed a used
bookstore. Her eyes caught on a familiar paperback in
the window. Eden stopped, her eyes zeroing in on the
Debbie Macomber cover with a cute little dog posing
on a purple bench.

*"What kind of trash is this?" He snatched the library
book from her hands and hurled it into the garbage.
"Not in my house. Not in my wife's hands."*

She shook the memory from her mind, gathered her
resolve, and entered the bookstore. A few minutes later
she walked back out, a copy of *Twenty Wishes* tucked
into her new purse.

Eden spent the next couple days running Miss Trudy
around, cleaning, and trying to plan a Thanksgiving
meal. She desperately needed it to turn out well. She'd
made too many mistakes this week. She'd turned some
of Beau's white T-shirts pink. She'd used the wrong
cleaner on the kitchen floor, making it sticky. And
she'd managed to break the vacuum cleaner somehow.
Each time she'd messed up, she'd expected it to be her
last day. But Beau took each mistake in stride.

He had asked for her W-4 form, but she told him
she'd left it at Paige's. She couldn't stall much longer.
She'd have to use a fake social security number and
hope she was long gone by the time the government
informed him of the error.

Eden lit the kindling in the fireplace and watched a log catch fire, then she turned on the radio, flipping stations until she found Christmas carols. She'd finally thought of a way to redeem herself. The turkey was thawing in the refrigerator, the potatoes were scrubbed and sitting on the counter, and Miss Trudy was napping. It was time to make this place festive.

She hauled the decorations from the attic and started to work. By the time the sun set, the house was a Christmas wonderland. A twinkling garland lined the mantel and staircase, and faux candles glimmered here and there. Miss Trudy had awakened from her nap halfway through and supervised. Riley had nodded approvingly when he passed through the living room.

She couldn't wait for Beau to see her handiwork.

• • •

Beau turned off his truck and stepped out into the cold wind. The barn was all set up with wreaths and garlands. The delivery truck had arrived from Bethel Farms, and he'd unloaded one hundred trees to supplement their own stock. He didn't mind these quiet days of preparation. But day after tomorrow the madness would start.

Customers pouring in. The smell of cut pine flooding the barn. Christmas carols following him everywhere. Children sipping hot chocolate, wrapped in scarves and layers of down. And the constant ringing of the sleigh bells as Marty Bennington guided the horses down the snow-covered trails would haunt him long after he turned the Closed sign at the end of each day.

Between the approaching season and Riley's news, Beau's mood was on the sour side. Riley had been avoiding him, and Paige hadn't come over for supper all week. Of course Kate's lack of culinary skills might factor in. Beau had insisted they order pizza tonight since she had her hands full with Thanksgiving tomorrow. His hopes for that particular meal weren't too high.

He didn't want to think about Christmas, but it was hard when he was pretty much surrounded by it all day. He just had to keep busy. It would soon be over and he could stuff the memories into the past where they belonged, just as his dad had.

He trudged up the porch steps, stomping his boots as he went.

Riley came out the door just as Beau reached the top step, and stopped short when he saw his brother.

"Should've left a few minutes earlier," Beau said. "You almost missed me."

"Yeah, too bad." Riley edged around him.

Beau grabbed his arm. "When are you going to stop being such an idiot?"

Riley jerked from his grasp and continued on his way. "Why don't you go to Paige's and leave me alone?"

"Maybe I will. She's upset about you leaving, too, or haven't you bothered having that conversation with her?"

"Yeah, I'll bet she's crying buckets," Riley said over his shoulder.

"What is your problem?"

The only answer was the slam of Riley's truck door. The engine revved, and the truck started down the lane. Exhaust curled from the tailpipe, vaporizing in the cold air.

Beau growled as he gave two hard stamps of his feet. Riley was so stubborn. He didn't know what had gotten into him. Ever since their dad died, he'd been withdrawn and moody. Beau wanted to slug his brother for the pain he was causing.

Beau opened the door and stopped in his tracks at the view. Ornate garlands ran up the staircase and along the mantel where familiar stockings hung—their names applied in Mom's familiar script. A Christmas tree stood in the corner, filled with ornaments he hadn't seen in years. The ceramic angel his dad had given his mom in her last days sat boldly on the end table, surrounded by red candles.

Christmas music wafted through the room, and the fire in the fireplace crackled and popped.

"What the heck is this?" He turned his glare on Aunt Trudy, who was knitting on the sofa.

"Look what I found." Kate bounced into the room, smiling, her arms filled with the three stuffed snowmen his mom had bought years ago when he and his brothers were little. "Oh, hi." Her smile fell as she studied Beau.

"Who said you could do this?"

Her gaze toggled to Aunt Trudy and back. "What?"

"These are our things." He grabbed the snowmen from her arms, one at a time. "Our personal things."

"I-I'm sorry, I didn't—"

"No, you didn't." He grabbed the angel and set it

in the box at his feet. Next went the candles and the floppy elf he'd made in the third grade.

"It-it's just Christmas decorations . . ."

He straightened, directing a glare at her. "*Our* Christmas decorations. Why don't you see if you can figure out how to cook a decent meal and do a load of laundry before you start snooping through our stuff?"

Her cheeks flushed, but he turned to the mantel, taking down the stockings next. He barely heard her and Jack leaving over the freaking Christmas music. He found the radio and snapped it off.

"Well, that was a fine thank-you," Aunt Trudy said.

"Thank-you? How could you let her do this?"

"Well, I'd hoped you'd be more reasonable than your father. It's been twelve years, Beau. Life goes on."

"It brings back bad memories."

"Is that really it? Or are you just holding on to something your dad started?"

"It about killed him—or are you forgetting that?"

"Your mother loved Christmas. She wouldn't want you boys remembering the one bad one when she worked so hard to give you all the good ones."

"So we're just supposed to forget?"

"Of course you don't forget. But you move on. We own a Christmas tree farm; it's not like we can escape the holiday. But, merciful heavens, did your stubborn daddy ever try."

Beau lowered the garland in his hands, frowning. "I can't believe you let her do this."

"She was halfway done when I woke from my nap, and she was smiling like she'd finally done something right."

Beau pulled the rest of the garland down and stuffed it into the box. He didn't want to be here anymore. And he couldn't even go over to Paige's because Kate had invaded her house too.

"I'm going to order the pizza."

An hour later he was in his room and on the phone with Paige. "Have you heard from Riley?" he asked after they'd asked about each other's days.

"He called this afternoon. He's hurting, Beau. I think he's running, but I don't understand from what."

"We had words tonight. Tomorrow's going to be a disaster."

"Maybe losing your dad has just made him feel like he's at loose ends."

"Maybe."

Riley didn't open up to him anymore—not that his brother had ever been an open book. He'd hoped they'd draw together after their dad passed, but Riley only seemed to drift further away.

"Why can't he just join the Coast Guard like everyone else around here?" At least he wouldn't be as far away. And he wouldn't be smack-dab in the middle of a war zone.

"It's always been the marines for Riley."

"I know."

"Did something happen at the house today? Kate seemed kind of upset when she came home."

"What'd she say?"

"Not much. She's been upstairs all night."

Beau wondered if there'd even be a Thanksgiving dinner. Or a caretaker for Aunt Trudy.

"She got into all our Christmas stuff in the attic, and when I came home she'd decorated the whole house. It was everywhere. Garlands, ornaments, everything."

"Oh no," Paige deadpanned. "How could she?"

Beau clenched his jaw. "I could use a little support here."

"Come on, Beau. You're not mad at Kate. You're mad at Riley. And you're really not even mad at Riley. You're just afraid."

He pulled the phone away and stared at it before returning it to his ear. "You're seriously telling me how I feel right now?"

"You always get mad when you're afraid."

Great. He loved being analyzed. "What exactly am I afraid of, Paige?"

A long thread of silence hovered between them.

"You're afraid of losing him. And you know what? So am I. But he has his own life to live, his own decisions to make. All we can do is support him and pray God keeps him safe."

"The way God kept Dad safe? The way He kept Mom safe?" Beau sighed hard. "I didn't mean that."

He ran his hand over his face. It felt like everything was falling apart no matter how hard he'd tried to hold it all together.

"God can handle your questions, Beau. And He can handle Riley. And Kate. And Thanksgiving."

He threaded his hands into his hair and squeezed until he felt a sting. "I was a real jerk tonight."

"Well . . . ," she said. "There's always tomorrow."

CHAPTER 9

Eden squinted at the directions she'd printed off, then put the bowl of butter into the microwave to melt. The turkey was all trussed up and waiting in the roasting pan. Paige was coming to help in a couple hours, bringing Micah with her. With any luck the meal would be edible, if not delicious.

The microwave dinged, and she began basting the turkey, stifling a yawn. She'd had a rough night's sleep. She wasn't even sure she was still welcome in the house after Beau's scolding. But she needed this job, so here she was.

The floor creaked behind her, and she looked over her shoulder. Beau appeared in jeans and a white T-shirt, his hair damp from his shower. Good to know he had at least one white T-shirt left.

"Morning." His voice was still rough from sleep.

"There's coffee over there." She put the finishing touches on the turkey, opened the oven, and reached for the roasting pan.

"Let me get that." Beau nudged her out of the way. The spicy scent of his cologne wafted over her.

He lowered the pan into the hot oven and shut the door.

"Thanks." Eden set the timer so she wouldn't forget

to baste the turkey. She washed her hands, then studied her to-do list, conscious of Beau nearby, pouring his coffee.

"Listen, Kate, about last night . . ."

She waved him away. "I'm sorry if I—"

"Don't. You didn't do anything wrong."

She looked up from her list. Sunlight flooded through the kitchen window, highlighting his face. She noticed the lighter flecks in his brown eyes and the subtle copper highlights in his black hair.

"I overreacted. I'd had words with Riley on my way in. And to be honest, we haven't done a real Christmas in a long time."

"I didn't know."

"I know you didn't. I was a jerk. I'm sorry."

She gave him a grateful smile. "No worries."

He lifted his mug, calling attention to his muscled bicep and the way his snug shirt stretched over his broad shoulders. She looked back at her list.

"Twelve years ago our mom was diagnosed with pancreatic cancer right after Thanksgiving. It was pretty advanced by the time they found it." He leaned against the counter, crossing his bare feet. "She went downhill so fast. From vibrant and strong to weak and so sick. It was hard to see her like that. Hard to lose her."

"I'm sorry. How old were you?"

"Sixteen." He took a sip of his coffee. "Dad was a wreck, and all I wanted was to make things better . . . but she died Christmas Eve."

The hurt she saw in his eyes made her want to pull him into her arms.

"We kind of just skipped celebrating the next year. Mom was the one who did all that—the decorations, the gift buying, the cooking. Without her, it just didn't get done. And honestly, the holidays brought back too many painful memories."

"But you have a tree farm . . ."

His lips twisted, shadows settling into that crescent-shaped dimple. "Ironic, huh? I guess we stayed busy with that and tried not to think about everything else. Aunt Trudy came to stay here, help out with us boys. But Christmas was never the same after that."

Eden set down her pen. "I lost my mom too. I was thirteen. She stopped at a gas station and was caught in a holdup. Just some random fluke."

A notch formed between his brows. "I'm sorry. Did they ever catch him?"

"Never did."

"Must've been hard."

"I was in denial for a long time. She just left for work and never came home. I don't know which would be worse: knowing the end is coming and you can't stop it, or having it happen suddenly and there's no time for good-byes."

"Since my dad died of a heart attack, I can pretty much attest that both ways blow." He drained the rest of his coffee.

"I guess you're right. But I do understand how something like that can change you. I'll take the rest of the decorations down."

"No, don't. It's time to move on. And your son deserves a real Christmas."

Maybe the holiday would provide a nice distraction for Micah. At least for a few weeks. "If you're sure."

"So what about your dad?" Beau asked. "He still living?"

Eden checked her recipe for the stuffing. "Um, yeah."

"Where does he live?"

"Oh shoot. I'm short a can of broth."

"I'll ask Paige to pick it up on her way over."

"Oh, that'd be great. Thanks."

"So your dad . . . where does he live?"

So much for diverting his attention. "St. Louis." She said the first thing that came to mind.

"Is that where you grew up?"

She bit the inside of her lip. "Um, no. Would you like some more coffee? I should've made a bigger pot today—wasn't thinking."

"I'll do it." He reached for the coffee beans. His shirt rose an inch above his waistline, showing a sliver of taut stomach. He was a beautiful man, she'd give him that. Tall, dark, muscular.

But he was Paige's boyfriend, not to mention Eden's boss. And she needed another man like she needed a thorn in her big toe.

. . .

"Need any help?" Riley pulled a Coke from the fridge.

The turkey was almost done, the stuffing and green beans were in the oven, and the rolls were ready to go in next. Heavenly smells filled the kitchen.

"I think everything's under control," Eden said.

Paige had stopped for more soda and broth, and now everyone was in the living room watching football and trying to keep Aunt Trudy out of the kitchen. Last she'd seen Micah, Paige was teaching him a card game in the living room.

The guys cheered from the other room, and the TV blared louder.

Riley popped the tab of his soda and took a drink. "You probably think it's pretty stupid, what I'm doing."

Joining the military to escape his heartbreak? "I'm the last person to criticize someone's decisions."

"Why, what'd you do?"

She looked into eyes that were shaped like Beau's, but green instead of brown. He had more angles to his face. He was barrel-chested and had thick arms, and everything about his physique said he was a man who could take care of himself. A man with both feet on the ground. But there was a vulnerability in his eyes that called for honesty. She was definitely getting brown vibes.

"What did I do?" She tossed the dish towel down. "Well, let's see. I married the first decent guy to come along just to escape my smothering father, and soon found out he wasn't as decent as I thought. Let's start with that one."

It was more than she'd meant to say, but hey. She had a secret on him, now he had one on her.

"No kidding."

"No kidding." The timer went off, and she pulled the green beans from the oven and put the rolls in.

Riley stared at the door leading to the living room. "It would kill him if he knew. He's always looked out for us. He'd sooner give his right arm than take something from me."

She gave a soft smile. "Like I said, I won't say anything. Anyway, I won't be here much longer." She gave him a look. "I guess you won't be either."

"I guess not." He gave her a half smile before wandering back into the living room.

. . .

Beau scraped up the last bite of mashed potatoes and leaned back in his chair, hand on stomach. "That was delicious, Kate."

"You did great," Paige said. "The turkey is perfect."

"I couldn't have done it without you." She squeezed her eyes in a wince. "Sorry about the stuffing . . . and the gravy."

"Everything was great," Beau said. Yeah, the stuffing had been dry and the gravy a little lumpy, but all in all, not bad.

Kate looked over at her boy. "Eat your veggies, Jack."

He pushed his green beans around his plate, his nose wrinkled.

"Just five of them, then you can have pumpkin pie."

"You don't want to miss Paige's pie, young man," Aunt Trudy said. "And those green beans will put some muscles on your bones. Just look at these boys. Made them eat their veggies every night."

"I used to feed mine to Bowser," Zac said.

Riley pushed back his plate. "Me too."

Aunt Trudy scowled at Beau.

"Don't look at me. I ate mine." He winked at Jack, making a muscle. "Should be obvious just by looking at us."

Riley humphed as he always did when his brothers claimed to be stronger. "Best meal I've had in ages, ladies. That beat Zac's wings all to pieces."

Zac winged his balled-up napkin at Riley. "Hey, watch it. I feed you the rest of the year."

But Riley would soon be gone. Not eating wings and shooting pool with them at the Roadhouse. Or rooting for the Pats on Sunday afternoons.

Beau had tried to apologize to him this morning. He knew he hadn't handled his brother's news well. And even though Paige's analyzing had annoyed him, he knew she was right. Nothing terrified him more than the thought of losing one of his brothers. When they were here, right under his nose, he could look after them. What was he going to do when Riley was thousands of miles away, dealing with IEDs and missiles? He couldn't even think about it.

Riley had accepted his apology, but things were still strained. He'd hardly looked at Beau all afternoon and had been subdued through an exciting football game against the Eagles.

After dinner they ate dessert, despite being full, and when the conversation at the table petered out, the guys shooed the girls off to the living room and started the cleanup process. Aunt Trudy settled on the sofa with her knitting, and Jack went off to a corner of the living room with a deck of cards.

In the kitchen Beau pulled another plate from the

sudsy water and scrubbed it. His fingers were turning to prunes before his eyes. How many dishes could one family go through in a meal?

Zac set another stack of dirty plates in the water, and Beau caught him with the spray.

"Dude. Control that thing."

"What's the score?"

Riley poked his head into the living room, then came back and dropped a handful of silverware into the water. "Cowboys are up by seven."

A few minutes later Kate and Jack popped in to say good night. She was probably ready to collapse after a full day in the kitchen.

Beau put a scoop of bubbles on Jack's nose. The boy's lips turned up into a smile before he ducked his head, rubbing his nose against Kate's leg.

The brothers finished cleanup in time to see the Raiders put up a touchdown, tying the game. When they broke for half-time commercials, Beau changed into more comfortable clothes and came back downstairs.

"Nice shirt," Riley said.

He glanced down. It was one of the casualties of Kate's laundry work.

He settled on the sofa and put his arm around Paige.

"So what do you guys think about Kate now that she's had some time to settle in?" Paige said.

"She keeps cooking like that," Riley said, "and I say we keep her around."

"Well, that's a fine thank-you," Aunt Trudy said, her needles clicking faster.

"Just until you're back on your feet." Zac dropped a kiss on her cheek. "Nobody can cook like you, Aunt Trudy."

"Suck-up," Riley said.

"That's not what I meant." Paige leaned forward, her long blond hair swinging over her shoulders. "I mean what do we know about her? Where's she from? Where's she going? Am I the only one who's curious?"

"What's it matter?" Zac asked. "She's nice enough."

"Now that you mention it," Beau said, "she has been kind of squirrelly when I ask about her past."

"She changes the subject when I bring it up too. I agree she's nice enough, but she's supposedly penniless, and she's wearing Joe's Jeans? It doesn't make sense."

"Who's Joe?" Beau asked.

Paige gave him a wry smile. "It's a brand. A very expensive brand. Like a hundred and fifty a pair. And that gray sweater she had on looked like cashmere."

Riley shrugged. "So she's got money somewhere. So what?"

"Paige is right," Beau said. "If she had money, she'd have an ATM card like anyone else. She wouldn't have been holing up in our outbuilding with her kid."

"And what kind of mom doesn't know how to cook a simple meal?" Paige said.

"Or do a load of laundry," Aunt Trudy said.

Riley crossed his arms. "Lay off her. It's none of our business."

Beau studied his brother's face. He seemed awfully defensive of Kate. Was he developing feelings? She was a pretty woman with her pixie blond hair and delicate features. Those eyes, like molten caramel, could stop a man in his tracks.

"Just relax," Zac said. "Beau checked her references and did a background check, remember?"

"Umm . . . ," Beau said.

Zac sent him a look. "Are you kidding me? Captain Thorough forgot the background check?"

"We were in a time crunch, if you'll recall."

"Maybe it's like that movie *Safe Haven*," Paige said, meeting Beau's eyes.

Beau frowned, not following.

Paige's eyes drifted around the living room to blank stares. "The one based on the Nicholas Sparks book? The heroine was abused by her husband and ran from him, only to land in this small town where she met this guy . . ." She shot Beau a look, giving him an elbow. "You took me to see it."

"I might've taken a short nap."

She gave him a long look. "Anyway . . . she could be running from an abusive husband or something."

"I haven't seen any signs of abuse." Unfortunately, he'd had experience with that as deputy sheriff.

"And her son doesn't talk," Paige added. "That happens to kids sometimes when they go through trauma."

"Wonder what happened," Zac said.

"Stop picking on the girl," Aunt Trudy said. "Riley's right. It's none of our business."

"It is if it puts us in danger," Beau said. She was living with Paige, after all. What if Kate had gotten herself into some kind of trouble?

"Maybe it's one of those custody things," Paige said. "Maybe she ran off with Jack, and his dad doesn't know where he is."

"She wouldn't do that," Riley said.

Beau frowned at him. "You've known her four days."

"If it were my kid I'd be going crazy," Zac said.

"You'd be surprised what people will do under stress. But that doesn't explain why Jack doesn't talk. You said something traumatic."

"Maybe his dad did something to him, and that's why Kate ran off with him."

Zac finished off his Coke. "Maybe she's involved in something illegal. Maybe she's running from the law."

"Maybe you should just sit the girl down and get some answers out of her," Aunt Trudy said.

"Or maybe you should all just leave her alone. She's doing the best she can." Riley turned up the TV, and the noise of the halftime show filled the room.

Beau remembered the W-4 he'd asked her to fill out. Maybe Kate really had forgotten it the past few days. Or maybe she was hiding something. If she was, then pressing might scare her away. And despite what Kate might be involved in or running from, he didn't want any harm to come to her or Jack. Maybe he'd do a little checking of his own.

CHAPTER 10

The weather had been mild the past couple days, and Eden finally insisted on getting Miss Trudy out in her wheelchair. The woman scowled at the contraption, but Eden bribed her with a stop at the Knitting Nook. After the yarn shop, Eden and Micah took turns pushing her along the boardwalk. She seemed soothed by the sea breeze and fresh air. Poor lady had been cooped up way too long. No wonder she was so cranky.

The sun sparkled across the quiet harbor, and snow clung to the pine trees along the rocky shore. Looking at the beautiful sight, listening to the waves ripple against the shoreline, Eden could almost forget the people who wanted her son dead.

When they returned home Micah pulled Miss Trudy's crutches from the back of the Explorer and brought them to the woman. They'd probably kept her out too long. The sun had gone over the hills, ushering in dusk, and Miss Trudy seemed tired as she maneuvered herself from the vehicle.

Beau was home from work, and Eden realized she should've had supper in the oven by now, if not on the table. She reached out to give Miss Trudy a hand.

The woman shooed her away. "I can do it myself."

The sound of a distant engine carried on the cooling air. Probably someone checking out the tree farm. People often wandered back to the house, ignoring the Private Drive sign. The first few times had scared her.

Eden walked alongside Miss Trudy, ready to steady her. The car rumbled closer as they navigated the porch steps.

The porch light flickered on, and Beau appeared in the doorway. "Well, look at you, out and about."

"We took a stroll on the boardwalk," Eden said.

"She made me ride in a wheelchair like an invalid."

Beau's lips twitched as his eyes flickered off Eden and back to his aunt. "You look good. Got some color back in your cheeks."

"It's called frostbite."

The crescent in his cheek deepened. "Now, Aunt Trudy, it's almost fifty degrees." His eyes swung past them. "You brought company."

Eden looked over her shoulder. The car pulled to a stop behind the Explorer. A white car with a sheriff emblem emblazoned across the side.

Eden's heart stuttered. Her breaths grew shallow. No. They couldn't have found her.

"Oh good," Aunt Trudy said.

The engine went silent, and a man in a tan uniform exited the vehicle.

Eden turned toward the door. But Beau stood on the threshold, his palm planted on the frame, blocking the way. The sheriff was coming toward the house. His car trapped the Explorer. Oh, how she wished her old beater were sitting out front. There was no escape.

She pushed Micah behind her as the man approached the porch.

"Howdy, Beau." He removed his hat, revealing a bald head. "Trudy."

"Sheriff, how you doing?" Beau asked.

The man strode up the steps, seeming even larger as he neared. He was enormous, taller than Zac even, with imposing shoulders and sharp eyes. He had a fiery red mustache above his firmly set mouth.

Eden stepped back into the shadows, pushing Micah with her.

"Kate, this is Danny Colton. This is Kate Bennet and her son, Jack. They're helping out around here while Aunt Trudy recovers."

He nodded Eden's way, his hazel eyes drilling right through her. "Ma'am."

"Hello." The word felt squeezed from her throat as her son peeked from behind her leg.

"Jack's a little shy," Beau said.

"Haven't seen you around town," the sheriff said.

"I just got here."

"She's from away," Beau said. "Just passing through. Came along at just the right time."

"I should go start supper." Eden pushed Micah through the door, wedging past Beau, waiting for the sheriff to stop her. Her heart beat up into her throat, and her mouth went dry.

"Heard about your accident, Trudy," the sheriff was saying as Beau pulled the door. "Let me know if I can help in any way."

"I can take care of myself just fine."

Eden took Micah's hand, pulling him into the kitchen. She sank into a chair at the table and attempted to steady her heart rate.

Micah's wide brown eyes were fixed on her, filled with questions. She wet her lips. "Why don't you help me get a salad ready, kiddo. Go wash your hands, okay?"

He scampered off to the bathroom as Miss Trudy hobbled through the door.

Eden straightened. "You need help?"

"No, I do not." She shuffled straight through the kitchen and into her bedroom, muttering about something. The mattress squeaked as she lowered herself onto it.

Eden looked out the window toward the porch. She could see the men's shadows as they stood talking. Why was he here? Had news of her escape made it this far north? She hadn't found anything in the local papers, but maybe their pictures had been distributed to law enforcement. Maybe even now he was quizzing Beau about her.

. . .

"I got your message and was on my way home." Sheriff Colton offered Beau a mint. "Thought I'd just stop by."

Beau squelched his smile, turning down the mint. "Appreciate that."

The sheriff took any opportunity to catch a glimpse of his aunt. The man seemed to have a crush on her, but he moved at the rate of frozen molasses.

Beau tugged the door closed and lowered his voice.

"I was wondering if you could run a background check for me, off the record."

The sheriff's eyes sharpened as he popped a mint into his mouth. "Kate Bennet?"

"Some things seem a little off, and with her staying at Paige's . . ."

"You want to make sure she's on the up-and-up."

"I'm sure she'll check out." Even as he said it, Beau had a gut check. She'd seemed nervous at Colton's arrival. But then the sheriff was a pretty intimidating guy. And if she'd been abused like Paige thought . . .

"I'd never forgive myself if something happened to Paige or my family because I'd been careless."

"Say no more. Happy to help. What do you know about her?"

"Not much. Says she's from the south, and her dad lives in St. Louis, but that's not where she grew up."

"That it?"

"Not much to go on."

"Can you get me her soc?"

"Yeah, I'll see what I can do." If she ever turned in her W-4. "But in the meantime, see what you can find?"

"I'll do that. Might be a few days—you know how things get around the holidays."

"I remember."

The sheriff set his hat back on his head. "I should let you get back to your evening."

Beau pocketed his hands against the cold. "Stay for supper. I don't know what Kate's fixing, but it's bound to be better than that frozen meal you're getting ready to microwave."

The sheriff's eyes lit up like the Christmas tree in the town square. "Well, thanks, Beau. Don't mind if I do."

· · ·

Kate was frying up ground beef when she heard the door open in the other room.

"Kate, would you set an extra plate for Sheriff Colton?"

"Oh. Sure." Her heart skittered across her chest. He was staying for supper? He seemed too old to be a friend of Beau's. He was more Miss Trudy's age.

Micah tapped her arm, and she looked down to the bowl of torn lettuce. "Good job, kiddo." She cleared the quiver from her voice. "Can you wash the tomatoes?"

He moved to the sink and ran them one at a time under the cold water.

Twenty minutes later she set the steaming spaghetti on the table. With a little help from Prego, the sauce had turned out tasty, and she hadn't burned the garlic rolls. Amazing, since her nerves were becoming more frayed as the minutes ticked by.

They settled at the table. The sheriff took Riley's usual spot next to Miss Trudy—directly across from Eden. After prayer they passed the food and dug in.

"Trudy, how long will you be on crutches?" Sheriff Colton asked.

"Not a second longer than they make me."

"Must be hard this time of year."

"Kate's been a big help," Beau said. "With the season under way we couldn't have done it without her."

Her cheeks warmed. She'd had more failures than successes at this point.

The sheriff's gaze softened as he turned to Miss Trudy. "Are you in physical therapy?"

"Is that what they're calling it?"

"Look at her," Beau said. "She's already getting around well on her crutches."

"Whoop-de-doo."

Sheriff Colton twirled spaghetti around his fork. "Say what you like, but my aunt had a tibia fracture. Took her a piece longer than you to start getting around. You're a strong woman, Trudy."

Miss Trudy's cheeks flushed. Eden wouldn't have believed it if she hadn't seen it with her own eyes.

"Stubborn as an ox is more like it," Beau muttered for Eden's ears only.

Eden caught her lip between her teeth.

"How'd you end up in Summer Harbor, Kate?"

She froze. "Um, my car broke down."

"Eddie at the garage is building a new engine for her," Beau said.

The sheriff nodded thoughtfully, then turned his attention to Micah. "What about you, young man? You have a nice Thanksgiving break?"

Eden edged closer to her son. "Jack's not in school yet."

"You don't say. I figured you for six at least."

"He's only five. Can you pass the rolls, Miss Trudy?"

Eden's hand shook as she took the basket.

"How are you enjoying the town so far?" the sheriff asked Eden.

"It's very nice. Friendly people."

"She's hardly been out of the house except to drive me to torture and back."

"Well, you'll have to rectify that," he said. "Not the best time of year to visit, but we have our share of holiday traditions. Christmas by the Sea is coming up. That's always a good time."

"You should take the boy for a sleigh ride, Beau," Miss Trudy said. "Bet he'd like that. Bet they both would."

Her son's eyes swiveled with interest between Miss Trudy and Beau.

"He loves horses," Eden said, remembering the collection of plastic horses he'd had before their world had fallen apart.

"That settles it, then," Beau said. "We'll do it after hours one night this week. I'll introduce you to Mr. Bennington, Jack. He owns the stables next door and knows everything there is to know about horses."

Jack's eyes lit up, and he seemed to have forgotten about the food on his plate.

"That's awfully nice of you," Eden said.

Beau took a roll from the basket. "He's a great guy. Never had kids of his own, but he never minded me and my brothers coming around—and believe me, we were a handful."

"You stayed on the right side of the law, that's all that matters," Sheriff Colton said, then turned his knowing eyes her way. "You have any brothers or sisters, Kate?"

She cleared her throat. "No, I'm an only. I'll bet it was fun having brothers, though." She turned her eyes to Beau. "Always someone to play with."

"They were energetic and rowdy," Miss Trudy said. "Always wrestling around and poking at each other, squirming through church service."

"Now, Aunt Trudy, you know you loved every minute."

The woman humphed. "The whole of Summer Harbor knew your daddy had his hands full, even with my help."

"Where did you say you were from, Kate?" Sheriff Colton gave a tight smile.

She shifted in her chair. "Um, from the south mostly. Moved around a lot." She pushed Micah's plate closer. "Eat your salad, kiddo. Just a few bites."

"I thought I detected a bit of a Mississippi accent," Sheriff Colton said. "That's where my daddy's from."

Eden tried for a steady smile. "It's mostly faded, I think. We weren't there very long. Did you grow up in the area, Sheriff Colton?"

"Sure did, ma'am. Fine place to live."

"Got yourself in your own share of trouble, as I recall," Miss Trudy said.

"They went to high school together," Beau explained. "And don't let Miss Trudy fool you. Sheriff Colton kept his nose pretty clean from what I've heard."

"'Cause it was always buried in a book," Miss Trudy said.

"Well now, I'm either a troublemaker or a book nerd. You can't have it both ways."

"You're a talented man—you somehow managed both."

"Sheriff Colton was actually an athlete," Beau said. "He played for the Celtics for a while."

"Very briefly," the sheriff added. "I was plagued with a bad knee and forced to retire."

The conversation turned to old times, allowing Eden to finish her meal in peace. She breathed a sigh of relief a half hour later when the sheriff set his hat on his bald head and left.

By the time Eden had supper cleaned up, Miss Trudy had turned in for the night, the outing having worn her out. Beau set down the *Harbor Tides* when she entered the living room.

"Dinner was good, Kate."

"Thank you." A surge of pride washed over her. She didn't feel it necessary to give credit to Mr. Prego.

"Mind if I drive you to Paige's? I need to take Aunt Trudy's car in for some maintenance in the morning. Paige said she'd drop you on her way to church."

"Oh, sure, that's fine."

The sooner the better. After the stress of the sheriff's visit, she was ready to fall into bed.

CHAPTER 11

Eden bundled Micah up in his thrift-store coat, then slipped on her own. The cold seeped through the cheap fabric as she made her way to Beau's truck.

He opened her door, and Micah scooted into the middle. After Eden buckled him in, he laid his head on her arm. Apparently Miss Trudy wasn't the only one she'd worn out today.

A moment later the truck started with a rumble, and Beau backed out. "Thanks for getting Aunt Trudy out today. I know she grumbles, but she's not used to being so dependent. It's hard for her."

"I don't mind. I'd probably feel the same way."

She felt Beau's perusal in the dark cab and shifted.

"I highly doubt that. You never complain. I hope you didn't mind the extra company tonight."

If only he knew she'd been on pins and needles the entire meal. She'd hardly tasted a bite. "Riley wasn't there, so it all evened out, I guess."

"You might have to get used to it. Sheriff Colton comes around now and then to see my aunt."

"Miss Trudy has a suitor?"

Beau's deep chuckle was the most appealing sound

she'd heard in ages. It wrapped around her like a warm hug, and she found herself hoping to hear it again.

"Not exactly. He comes around, tries to flirt. They bicker back and forth for a while like a couple kids, and then he leaves."

"That's kind of cute."

"It would be if it hadn't been going on for so long. Now it's just getting pathetic."

She liked the idea of Miss Trudy having an admirer even as she wished it weren't the sheriff. "Has he asked her out?"

"I don't think so. The man can handle hardened criminals in his sleep, but sit him down across from my aunt, and his courage shrivels up like an old grape."

"You have to admit it's sweet."

He turned out onto the road, his lips curving. In the darkness of the cab, she was more aware of him. Of his masculine scent, his muscular build, his strong hands curled around the steering wheel.

"I thought he might make his move after my dad died. He came around a lot, checking on us, but . . ." He shrugged.

"You seem to know him well."

"I should. I was his deputy for two years."

Eden's breath froze in her lungs. How had she not known this? Only she would end up working for a former law enforcement officer!

"I-I didn't know."

"After my dad died I tried doing both jobs for a while, the deputy thing and the farm. It was manageable until the season neared. I had to make a decision."

"And you chose the farm."

He lifted a shoulder. "It's been in my family three generations. Aunt Trudy owns half and is dependent on the income it generates, such as it is."

And he chose his family over his own desires. She was starting to see a pattern. "How does it survive when it's so seasonal?"

"Christmastime is pretty lucrative, plus we make maple syrup in the spring. We get lots of school field trips and a few tourists. Dad talked for years about doing something in the autumn—hayrides, bonfires, that kind of thing, but he never got around to it. I'm going to implement those changes next year. Plus, I'm planning to sell wreaths and baskets through our website."

"I didn't know you had one."

"It's pretty basic. I'll have plenty to keep me busy over the winter when I'm not working on the pipeline or thinning the sugar bush."

Too bad she wouldn't be there longer. She could design one heck of a website for the farm. She wouldn't use the typical red and green. She'd use blue to suit Beau but tone it down a bit—the color of a shadow falling on the snow. She'd add a little white and silver to complete the look. The home-page photo would be of the main barn while snow was falling. And there'd be an events page, updated regularly, and a guest book for satisfied customers to sign.

"Do you miss being a deputy?" she asked.

"I do. Not that a whole lot ever happened around here. But I liked looking out for people. Even the ones who ended up in trouble—they had a story, and that mattered."

"What do you mean?"

He lowered one hand to his leg, driving with the other. "Like Mr. Flannigan. He gets arrested for drunk and disorderly practically every Saturday night. He lost his wife and kid in a boating accident a few years ago and blames himself. We lock him up for the night and release him the next day. It's more to keep him safe than anything else. Then there's Scott Lewis on the other side of town. He's eighteen. Gotten in more fights than you can count. His mom abandoned him here with his grandma when he was a kid. Never knew his dad. He's angry and needs to find a better release."

Their eyes aligned, his burning into hers for a long moment. She couldn't seem to break the hold of his gaze.

"People have reasons for the things they do." His voice was low and husky.

Afraid he'd see more than she wanted to reveal, Eden wrenched her eyes away. The shadowed landscape passed her window in a dark blur.

She'd have to be more careful with him. His experience as a deputy had no doubt made him suspicious and observant. She'd already given him a false city where her dad lived. It wouldn't take much to check that out. And the sheriff had picked up the remnants of her Mississippi accent.

She supposed the speech therapy Antonio had insisted on hadn't quite done the trick. She couldn't believe she'd gone to such lengths to please her husband. And for what? He hadn't loved her. Hadn't cared about her. He'd only wanted someone to control. Someone to have on his arm at hospital fund-raising events. And she'd blithely gone along. By the time she'd opened her eyes, it had been too late.

"Kate . . ." Beau's deep voice beckoned her from her thoughts.

Desperate to leave them behind, she met his gaze head-on and sensed she'd fallen right into a trap.

"Are you in some kind of trouble?"

Her heart stuttered even as she breathed a laugh. "What—what do you mean?"

She clasped her chilled hands together. They got cold when she lied, and lately they were cold a lot. She looked down at her son. His eyes were closed, his lips relaxed in sleep.

"If you're in some kind of trouble, maybe I can help. I have resources."

"*No.*" The very notion sent fear rippling through her.

She'd trusted the law to keep them safe once upon a time. She'd been naive and foolish. She'd let her guard down and put her son's life in danger. Never again.

She looked out the window and let the familiar words slip out. "We were just traveling and had some bad luck. That's all."

He slowed for a stop sign, then continued toward town. Silence hung heavily between them, thickening the air.

"You're not alone here, Kate."

He meant to reassure her, but alone was exactly what she wanted. Just her and Micah, totally free. The concept seemed like an elusive dream sometimes.

"Your family's been very kind. By Christmas I'll have my car fixed and a little extra socked away. Then Jack and I'll be on our way."

She felt his eyes on her, felt the burn on the back of her neck. He sighed softly.

She wasn't fooling anybody. She wished he'd press the gas pedal harder so she could escape those knowing eyes.

He said no more as they entered town and crawled through Paige's neighborhood. Micah stirred as they turned into the gravel drive.

She ran her hand through his soft curls. "We're here, kiddo."

Beau put the truck in park and helped Micah with his seat belt.

Paige's car wasn't in the drive. She was having a girls' night out with her coworkers and had told Eden she'd be late.

She opened the door, and Micah hopped down. "Thanks for the ride."

"Anytime. Hey, while we're here, why don't you grab your W-4 form."

Eden's heart sank. "Oh. Sure. I'll be right back."

She told Micah to find his pajamas while she grabbed the form from her nightstand drawer. She quickly filled it out, pausing at the line for her social security number. She closed her eyes, the pen hovering over the space.

Her heart in her throat, she jotted the correct numbers for the first three digits followed by six random numbers. She snapped up the paper and ran it out to Beau.

"Here you go." She handed it through the open window.

"Thanks. See you in the morning."

"See you."

Once the front door was shut behind her, the truck rumbled out of the drive. She gave Micah his bath and settled him in bed. After reading him three books, she tucked him in and kissed him good night.

"Love you, kiddo."

Once he was tucked in, she took her Debbie Macomber book into the living room and settled in the recliner. She hadn't started the novel yet. It seemed like enough just to have it. She ran her fingers over the cover.

A thump sounded outside, and she jumped. Voices followed, and she realized it was only the family next door returning home. She pulled the afghan around her until she was bundled like a cocoon.

Saturdays always made her extra jumpy, even all these months later. Every week she'd hoped Antonio would forget, but he never did. She remembered the last one like it was yesterday . . .

Her skin crawled as she slipped between the luxurious sheets. Maybe if she went to bed early he'd think she was sick. Heaven knew he wouldn't touch her if he suspected he might come in contact with a cold germ. He even avoided Micah if he had so much as a sniffle.

She flipped out the lamp and lay on her back, her heart thudding so hard the bed shook with it.

It's a small price to pay, she told herself for the

hundredth time. On the surface the words were true, but sometimes it seemed like Antonio wouldn't be happy until he had her soul.

She checked the time. 9:47.

He'd be downstairs right now, sipping his scotch while he finished the business section of the Miami Herald. In a few minutes the ice would tinkle loudly against the highball glass as he finished the last drop. Then she'd hear the tap of his shoes on the travertine, and the shower would kick on in the master bath.

She clutched the sheets against her satin pajamas, drew a breath in through her nose, and blew it out slowly over her drying lips. How had she ever thought Antonio was the answer to her problems?

She thought of her dad back in Hattiesburg, her heart aching to see him. Maybe his rules had been strict, but he loved her. She'd left the smothering nest of her father for the alluring promise of freedom.

Antonio had been wonderful at first. He'd swept into her life with his dreamy-smelling cologne, expensive suits, and attentive green eyes. She'd been caught up in the fairy tale, hardly able to believe someone of his stature would take notice of her. After the wedding he'd gradually become more controlling.

Bu it wasn't until she was pregnant with Micah, until she fought him over the nanny, then questioned the mysterious deposits into their banking account, that he'd begun shutting her out. That had been the end of normality and the beginning of the threats. Threats she knew Antonio had the money and power to carry out. If she wanted any part of her son's life, she was stuck in this nightmare.

"You won't go," he said sometimes. "No one else will want you." And other times he played on her fear of losing Micah. "If you leave, you'll never see him again. I'll make sure of it."

The walls began to feel as if they were closing in so tightly they pressed against her lungs. He began insisting she wear only muted colors—black, gray, brown—and they had to fit loosely. Skirts had to be to the knee, tops buttoned to her neck.

She began to feel so isolated. Antonio didn't like her old friends from Hattiesburg, and the shame of having to lie about her marriage prevented her from making new ones. She was alone. So very alone. She hosted formal dinner parties for his colleagues, and heaven help her if anything went wrong.

"Have you even read Proverbs 31?" he'd rail later. "This is your job, Eden. I'm not asking much." The rant would go on the rest of the night until she felt as small as a speck of dust.

She stilled as the haunting sounds of Antonio's footfalls reached her ears. She held her breath until the water kicked on. It would be a quick shower. He would emerge from the steamy room, reeking of Neroli Portofino soap, a smell that now only turned her stomach.

Her road to freedom had been set with a trap, and the bait that held her hostage was the little boy she loved more than life itself.

CHAPTER 12

The house was quiet with the family gone to church. Only Miss Trudy remained behind, and she was watching her favorite television pastor, her knitting needles clacking away.

Micah was building a Jenga tower on the kitchen table as Eden finished breakfast cleanup. She stifled a yawn as she hung the towel on the peg. A nightmare had woken her at three thirty, and she hadn't been able to go back to sleep. The dark cloud had hovered around her all morning, making her jumpy and irritable.

She'd lain in bed thinking of her dad, missing him. She'd bought a disposable phone on a whim last week. She knew she couldn't call him. Marshals Walter and Brown had drilled that into her the first weeks at the safe house. She couldn't contact anyone. Not her dad, not her old friends. It would only put their lives in danger. Put all of their lives in danger.

The thought of her dad worrying about them made her heart squeeze tight. It wasn't fair. Look what she'd done.

I'm sorry, Daddy. She rubbed the spot over her aching heart. *I miss you so much.*

She missed his sturdy hugs, his rugged laugh, his warbly voice. What she'd give just to hear it again. Was he okay? Had the stress of her situation caused health problems? What if he'd had another heart attack? What if he'd died? Would the marshals even have let her know?

Anxiety zipped through her veins like electricity, lighting up every worry zone in her body. The phone burned a hole in her pocket.

No, Eden. You can't.

She looked at the kitchen clock. He'd be at church right now, if all was well. He'd always gone, despite his phobia, coming in late and sitting in the back pew.

But what if all isn't well? What if he's ill? Ill and alone because of your stupid mistakes? Or what if Antonio's "friends" had paid her dad a visit? Had tried to extract their whereabouts after they'd run? Why hadn't she thought of that until now? She'd been so busy trying to keep Micah safe, she'd forgotten about her father.

She glanced at Micah, still mesmerized by his Jenga tower, and slipped out the back door before she could second-guess herself.

He wasn't home, she reassured herself. It was a disposable phone—untraceable. She wouldn't talk to him. Only listen to his voicemail. She needed to hear his voice. She'd hang up before it cut off, and no one would be any the wiser.

She huddled against the cold on the back stoop, her fingers trembling as she pushed in the familiar numbers. Her pulse jumped, racing ahead of her shallow breaths. She lifted the phone to her ear and waited.

It rang once. The thought of those men getting hold of her dad tightened an invisible cord around her neck, sucked the moisture from her mouth.

The phone clicked. Her dad's voice filled her ear. She listened to the message, her eyes stinging at his familiar inflections. His Southern accent sounded heavier than she remembered, his tone warmer. Her eyes filled, and she blinked back the tears. The message was winding down, and she had to hang up before the beep sounded.

She waited until the very last moment and disconnected. She kept the phone to her ear as if she could hold him there for just a few more seconds.

"I miss you, Daddy," she whispered. "I love you. We're safe. Don't worry about us. Be careful."

Her breath vaporized before her, disappearing as quickly as a wish on the wind.

· · ·

Eden slid into her coat. She was ready for her afternoon off, eager for some quality time with Micah. And she was desperately in need of a nap—if she could get her son to cooperate.

"Hey, Kate," Beau said as he exited the kitchen. "Can you help me with something before you leave?"

He looked like he was fresh out of a J.Crew catalog, in his plaid button-down and fitted khakis. The Callahans sure weren't hard on the eyes.

"Um, yeah." She started to take off her coat.

"Leave it on. I need you outside."

"You both can't leave," Miss Trudy said. "Who's going to babysit me?"

Beau put his hand on Eden's son's shoulder. "Jack, you up for the challenge?"

He looked up at Beau and nodded solemnly even while Miss Trudy scowled.

Beau winked at his aunt. "There you go. Problem solved."

They scuttled out the front door before she could complain.

"That was ornery." Eden followed him around the house.

"Ornery's my middle name."

Her shoes made tracks in the few inches of snow. "Where are we going?"

"To the barn. There's something I think Jack might like, but I wanted to check with you first."

The barn was a short walk from the house. She had yet to step foot inside it. The door opened with a squeak, and a musty smell filled her nostrils. The shadowed, dank building wasn't a place she wanted to spend any time. She sneezed at the dust their feet scuffled up.

Something about the atmosphere dredged up the nightmare from the night before. Was it the smell? The darkened interior? The male body so near to hers?

She stopped when Beau did, trying to shake the dark feeling that had come over her.

"There's a sled right up here," Beau said, reaching up on a high wooden ledge. He pulled something forward. Boxes tipped to the side as he worked to free the object.

"I guess it's been awhile. It's wedged under a bunch

of crap. No telling what all's up there. My dad was kind of a pack rat."

She reached up to help, catching hold of a red runner as he tried to clear the boxes away. It was almost free. She tugged on the runner, and it came loose easily. She stumbled backward. A large box fell with it, and Beau batted it away from his head, letting loose of the sled.

Its weight fell toward her, and she pushed it aside as she went down. Beau reached for her, but it was too late.

She landed with a hard thud on the wood floor, Beau following a millisecond later, sprawling over her, his hands landing beside her shoulders, his weight pressing down on her.

She blinked at the ceiling, her breaths ragged, as she assessed the damage. Her back had taken the brunt of the fall.

Beau leaned away, his sharpened gaze on her face. "You okay? Did you hit your head?"

His body felt like a thousand-pound weight pinning her down. Her arms were trapped against her body. Suddenly it was Antonio's body pressing against her. His greedy hands touching her in ways that turned her stomach.

Panic flooded through her, and hysteria built inside. She pushed against his weight. "Get off. Get off me!"

Beau rolled to the side.

Eden scrambled across the floor crab-style until she hit the sled. Her breaths plumed in the cold shed, her heart beating out a frantic rhythm. Beau's eyes fixed on hers, recognition dawning in the shadowed depths.

. . .

Beau didn't know exactly what he'd done wrong, but he felt like all kinds of jerk. The past few seconds rewound in his head to the panic that had burned in Kate's eyes in that instant before she'd pushed him away. Something had happened. Something more than a clumsy fall.

Her chest rose and fell quickly as she scrambled to her feet.

He rose, too, moving warily. "I'm sorry. Are you okay?"

She backed away, not meeting his gaze. "I-I'm fine. I have to go."

"Kate . . ."

But she was already rushing toward the door and through the snow. He watched her go, wondering what the heck had just happened.

CHAPTER 13

Eden's heart sped up at the sound of the doorbell the next evening. She left Micah in their room drawing on an Etch A Sketch and went to answer Paige's door. After peeking through the sidelight, she opened the door.

Beau wore a striped button-down under his L.L.Bean jacket. His hair was wind tousled, and he smelled like heaven.

This morning she'd woken feeling like an idiot for her reaction in the barn. She'd planned on a full day before having to face him again.

"Come on in." She moved aside, careful to give him a wide berth. "Paige got stuck at work. She'll be here in a few minutes. She tried to call."

"Ah. I left my phone charging at home."

They stood for a beat, awkwardness swirling around them like snow flurries caught in an updraft. She shifted her bare feet on the cold wood floor. She'd tuned Paige's TV to a station that played Christmas carols, and the playful melody of "Baby, It's Cold Outside" filtered through the room.

She felt stupid offering him a seat or a cup of coffee.

He'd probably spent more hours here than she. The sun had set, and only the hall light filtered into the living room.

She flipped on the light as he unzipped his jacket.

"Would you like—"

"About last night . . ."

They spoke at the same time.

Eden gave a wry huff. "That's starting to become our phrase." Her smile wobbled on her lips when he failed to respond to her attempt at levity.

"Maybe it's just as well Paige is late. I think we should talk."

"Listen." Eden tried for a smile, dodging his knowing eyes. "I was just feeling spooked last night. I had a nightmare the night before, and the barn was all dark and creepy, and I got caught off guard when you—"

"Is it your husband?"

Her eyes darted to his, her fake smile falling away. She swallowed hard. "What?"

"I'm sorry to be so blunt, but after the way you reacted—" He straightened his shoulders, an action that made him even taller. He pinned her with a look, and she couldn't drag her eyes away.

"I have Paige, my family, to think about, and you haven't exactly been an open book."

"I'm a private person."

"You didn't answer my question. Are you running from your husband?"

She moved toward the divider between the living room and dining room, putting space between them. She had to allay his suspicions or he'd go snooping into her past. She leaned against the wall and saw that he had followed, seeming to shrink the space in half.

"You don't have to worry about my husband," she said. "He's—he's dead."

Beau's eyes sharpened even as his head tipped back a fraction of an inch.

"And no, I didn't do it."

"That's not what I was—" He pressed his lips together. "Okay, maybe it was." He gave her a sheepish look. "Blame my law enforcement background. I'm sorry for your loss."

Truthfully, his death had only been a loss for her son, but she had a feeling Beau already knew that. "Thank you."

She looked toward the stairs, wishing for the buffer of her son, needing to escape Beau's questions, his scrutiny.

She pushed off the wall. "I should go check on Jack. I'm sure Paige'll be here any—"

He caught her arm gently as she passed. "We're not finished with—"

The front door flew open. "Sorry I'm—" Paige's eyes toggled from Beau to Eden, then fell to his hand, still on Eden's arm.

Beau's hand fell away. "Hi, hon. Get caught up with an emergency?"

Paige's expression shifted. "Um, yeah. That and some paperwork. I tried to call."

"I have to check on Jack." Eden tried for a smile, relieved for the chance to escape. "You guys have a good time," she said before beating it up the stairs.

. . .

They made it all the way to the corner booth of The Wharf before Paige broached the subject. They'd already covered her workday and Beau's day off, which had consisted of restocking the cut trees and finishing some accounting for the farm he'd been putting off.

It had been at least a month since he'd taken her out. He'd been so busy getting the farm up and going, and she'd been so swamped at the pet shelter. They'd made do with suppers at the farmhouse and impromptu Roadhouse gatherings. Still . . . a month. He deserved the Worst Boyfriend Award.

"So," Paige said, raising the menu. "It looked like you and Kate were in the middle of an intense conversation when I walked in."

Paige perused the menu as if nothing was amiss, but he'd have to be stupid to miss the carefully casual expression on her face.

"I think you're right about her. Something's off. I asked Sheriff Colton to check her out. He has her soc number, so hopefully we'll know something soon." He also suspected the sheriff would check her plates at the garage.

He didn't tell Paige that all three of Kate's references had been wrong numbers. Then he wondered why he withheld the information.

"That's good. Have you asked her point-blank if she's in some kind of trouble?"

"I have. Not that I've gotten much of an answer. She

admitted that her husband passed, so that eliminates that theory."

"If she's telling the truth."

"I'm pretty sure she was." Being a deputy had made him good at reading people. Or maybe he just wanted to believe her.

"But she's still evasive?"

"Very much so."

The server returned and took their orders and their menus, leaving nothing but a flickering candle between them.

"It could take awhile for Sheriff Colton to work his magic," Paige said. "And even if she is hiding something, you may not learn anything relevant, not if there's nothing on the record."

It wasn't a new thought. "I know."

Her blue eyes softened in the candlelight. "Beau . . . maybe you should just let her go. Aunt Trudy's getting around pretty well now, and maybe we can work out some kind of ride arrangement for her therapy appointments."

The thought of turning Kate and Jack loose with so little didn't sit well with him. He suspected now more than ever that she was in over her head with something, and it wasn't his nature to let her fend for herself. She didn't even have the money to get her car fixed yet.

But it wasn't fair to Paige to have a stranger potentially jeopardizing her safety. He wasn't crazy about that himself.

"Maybe we should move her out to the farmhouse.

Aunt Trudy's room upstairs is—What?" he asked at the sudden shift of emotion on Paige's face.

"It's not your job to protect her, Beau." Her voice was firm.

"I'm trying to protect *you*. Aunt Trudy's nowhere near ready to take over the house again, and her therapy takes time. Not just the appointments, but the stuff she does at home."

She studied him until he felt as if he were under a microscope. He had no reason to feel guilty. He hadn't done anything wrong.

But if he were gut-level honest, he was more aware of Kate than he should be. And as much as he'd like to chalk that up to his investigative tendencies, he knew deep down it was more than that. He didn't have feelings for her—just an attraction. But that was normal, right? She was a pretty woman, and he was a healthy young male.

"What's your gut telling you?" she asked.

For a moment he thought Paige had read his mind. Then he realized she was talking about Kate's past.

"I think she's running from something. But that doesn't mean she's in danger. People run from all kinds of things."

"But it doesn't mean she's *not* in danger. What did she say tonight? She seemed kind of frazzled."

Beau leaned back in the booth. "Something happened last night. We were in the barn, and she got kind of spooked. We were trying to get the sled down, and I ended up falling on her. She freaked out and starting pushing me off, and then—"

"Wait. You were on *top* of her . . . ?"

His gaze hardened. "You're missing the point."

Was it just him, or did it seem like Paige was reading into things? Maybe his conscience was giving off guilty vibes. She wasn't the jealous type—at least he didn't think so. They hadn't been a couple all that long, and frankly, she'd had no reason to be jealous.

Not that she did now.

"There's nothing to be jealous about."

"I'm not jealous."

"You know how I feel about you." Maybe they hadn't exchanged "I love yous" yet, but he'd come close to saying it. And he was pretty sure she was only waiting for him. He wasn't sure what held him back.

He didn't want Kate coming between them, even if it was only in Paige's mind. "I actually think Riley might like her."

She scoffed. "She's totally wrong for him."

Beau shrugged. "Well, he's pretty defensive of her. And I've walked in on them talking a couple times. They stopped when I came in like I'd interrupted something."

She shook her head. "He was probably fishing for information, like you."

"I don't think so."

"Well . . . he's leaving soon anyway." Sadness settled over her features at the acknowledgment. Her shoulders slumped as she picked at her napkin.

Awhile later their food arrived, a welcome interruption. Paige gave Beau a thin smile over the steaming seafood platters. So much for their night out. The date had been hijacked by people who weren't even in the room.

CHAPTER 14

"Time to put the toys away, Jack," Eden said.

Eager for the promised sleigh ride, Jack couldn't move fast enough. While he scrambled for Legos, she stopped by the Christmas tree to retrieve a fallen ornament. She hung the paper angel on a high branch, smiling at the crayon face one of the Callahan brothers had no doubt drawn in some elementary school class.

She remembered the Christmas trees they'd had when she was married to Antonio. He'd hired a decorator to come in every year. The enormous artificial tree gleamed with extravagant ribbons and rich burgundy and gold ornaments, probably hand-painted in some exotic country.

She preferred this look, she thought, standing back to survey her handiwork. The smell of pine in the air. Memories attached to each ornament. Maybe they weren't her memories, but they meant something to someone.

The front door opened and Beau stuck his head in. "Ready?"

"We'll be right out," she said.

Eden helped Micah with the rest of the Legos, then told Miss Trudy they'd be back soon.

They met Beau in the front yard, where he waited with a red sleigh and two horses, one white and one black. The sun had set, and the darkening sky was swathed in pinks and purples.

The black horse nuzzled the palm of Beau's hand.

He smiled at Micah as they approached. "Jack, come meet Salt and Pepper, our escorts for the evening."

"They're beautiful," Eden said.

Micah held his hands up to Beau, and Eden almost gasped. Without hesitation Beau scooped her son into his arms and began showing Micah how Pepper liked his nose stroked.

She watched in wonder as Micah boldly followed his direction. He hadn't reached out to anyone but her since his dad was killed. Not even Walter, and they'd had ten months to bond. Maybe he was finally beginning to heal. Maybe he'd be okay someday. Maybe they both would. She had to believe that.

"Want to give Pepper a treat?" Beau pulled a handful of carrot sticks from his coat pocket.

Micah wrinkled up his nose, and Beau laughed. "Believe it or not, Pepper considers carrots a treat."

Eden watched Micah feed Pepper the carrots, then Beau let him give Salt peppermint candies.

Beau popped one into his own mouth, and Micah smiled as he followed suit.

"All right, now they're ready to work. Want to ride in the front seat with me or the back with your mom?"

Micah pointed to the front, where he could be closer to the horses, and Beau set him in the red sleigh while Eden climbed in behind them. Beau tucked a blanket around Micah, then handed her a thick blanket and helped tuck it around her as well.

He smiled up at her. "Warm and cozy?"

"Surprisingly, yes. What's this thing made of?"

"Magic." He winked.

The sled rocked as he climbed up beside Micah and snapped the reins. "Here we go."

The bells around the horses' necks jingled as Beau guided them toward the lit trail that wove through the pine forest. The sleigh's runners shushed through the snow.

Beau chattered to Micah about the horses, but most of it was lost on the wind. Eden tucked her hands under the blanket, reveling in the smile that bloomed on Micah's face. He'd had precious little to smile about lately. Her eyes flittered to Beau, and her heart squeezed at his kindness.

God, please. I want Micah to have more moments like this. I want him to know life can be good again. Help me to be able to give him that.

As they entered the forest, the trees sheltered them from the wind, and the heavy scent of pine saturated the air. She snuggled into the cushioned bench and watched the landscape pass.

Awhile later, Micah startled her when he shot up straight in his seat, pointing to the right. Eden's heart nearly burst out of her chest until she saw four deer pawing through the snow.

One of them looked up, and seconds later they scampered away, disappearing among the pine trees.

"Good eye, Jack. They like to feed on the spruce and fir twigs in the winter. Sometimes they damage the smaller trees, and we have to put out repellent. Have you seen a moose yet?"

Micah shook his head, looking up at Beau with wonder.

"Stick around long enough, and you will." He launched into a story about a bull moose that lived on their property when he and his brothers were little.

Eden was content to let Beau carry the conversation. He handled Micah's muteness well, asking questions, content with a nod or a shake of his head. And he talked about things that would interest a young boy. Her son hung on to every word.

Before long they'd meandered through the whole farm and circled back to the house. Darkness had fallen, but the porch light spilled across the yard.

"Whoa." Beau pulled back on the reins, and the sleigh came to a stop. He climbed off and lifted Micah down, then extended a hand to Eden.

She slipped her gloved hand in his and stepped down. "Thank you so much." Beau dropped her hand as Micah tugged on her coat. "Jack says thank you too."

"No problem." That smile, directed at her, made her knees a little wobbly.

He turned to Micah, ruffling his hair. "Get some rest. See you in the morning."

. . .

Beau popped in his earbuds and started his country playlist. The upbeat rhythm of "Ready Set Roll" came on, breaking the stillness of the morning.

Set for music, he slit the twine on the Frasier fir and leaned it against the wooden rack. The farm didn't open for a couple hours, but he had plenty to do. The cut tree lot had been picked through, and they'd gotten a fresh load of trees this morning. This was usually Riley's job, but Beau had needed to get out of the house.

Things had been strained between him and Paige since their date two nights ago. They'd sent a few short texts, but his one call to her had gone to voicemail. He knew she was upset over Riley leaving soon, and he hated that he'd added to her stress.

On top of that, he kept thinking about Kate. It had felt good the other night to take her and Jack out for a sleigh ride. Just seeing the boy's smile had been reward enough, but when Kate had looked up to him, gratitude shimmering in her honey-brown eyes, he felt like he'd just hung the moon.

He kept seeing that look when he closed his eyes at night, kept remembering the feel of her gloved hand in his as he'd assisted her from the sleigh. And then he'd push the memory from his mind and chide himself for thinking of her at all when he already had a wonderful girl.

What was wrong with him?

The sound of an engine purred over the music, and he looked up to see Sheriff Colton's patrol car approaching. Snow crunched under the tires as he pulled into the lot.

Beau sheathed his knife and pulled his earbuds, meeting Colton as he got out of his car. "Morning, Sheriff."

"Beau, you're out early. Thought I'd catch you still at the house."

Hoped, was more like. "I'm sure Aunt Trudy's up and about if you want to stop by and say hi."

The sheriff shifted, his cheeks going ruddy, as he gestured inside the car. "Well, I did bring some dough-nuts for the family."

Beau's lips twitched. "Nice of you. Got a custard in there?"

"You know it."

He grabbed the box and let Beau help himself to the chocolate iced custard. They used to stop by the Sugar Shack on a regular basis for their favorite doughnuts and a tall cup of java.

Beau bit into the tasty confection. He didn't mind being a cliché if it tasted like this.

"How's the new deputy?" he asked.

The sheriff scowled, his red mustache twitching. "He's no Beau Callahan, that's all I can say."

"I heard he gave Pastor Daniels a ticket for jay-walking."

"Yep."

"And Alma Walker a ticket for doing 37 in a 35."

"He's a regular Barney Fife."

Beau chuckled. Alma was eighty if she was a day, and it had been her first ticket. "She was pretty riled up about it. Gave me an earful at Frumpy Joe's."

Colton scowled. "You got nothing. She read me the

riot act over the phone for twenty minutes. What am I supposed to do? I can't undermine my deputy, and she *was* breaking the law. Technically."

"He'll settle in. He's just a smidgen overeager."

"Well, I hope he calms it down before I have a town riot on my hands." He shook his head. "Pastor Daniels . . ."

"Well, let me know if I can help." Beau took the last bite and licked the chocolate off his index finger. He wished he had a nice cup of hot coffee to wash the doughnut down with.

The sheriff leaned against the car, crossing his burly arms. "So I looked into that housekeeper of yours."

Beau swallowed the bite. "And . . . ?"

"Unless your Kate Bennet is really Arnold William Davis and a plumber from Topeka, Kansas, she gave you a false soc number."

All the breath left Beau's lungs. "Well, rats. I was afraid of that." She *was* hiding something, and it couldn't be anything good. "Maybe it was an accident," he said halfheartedly.

"I think we both know better. I ran her plates, and they belong to a James Edward Boyd of Augusta, Georgia. I could run a search on her name, but I highly doubt she's using her real one. There's always fingerprints, but unless she's in the system . . ."

"True."

"You could always snoop around her things. She's got to have a driver's license, a birth certificate for her kid . . . something."

Beau shook his head. "Everything she had was stolen when she got to town."

The sheriff's eyes sharpened. "Why didn't I hear about this?"

Beau stuffed his hands in his pockets. "She didn't report it."

"Pretty much tells you all you need to know, don't you think?"

"Not necessarily."

The sheriff cut him a look.

So he was being defensive. Seemed he and Riley had something in common besides their taste for buffalo wings.

"She's either running from the law or she's hiding from someone. A set of fingerprints might narrow it down."

Beau rubbed his neck. And what if she was guilty of some crime? He didn't think Kate was capable of anything heinous, not unless she was protecting herself or Jack. And he couldn't stand the thought of bringing more trouble on her. What would happen to her son? They didn't seem to have anyone they could count on.

The sheriff reached for his door handle. "Well, you think on it and let me know."

"Will do. Thanks for your help."

A minute later Beau watched the patrol car ease down the lane and wondered what he'd gotten himself into with Kate.

Kate. Was that even her real name? Maybe it was. Maybe she'd only used a false soc number to throw the government off her trail.

If it was her real name, he knew who could dig a little deeper into her past.

He pulled his cell from his pocket and dialed as he entered the shelter of the barn.

Abby picked up on the second ring. "Hey, Beau. Good to hear from you."

"How's married life treating you, cuz?"

Abby had remarried Ryan McKinley after they'd visited Summer Harbor several months ago. They'd spent the weekend pretending to still be married for her parents' benefit, and apparently the pretense had rekindled their feelings. They lived in Chapel Springs, Indiana, now.

"Couldn't be better. My agency's up and running, and Ryan's school year is going great. They had a pretty good football season."

Beau paced across the pine-needle-strewn floor. "I heard. Ryan sent me a pic when they won regionals."

"Yeah, he was stoked. We hoped they'd win state, but maybe next year. So . . . I'll bet you're crazy busy with the farm. I heard you got a bunch of snow recently."

"That's winter in New England. But, yeah, the farm's doing great."

"How are Riley and Zac? They never call. Tell them they're deadbeat cousins."

Beau smiled. "They're helping out here as much as they can, and Zac's got his hands full with the Roadhouse."

"I can't believe that woman ditched him like that."

"He's still pretty heartbroken." Beau had wanted to wring Lucy's neck a hundred times for the heartache she'd left behind.

"Did he ever get any answers?"

"Not really. He's trying to move on."

"What about Riley? What's going on with him?"

"I guess you haven't heard . . . He enlisted. He's headed off for boot camp in a few weeks."

"I'll be darned. I can't believe it. Coast Guard?"

"Marines."

"That's right. He used to talk about it."

"It was a real shock, to be honest, and I'm still not keen on the idea. I mean, why now? Right after losing Dad and everything?"

Abby was quiet for a beat too long.

"What?"

"He's a big boy, Beau. He can take care of himself. Maybe he just needs to stand on his own two feet, be his own man, you know? There in Summer Harbor, he'll always just be the baby Callahan brother."

"Maybe you're right. I still don't like it."

Beau caught her up on Aunt Trudy, who wasn't Abby's aunt since Abby was his cousin from his mom's side. Once they finished with small talk, he brought up the reason for his call.

"I was wondering if I could get your help with something. If I wanted to look someone up—do a little digging—how would I go about it?"

"You'd give me the name and everything you know about this person and let me do my PI thing."

"I'll pay you for your time."

"How about you send me a couple fresh lobsters, and we'll call it even."

"You don't even like lobster."

"Well, Ryan does, and I like to keep my man happy."

"Done." He filled her in on everything he knew about Kate. She tapped away on her keyboard as he talked.

"That's not much to go on," she said when he finished. "Do you have her soc number . . . a birthday or address . . . anything?"

"Sorry, that's all I got."

"Who is she, anyway, if you don't mind my asking?"

"That's what you're supposed to find out."

"Funny guy. You know what I mean."

"I hired her to be Aunt Trudy's caretaker while she's recovering. Honestly, I'm not even sure she's given me her real name."

"She's not staying there, is she?"

"No . . . She's staying at Paige's."

"Beau . . . if she's raising suspicions, and clearly she is, why is she staying at your girlfriend's house?"

He was starting to wonder the same thing. "She might be hiding something, but my gut says she's not dangerous."

"Well, I trust your gut, but that doesn't mean she's not *in* danger. And if she's in danger that puts Paige in danger."

"I know, I know." How could he have let this happen? "I'd feel better about moving her into the farmhouse, but Paige wasn't too crazy about the idea."

"I take it Kate Bennet is young and attractive?" There was a smile in Abby's voice.

"You said it, not me."

Abby laughed. "Well, you could always fire her."

Beau stopped pacing and looked up at the rafters, heaving a sigh.

"Let me guess, you don't have the heart to put her out on the street."

"Just do your PI thing and leave my heart out of it."

"Such a softie. Don't worry, I won't tell anyone."

A few minutes later Beau hung up the phone. How was he going to get Kate out of Paige's house and into the farmhouse?

CHAPTER 15

"What are you doing?" Beau's voice was full of reproach.

Eden turned from the sink as he entered the kitchen, studying his face for signs of displeasure.

She relaxed at the sight of his playful grimace. "Um, the dishes?"

He wore a black Henley, worn jeans, and a day's scruff. He'd lost his shoes after church, and one of his toes poked through a hole. Antonio would never have stood for that.

"I told you to leave them," he said. "You're officially off the clock."

"I don't mind."

"Well, I do." He snatched the dish towel from the peg and took the clean bowl from her hand.

Eden reached into the water and came up with a plate.

They'd invited her and Micah to stay for the Patriots game. She'd watched the Saints with her dad, and he'd taught her the game. But Micah hadn't watched football before. It was only half time, and her boy was already fully engaged. It was good for him to have some guy time.

Paige had to leave after lunch to work on her float for the parade, and Beau had promised Eden a ride back after the game. She had to admit it was fun observing the guys as they watched. Riley darted to his feet at every bad call, shouting at the referees. Beau leaned forward in his seat, his elbows digging into his knees at the critical points, then fell back against the sofa when the moment passed. Zac wrung his big hands.

Miss Trudy pretended not to care at all, but her needles paused every time the Pats entered the red zone.

"You all take your football pretty seriously. I thought Riley was going to have a coronary at the horse-collar call. Though it *was* bogus."

"You know football?"

"Well enough." She handed him the plate.

"Does Jack play any sports?"

"Not on a team, no. He used to played soccer with his friends. He seems to like watching football, though."

"He's catching on fast."

Kate angled a look his way. "How can you tell?"

Beau smirked. "He's nervous at all the right times."

"He fits right in around here then."

She scrubbed at a spot on the next plate, gave it a thorough wash, then rinsed it under the faucet.

"So, Kate . . . I was thinking that maybe it would make more sense if you and Jack moved in here at the farmhouse. Aunt Trudy's room upstairs is empty, and that way you wouldn't have to shuttle back and forth every day."

Something inside plummeted. Had she gotten on Paige's nerves? She tried to clean up after herself, and Micah hadn't had many nightmares. She tried to quiet him as quickly as possible when he did.

Even so, she'd sensed a distance in Paige since the night she'd come home in the middle of Eden's conversation with Beau.

"I guess we've kind of intruded on Paige's space. I hope she's not upset with me."

Beau's dish towel paused midswipe. "No. No, it's not that at all."

"Then what is it?"

His lips parted, then closed.

She hadn't noticed how close he was standing. But now that she had, she could smell the scent of his cologne over the lemony fragrance of the dish soap and see the lighter flecks of brown in his eyes.

"Look, I'm going to be honest. You've given me reason to believe you're in some kind of trouble—"

She started to speak.

He held up his hand. "I know you want to keep your past to yourself. But I'm not comfortable with you at Paige's when I don't know what's going on. And if my gut's right, and you are running from something or someone, you and Jack'll be safer here."

He was right. Her breath eased out in a rush. She'd done her best to cover her trail, but these weren't amateurs she was running from. She had been putting Paige in harm's way. And even if she moved into the farmhouse, she was potentially endangering Miss

Trudy, not to mention Beau and Riley. And after they'd been nothing but kind to her.

She felt a pinch in her chest, and her breath seemed stuffed into her lungs. "Maybe we should just go." She didn't have enough money yet to pay for the repairs on her car, but maybe Eddie would take installments.

Beau set his hand on her arm, and it was as if the barrier of her cotton shirt didn't exist. Every cell there flared to life. The skin beneath his hand burned and tingled. Their eyes aligned, and she could see he felt it, too, in the way his expression shifted.

His hand fell away. "Please don't. We need you. And I wouldn't feel right sending the two of you off on your own. Not when I can protect you."

Her spirit balked at that notion. "I can take care of us just fine. Maybe I wasn't doing such a good job of it when you found us, but I've got some money saved now."

"Aunt Trudy needs you. And I think having Jack around has kept her mind off her injury. I don't want you to go." Something flashed in his eyes, but it was gone in an instant.

Zac burst through the kitchen door. "Dude, I thought you were getting the crab dip."

"Get your own dip. I'm helping with the dishes."

Zac opened the fridge as Miss Trudy hobbled in on crutches. "What's a woman got to do to get a drink around here?"

"Sorry, Aunt Trudy," Beau said over his shoulder. "Got distracted."

She looked between Beau and Eden. "I see that." Her eyes swung toward the ceiling above them. "I also see you're standing under the mistletoe."

Eden looked up, and sure enough . . . a sprig of mistletoe dangled from a hook above the sink.

Her eyes flitted off Beau, her face warming. "I didn't hang it there."

Beau tossed a sour look at his brother's back. "Zac's just being cute. It's a game we used to play with our parents when we were little."

Zac shut the fridge door, smirking. "Nah. I just wanted to catch Paige unaware."

Beau threw the towel at Zac, hitting the back of his head as he scooted out the door.

"Like you ever do the dishes," Beau called after him.

His gaze bounced off Eden as he pulled another dish towel from the drawer and took the wet plate she'd been holding suspended in midair.

"Well, boy," Miss Trudy said, "don't be rude. Give the lady a kiss."

Beau narrowed his eyes at his aunt. "*You* moved it."

Miss Trudy sniffed as she shuffled to the fridge. "I need a little entertainment around here. So sue me." She withdrew a bottled water from the fridge and cracked open the lid, leaning on her crutches.

After taking a swig and replacing the lid, she gave Beau a long, dark look. Apparently Miss Trudy wasn't leaving until she got her way.

Beau must have reached the same conclusion.

"Fine." He turned to Eden and gave her a sheepish look.

Her eyes settled on his lips. How had she not noticed how beautiful they were? Curvy on top and lush on the bottom. Lips so perfect God must have come down and sculpted them personally.

He leaned in and set a kiss on her cheek.

Except she miscalculated and turned her head just the tiniest bit. His lips landed on the corner of hers, soft and gentle.

Her pulse skittered like marbles across a hardwood floor. His breath fanned her cheek as he slowly withdrew. His eyes aligned with hers, holding her transfixed. Something flickered there, something that sent a low hum buzzing through her veins.

Then he blinked, his lids like shutters, slamming down over his eyes. He returned his attention to the plate he was drying.

Eden turned to see the tip of Miss Trudy's crutches swinging out the door.

Beau cleared his throat. "She gets ornery when she's bored." His voice was thick and husky.

"I'll keep that in mind."

Moments later he dried the last dish and returned to the living room. But Eden's heart still raced when she joined the family well into the third quarter.

• • •

He shouldn't have done that.

That had been his mantra for the last quarter of the game. A game he was barely even following anymore. He was more aware of Eden's leg ticking back and forth a few feet away than he was of which yard line the Pats were on.

It was just an innocent kiss. A mistletoe kiss. A kiss on the cheek. Like kissing his cousin Abby.

But it hadn't really been like any of those things, because he'd caught the corner of Kate's mouth, making it just shy of really wrong. And—let's get real—kissing Kate hadn't been anything like pecking his cousin on the cheek.

"Come on, man!" Riley said, jumping to his feet. "Do you believe that?"

Beau zoomed in on the TV, trying to figure out what was going on. A possible interception, apparently.

"Sit down before you spill your Coke," Aunt Trudy said.

Riley slowly sank to the edge of the recliner, his eyes glued to the screen.

"It hit the ground," Zac said.

Riley shook his head. "No, it didn't."

Beau's eyes swung to Kate for the dozenth time since she'd rejoined them. But this time her eyes were on him. Caught, he turned back to the TV where a replay was in motion.

"See," Riley said. "Interception!" A few minutes later the referee corroborated the call.

The game continued, the Pats holding their lead into the last minutes of the game.

Beau couldn't keep his mind on it, however. His thoughts kept returning to Kate and his offer to move her. She'd never agreed, but she hadn't said no either. She'd only mentioned quitting, and he didn't want that, despite the way she was getting under his skin. He could handle his attraction to her. It was only a few more weeks, and first chance he got he was confiscating that stupid mistletoe.

He glanced over at her, wondering what she was thinking about, so quiet over there in the corner of the sofa. Maybe about how to break the news that she was quitting. Or maybe she was plotting to take off with no warning at all.

He'd already caused problems with Paige by telling her he was moving Kate into the house. Not that she'd said much. She wasn't the type to rant and rave, but she'd protested in her own quiet way.

He wanted to keep Paige safe, but he needed to keep Kate and Jack safe too. Maybe they weren't family, but God had dropped them into his life, and he felt responsible for them.

When the game finally ended, Kate and Jack donned their coats and followed him to his truck. He waited until they were on the road to broach the topic.

"So, about what we were talking about in the kitchen . . . ," he said, going for vague since her son was with them. "Are you okay with my suggestion?"

It had begun to snow during the game, and he turned on the wipers to clear the windshield.

"I guess if it would make you feel better . . . and if you're sure we shouldn't just leave."

"Like I said, we need you here. Don't go and bail on me during our busy season." He smiled across her son's head.

She bit her lip, drawing his attention to the fullness

of her lower lip. The memory of their kiss made his heart lurch.

Guilt pricked hard, and he jerked his eyes back to the road.

"Okay, then," she said. "I guess so, if you're sure. When?"

"Might as well do it tonight."

As they entered Paige's neighborhood, Kate explained to Jack what was happening. He took the news calmly, and once they were inside he helped gather his things. Kate went behind, pulling the bedding and tidying up after them.

By the time they had the truck loaded with their meager belongings, Paige still wasn't home, and Beau was only glad that he didn't have to face her one more time today.

CHAPTER 16

Settling in at the farmhouse was done in the blink of an eye. All of their belongings fit inside a duffel bag. Riley and Beau carried in a twin bed from Riley's room, and an air mattress appeared on the rug beside the bed. She was directly across the hall from Beau and next door to Riley.

They'd settled into the household quickly, but nighttime was a challenge for Eden. The farmhouse came with a multitude of foreign noises. She hadn't noticed them during the day, but at night, when darkness ushered in memories best forgotten, her restless mind summoned all manner of potential danger.

On Friday night she and Micah stayed up late watching a Superman marathon. They were getting up early the next morning for the Christmas parade, but he'd been so excited to watch his favorite cartoon, she'd given in.

Micah had already fallen asleep when a clicking noise sounded. She reminded herself it was just the furnace, but she gave up on falling asleep and crept from the bed. She tiptoed down the hall, convincing herself as she padded down the stairs that the scratching noise she heard really was a branch brushing the house. She was being paranoid. She was safer here than she'd ever been at Paige's.

But just one mental image of Walter's brutal murder was a stark reminder of the danger they were running from. The likes of which, she was sure, Beau had never encountered as a deputy.

All was quiet as she passed Miss Trudy's room. The woman had gotten her cast off today and had a less restrictive brace put on. It had to be more comfortable.

Eden wakened the computer as she sat at the built-in desk. She did a quick check on the trial, but she couldn't find much, so she moved on to the next thing. She needed a fake ID and documents for both of them. The money she'd saved would be gone tomorrow when she paid for her car. But she needed to know how much the documents were going to cost.

She did a Google search and followed the links. She'd need a driver's license and birth certificates for both of them. A social security card. She typed the question into the search engine.

She found the answer and sighed. She might have to wait until they were tucked away at Loon Lake. There was no rush, really. She'd been thinking about what Karen had said about selling the place. If things worked out, maybe she could buy it.

A sound startled her, and she jumped.

Beau crossed the kitchen with his familiar masculine grace, stopping short when he saw her at the desk.

Eden exited the website and pushed back, her heart

beating like a drum. She didn't think he could have read the screen from there.

"Can't sleep?" Her voice was barely more than a squeak.

He strolled to the sink and pulled a glass from the cupboard. "Thirsty."

It was only as he stood in front of the kitchen window, the moonlight spilling over his shoulders, that she realized he wore only dark pajama bottoms.

The blue light from the computer screen glowed on the rugged planes of his back. Shadows played in the dips and curves of his shoulders as he filled the glass with tap water.

Remembering the mistletoe, a foolish part of her wanted to join him by the sink. But a quick peek above him showed the sprig was gone. She wondered if he'd swiped it. That put a damper on her little fantasy.

He turned with his glass full of water, his eyes dipping to the computer. "Looking for new recipes?"

She shrugged, not wanting to lie. "Couldn't sleep. I hate tossing and turning."

He gave her a rueful look. "It's not the best mattress."

"It's fine. And Jack is sawing logs on the air mattress."

Beau smiled, leaning back against the counter. "Kids can sleep anywhere."

"Isn't that the truth." Micah had been doing just fine on the cold floor of the shed, in a small pile of hay, until Beau had stumbled upon them. Of course, they'd had two days on the road leading up to that.

"We used to camp on the beach sometimes." Beau's voice rumbled low in the quiet of the kitchen. "Dad would take us down to Lighthouse Pointe, and we'd hang out there for the weekend. Looking back, I think the trips were his way of giving Mom a break. We had fun, though. We'd build outrageous sand castles and go kayaking in the bay and tide pooling."

"What's that?"

"The low tide leaves pools of water in the crevices of the rocks along the shore. All kinds of marine life get trapped in the pools: mussels, sea stars, anemones . . . sometimes even crabs or lobsters. Our own personal aquariums. We'd go clamming too and have clam-bakes on the beach for supper."

"Sounds like I'm here the wrong time of year."

"Summer's pretty awesome. But winter has its merits too. You'll see tomorrow. Christmas by the Sea is great. Everyone in town turns out for the parade and to see Santa come in on the barge."

"Santa arrives on a barge?"

"We Mainers do things our own way. Wait till you see the lighting of the tree. It's made of lobster traps and decorated with buoys."

Eden leaned back against the chair back. "Jack will love it. I haven't been to a parade in years."

"We get hot chocolate from Wicked Good Brew and stake out a spot on Chapel Street near the end of the parade route. It's sheltered from the wind there. Last year it was snowing and in the single digits. Hopefully it won't be so brutal this year."

"We'll dress warm."

"Jack can take a turn on Santa's lap. Is he still a believer?"

Eden lifted a shoulder. "He was last year." But this year he'd lost his dad and his voice. She wasn't sure if he believed in anything anymore.

"Well, he'll have to put in a request or two. Although I guess that'll be tricky for him."

"I'll have to help a little. How long do the festivities last?"

"Just the weekend. There's ice-skating on the square and a gingerbread house contest. My aunt Lillian won last year with a lighthouse."

"I didn't know you had another aunt."

"My mom's sister—she's a librarian. We're not as close to her. Our uncle's not very pleasant to be around, and she's kind of under his thumb."

Eden felt an immediate bond with Aunt Lillian.

"We're close to their daughter, Abby, though. She used to go along on some of those campouts."

"I haven't met her yet."

"She lives in Indiana now. Married my best friend from college."

"Where'd you go?"

"Boston College. Bachelor's in criminal justice, though it wasn't technically necessary for a deputy position. Dad didn't go to college, so he really pushed us to get a degree."

"Makes sense."

"Did you go to college?"

"I wish. Married straight out of high school. I wasn't even pregnant—just stupid." She bit the inside of her lip, instantly sorry for offering personal information, but he didn't press her.

"Love'll do that to you, I guess."

She was pretty sure what she'd felt for Antonio hadn't been love at all, though she'd thought it was at the time. In reality she'd seen him as her knight in shining armor. The armor had lost its luster pretty quickly.

Beau was regarding her with a curiosity that sent up a warning flare in her gut. As much as she was enjoying this quiet moment with him, she needed to escape before his curiosity turned into more questions.

"I think I'm ready to turn in now." She pushed to her feet.

"Good night," Beau said.

She padded past him and up the stairs, then slid between the cool sheets. But it was a long time before sleep came to claim her.

CHAPTER 17

Beau stuffed his hands into his pockets, peering through the crowd at the first vehicle in the parade. Sheriff Colton waved to the people lining Chapel Street as he passed by. He spotted the Callahans in the crowd and gave a nod. In her wheelchair up by the curb, Aunt Trudy raised her chin and looked away.

Behind the patrol car the Bristol High School marching band belted out a happy Christmas carol as they marched in formation down the street. The drum cadence made his insides vibrate. He looked over at Jack to see his response to the hoopla.

The boy was perched on Kate's hip, trying to peer around the people in front of him. Beau touched Jack's shoulder and raised his voice above the blaring horns.

"Want to sit on my shoulders?"

The boy nodded, reaching out.

Beau hoisted him up and wrapped his arms around his lower legs while Jack's hands settled on top of his head.

"Thanks," Kate said.

"Hard to believe I used to hold Riley like this."

Kate laughed, probably picturing his tank of a brother up there now. With her eyes lit, her cheeks flushed with happiness, she looked like a different woman, and he found himself wanting to see this relaxed Kate more often.

"Where's Paige?" she asked.

"She's on the Perfect Paws float—it'll be coming up here in a bit."

"That's right. She's been working on it this week."

"It'll be packed with animals needing homes, wait and see."

The last of the marching band passed, ushering in Miss Maggie's School of Dance. Little girls in parkas and boots sashayed past with varying levels of skill, all of them pretty darn cute.

Kate touched his shoulder, gesturing toward the coffee shop. "I think I'm going to grab a coffee real quick."

"Running on empty?"

"The hot chocolate was good but lacking caffeine, and the line's down now." She held her hands out to her son. "Come on, Jack. We'll be quick."

Jack's legs squeezed tighter around Beau, and his hands pressed flat against Beau's forehead.

"We'll be fine," Beau said. "We'll save your spot."

Kate looked at her son, her eyes assessing, then back at Beau. He felt a squeeze in his chest at the easy smile that lifted her lips.

"All right. Be right back."

Beau watched her weave through the crowded sidewalk, feeling almost heady at her trust in him. She hardly let the boy out of her sight. He told himself that the coffee shop was only two stores down, but it didn't stop the ribbon of warmth that unfurled in his chest.

Jeez. Butch up, Callahan.

Beau gave a little hop, adjusting Jack on his shoulders, and the boy's hands tightened in his hair, pulling at the roots. He should take them to junk food alley tonight after the Christmas tree lighting. They had to try the Needhams and cranberry almond bark.

Two horses clopped by, pulling Mr. Bennington in a wagon filled with a bunch of kids. Beau wished he'd thought to ask if Jack could join them in the wagon.

"Look, there's Salt and Pepper," Beau said.

A roar of motors announced the arrival of the ATV club, overtaking the happy strains of "Jingle Bells." Riley rode in the middle of the bunch. He offered a two-finger salute in their direction, an action he'd picked up from their father.

Beau's gut tightened. Times like this he missed his dad so much he ached with it. The winter festivities felt different without him. So did the tree farm. He'd had a dry sense of humor and a stoic way about him. Beau missed his quiet presence in his life. Hardly an hour went by at work that he didn't think of him.

Tell him we miss him, God.

The ATVs passed, and the local middle school band came next, belting out "Rudolph the Red-Nosed Reindeer." A tractor followed, pulling a flatbed trailer filled with dancing snowmen and a lobster wearing a Santa Claus hat. The lobster spun in a circle, claws flailing, until the tractor braked. The lobster fell flat on his tail.

The crowd chuckled as the lobster made a comedy act out of the incident, and Beau could swear he felt the echo of Jack's laughter against the back of his head.

Beau turned, watching for Kate's return, wanting her to experience her son's joy. He was turning back to the parade when a loud pop reverberated down the street. The sound registered an instant before Jack began scrambling from his shoulders.

Beau grabbed the boy as he clawed frantically down his body. "Jack! Whoa, buddy."

The boy fought for freedom, but Beau hung on tight. He had a feeling the boy would bolt if his feet hit the ground.

Beau eased back out of the crowd, fighting to maintain control of Jack. It must have been a backfire. The kid's body trembled, his hands pushing, his feet clambering.

"Jack, it's okay. It was just a car."

The boy's body trembled, and panic filled his face as he fought, bumping the people around them.

When Beau stopped in front of the brick storefront, he tightened his grip. "Jack! Did you hear me? It was just a car. You're safe."

Jack's legs stilled, his hands clutching at Beau's shirt. His wild eyes found Beau's.

"It's okay. You're okay. I got you."

Jack's eyes flitted away to the crowd, scanning, darting. His body was rigid and unyielding.

What could he say? What did he know about kids, much less a kid who was freaking out?

Beau took Jack's chin and pulled it toward him firmly

until the boy's eyes locked on him again. "It's okay. Was it the sound? That was just a car backfiring. That happens when unburned fuel gets into the muffler. You know what a muffler is?"

Jack continued to stare wide-eyed, unblinking. But he'd stilled, and some of the panic was gone from his eyes.

Keep talking.

"It's that part on the back of a car where the pipe comes out of the bottom. The heat of the exhaust system causes the fuel to combust—uh, to catch on fire—and that makes a really loud popping sound. Sometimes it sparks too. But it's harmless. That's all that noise was."

Jack's body quaked against him, but the panic was fading, and his body was less rigid.

"Okay, buddy?" Beau pulled him into a hug.

Jack came willingly, his arms clamping tight around Beau, and he buried his face in Beau's neck, his chest rising and falling rapidly.

"Daddy!" The word sounded as if it had clawed its way to the surface.

Beau would have thought he'd imagined it if he hadn't felt the word echo against his chest. His heart ripped in two. He tightened his arms. What had happened to this kid?

God, his heart cried, but he was lost for words.

"Let's go find your mom, okay?"

He rubbed the boy's back as he skirted people, his eyes straight ahead, focused on the coffee shop entrance. His mind spun with questions and theories, but he pushed them aside. All that mattered now was Jack.

Up ahead he saw Kate push through the door, coffee in hand. She held the door open for a patron, a smile on her face.

When she saw him hurrying toward her, their gazes connected and locked.

Her smile fell as she rushed forward. She dropped the cup, reaching for Jack. The same panic he'd seen on Jack's face traveled over Kate's.

"What happened?"

At the sound of her voice, Jack let loose of him and tumbled into Kate's arms. He clung to her like a barnacle on a boat.

"What happened?" she asked again, her wild eyes darting around, her feet twitching like she was poised for flight.

He took her arm. "He's fine. A noise startled him. A car backfired, and he just . . . freaked out."

"Are you sure?" She looked over Jack's head, scanning the pressing crowd. "Are you sure that's all it was?"

His hand soothed her arm. "I'm sure. It's Gil Flannigan's Oldsmobile. It's been backfiring as long as I can remember."

Jack's little body still trembled against Kate. She was murmuring something into his ear, rubbing his back.

People bustled to and fro on the sidewalk, skirting the parade crowd, jostling them. Another band was passing, the horns blaring.

He needed to get them out of there. He tugged her arm. "Come on," he called over the music. Setting his hand on her back, he led her in the opposite direction toward the end of the parade route and around the corner.

The walkway to the chapel was clear of snow, and the salt crunched beneath their shoes. He led her up the three steps, opened the heavy wooden door, then guided her through the bright vestibule and into the sanctuary.

The door clicked behind them, shutting out the chaos. He led her to a padded pew, and they sank down on it.

She was whispering words he couldn't hear into Jack's ear, drawing her fingers through his curls.

Giving them a moment, Beau let the silence fill him. The hanging pendants were off. The only light spilled through the stained-glass windows, giving the room a soft amber glow.

He'd never sat in the sanctuary when it was empty. It felt different than it did on Sunday mornings when the strains of the pipe organ filled the room and voices lifted to heaven in praise.

It was peaceful, calming. He looked back at the pair beside him. Jack was still wrapped around his mom, but he wasn't shaking anymore. Kate continued to whisper in her soothing voice, cheek to cheek with her son.

This is exactly what they needed.

He wasn't sure how long they sat there before she finally spoke. "I think he fell asleep."

Beau peeked over her shoulder. The boy's eyes were closed, his lips lax. "Think you're right."

She looked around, as if seeing her sanctuary for the first time. "Is this where you go to church?"

"Yeah. They keep the doors unlocked during the daytime. Pastor Daniels is usually around, but he's probably watching the parade with everyone else."

"It's peaceful." She drew a deep breath and blew it out, ruffling Jack's hair. He didn't so much as stir. "We haven't been to church in months."

He heard the longing in her voice. "You should go with us sometime, now that Aunt Trudy's getting around better. Tomorrow."

"Maybe."

"The people are nice. Welcoming. There's a great kids' program."

Her eyes shuttered, and he knew he'd lost her. She wouldn't leave Jack in a class. She'd barely left him with Beau for two seconds—and when she had, look what had happened.

Beau's eyes fell on the kid's face, his heart melting as he remembered the panic in his eyes.

"What happened back there?" he asked.

Kate ducked her head, burying her nose in Jack's curls.

He hadn't wanted to press her, but his mind had been busy while he'd been sitting here, and he didn't like the direction of his thoughts.

"He thought it was a gunshot, didn't he?"

She continued to rub Jack's back. She swallowed, closing her eyes.

"Come on, Kate. Give me something."

She turned toward him, her eyes searching his. What was she looking for? Trustworthiness? Compassion?

She turned away, her eyes fixing on the altar. "His

dad was killed," she said softly. "He saw the whole thing. Right there in our driveway."

A fist tightened in his gut.

Kate stared into the distance, seeming to float away to another time and place. "Jack watched the clock every night, waiting for him, and as soon as his car would stop in the drive I'd let him run out. They had this game where his dad would swoop him up in his arms and swing him around like he was an airplane. He'd laugh and laugh. One night I was in the house when Jack ran out to meet him. I heard the sound and—"

She swallowed again, her eyes finding Jack's face. Her mouth closed as if thinking better of saying any more.

"It's been so long since I've heard him laugh." Her voice was a thready whisper.

He couldn't imagine. It had been hard enough when his own dad had died. He couldn't imagine a kid losing his father so young, and in such a brutal way—right in front of him.

"I'm sorry," he said.

. . .

Eden readjusted Micah on her lap so he'd be more comfortable. He didn't even stir. They'd gone to bed late last night and gotten up early to stake out a spot for the parade. That combined with the trauma must have just tuckered her little guy out.

"Is he behind bars?" Beau asked. "The guy who shot your husband?"

Her eyes flashed off his. She'd never seen the man in person, but she was sure Jack would never forget his face. And they'd never be safe until he was behind bars.

"No." She heard the defeat in her voice. Though she prayed he would be soon.

"That must be doubly hard after what happened with your mom."

Her eyes cut to his. She couldn't believe he'd put that together in the space of a breath. It had taken her weeks to understand why she'd been so determined to see Antonio's death avenged. Why she was so torn about running with Micah even though Fattore might get off scot-free without his testimony.

"I hate it. I hate that he might get away with it."

"Did Jack see him?"

"Yes."

"Did they do a drawing?"

She glanced down at Micah. "I don't want to talk about this right now." She felt a prick of guilt for using her son as a shield.

"He's sound asleep. Are you in danger, Kate? Is someone after Jack because of what he saw?"

She pressed her lips together. Her feet itched to run from the sanctuary, but what good would that do? She'd have to face him sometime.

"If you're in danger, then so is my family. I deserve to know the truth. I'm not going to fire you. I just want to help. Sheriff Colton and I can—"

"*No.*"

His brows knotted. "Why do you keep doing that?"

"You can't tell anyone anything. Please." She'd already said too much. *You're so stupid.*

"Don't you trust me?"

She gave a hollow laugh. "Why would I? I hardly know you."

"I think you know me well enough to trust me."

"I can't trust anyone!"

He frowned. "That's not true."

She closed her eyes, shook her head. Her heart was beating a million miles per hour. "You don't know what we've been through."

"Then tell me."

"I can't do that without jeopardizing our safety!" Her voice echoed through the room.

She tried to slow her breathing, calm herself down before she said something careless. Her arms tightened protectively around Micah.

"Kate—Is that even your real name?"

The walls were closing in. The room that had felt so peaceful before felt like a prison cell now. Maybe they should leave town. Her car was fixed. They'd leave in the middle of the night.

"He said something."

Her gaze drifted to Beau, not quite hearing his words, already making plans for their departure.

"Jack . . . ," Beau said. "He spoke earlier after the car backfired."

"What?" She searched his eyes, fully alert now. "What did he say?"

Beau gave a tight smile. "He said, 'Daddy.'"

Eden's breath left her body. Her poor baby. Her eyes

stung, and her chest felt so tight she couldn't breathe. He must miss him so much. Maybe Antonio had been a terrible husband, but he'd been a good father.

Hearing the car backfire had unlocked the word from Micah's heart. But he'd spoken. That was good, wasn't it?

"How long has it been?"

She shook her head. "Months."

"Have you considered therapy?"

"We did that for a while until we—" Her eyes flitted off him. "Until we had to leave. I'll get him back in again when we settle. Or maybe he'll start talking again on his own."

Although, who was she kidding? He'd need years of therapy to deal with the violent scene he'd witnessed. She'd do whatever it took to get her happy little boy back.

"Let me help you."

"Stay out of it, Beau. If you want to fire me, then do it. If not, then leave it alone."

She looked into eyes as dark as coal in the shadows of the sanctuary. But they were filled with compassion. She remembered the way her son had clung to Beau as he'd rushed toward her. Remembered the way Beau's hand had cradled his head.

Her son had sought safety in his arms. Had trusted Beau with his first word in months. His response to the noise had shown he was a long way from healing. But this place, these people, were good for him. And they were as safe here as anywhere. As long as Beau didn't go poking around and alert someone to their location.

They would stay. Just a few more weeks, because that was the best thing for Micah. She looked into Beau's warm eyes. They tugged at something deep inside her. As much as she'd fought him, as much as she'd tried to build a wall around herself, her feelings had crossed over some invisible line.

"I want you to stay," he said.

The low hum of his voice made her pulse race, her heart squeeze. The tenderness on his face cut right through her. No one had looked at her that way in such a long time. She instantly remembered the feel of his lips on her cheek. The warmth of his breath. The flare of longing in his eyes.

"Please," he added, calling her attention back to the present.

The moment pulsed between them, an electric thread connecting them.

"Okay." She struggled to ignore the attraction humming between them. There was no future here. Not with Beau, and not in Summer Harbor. Staying might be the best thing for her son, but Eden wondered if it might end up being her own undoing.

CHAPTER 18

Beau pushed open the chapel door, letting Kate through. He blinked against the brightness. The parade had ended, and the crowd had disbanded. He nodded at neighbors as they fell into the foot traffic on the sidewalk.

Kate adjusted Jack's weight. "I hate to be a bother, but could we get a lift back to the house? I'd like to let him sleep a little longer, but he's too heavy to carry."

Beau had wanted to show them a good time today. Kate worked so hard, and Jack had suffered so much. Beau wanted to erase the trauma of the morning. Besides, he didn't like the idea of their being alone at the house.

He reached out for Jack. "Let me take him. He was looking forward to sitting on Santa's lap."

Eden paused a beat before passing her son into his arms. "Thanks."

Jack's light weight settled against his chest, his body like a limp rag doll.

"Where are the others?" she asked.

He suddenly remembered their plans to meet at the end of the parade route and felt his pocket for his phone. He'd left it charging in the truck. He checked his watch. Almost an hour had passed in the chapel.

"Crap." He quickened his pace. "We were supposed to meet up with them after the parade."

The crowded sidewalks challenged their brisk pace. The three-block walk seemed to take an eternity. He was stopped by neighbors he hadn't seen since fall: Lydia and Merle Franke, who farmed a cranberry bog north of town and Margaret Lefebvre, who ran the Primrose Inn. She raved about the wreaths she'd purchased at the farm.

When he finally got free, he realized the staff he'd left at the farm also had no way of contacting him. He made a mental note to grab his phone and check in with them soon.

He finally spotted his family and Paige over the crowd, waiting by the lit-up Christmas moose in front of the Mangy Moose Gift Emporium.

Riley was squatting next to Aunt Trudy's wheelchair, fussing with the wheels, Zac was sipping a hot drink, and Paige was checking her phone.

She looked up just then, spotting them as they emerged from the crowd. Her smile fell as her eyes toggled between Beau and Kate. Her lips tightened, and he suddenly realized how they must look.

"Sorry we're late," he said as they joined the group.

Riley rose to his feet, scowling at Beau. "We've been texting and calling."

"I left my phone in the truck."

"It was my fault," Kate said. "I had a problem with Jack."

Five pairs of eyes swung to the boy, sleeping peacefully in Beau's arms. Riley's eyes narrowed on him.

Guilt pricked hard, but Beau shoved it down. He hadn't done anything wrong. He stifled the urge to supply further details. He couldn't say much without divulging all Kate and Jack had been through.

"Well," Aunt Trudy said. "I don't know about you all, but I'm ready for a big, gooey cinnamon roll from the Sugar Shack."

They started strolling that direction, Paige coming alongside of him, taking the lead, and Zac pushing Aunt Trudy's wheelchair behind them. Kate fell back in line with Riley.

Waves of disapproval were rolling off of Paige. He realized he hadn't even seen her go by on the float she'd worked so hard on. He felt like a real jerk. He wanted to smooth things over before the morning's events ruined their entire day.

"I'm really sorry we kept you waiting," he offered.

"I was worried."

"I meant to grab my phone when I got out of the truck. I forgot to charge it last night."

The clatter of people and passing cars was not enough to disguise the silence that hung between them. Somehow he knew it didn't help that Kate's son was still draped over his shoulder. But what was he supposed to do? Let Kate traipse all over town with him?

"Should I be?" she asked quietly.

He looked at her over Jack's head. "What?"

Her blue eyes fixed on him. "Should I be worried?" She wasn't talking about the potential danger Kate might be exposing them to. His gut tightened at the hurt in her eyes.

"Of course not," he said.

Guilt pricked him hard again. He swallowed, looking away, glad they were almost to the bakery. Even if he hadn't done anything wrong, his feelings for Kate were growing. Feeling protective was one thing, but he felt more than friendship when she looked in his eyes. More than attraction when she trusted him with her son.

She's leaving soon. Then things will get back to normal. He loved Paige.

Didn't he?

But things had seemed off lately. Before Kate's arrival even. He was hesitant to explore the thought further, mainly because he could see where this might be heading. But now wasn't the time. Riley was leaving next Friday. The marines were a tough gig. He'd need his head in the game.

Beau sighed. He'd known getting involved with his brother's best friend would be complicated.

The Sugar Shack was in an old brick storefront with large display windows. The logo arched across the glass in script, and a steaming blueberry pie rested under it.

Jack stirred as they reached the door, looking up at him with sleepy eyes.

Beau paused by the door. "Hey, buddy. We're getting cinnamon rolls. You hungry?"

Jack nodded and Beau let him down, then held the door for the others. The smell of yeast and cinnamon wafted out.

Kate took Jack's hand as she entered. "Have a nice nap, kiddo?"

The lobby was packed. Beau stopped Paige with a hand on her arm and reached into his wallet. "I'll just wait out here." He handed Paige a twenty. "Surprise me?"

She returned his smile with a tight one of her own. "Sure."

He sank into a wrought-iron chair at a patio table, glad for a break from the tension between them. This wasn't the morning he'd planned.

Riley had hung back, too, and he dropped into the seat across from him. He gave Beau a dark look, his lips thinning, then folded his arms over his wide chest. His guns popped under his jacket sleeves.

"What?" Beau asked when he couldn't stand it anymore.

"Seriously?"

Beau exhaled hard, his breath vaporizing. He pocketed his cold hands. He wasn't going to play dumb. "You're making too much out of this. It's not like we sneaked off to be alone. It's true what she said. Jack freaked out at a loud noise, and we took him into the church until he calmed down. He fell asleep. End of story."

Riley stared back, seemingly weighing his answer and finding it lacking. "It just seemed awful cozy, watching you come down the sidewalk like a little family—"

"I know how it looked, but nothing happened."

"Paige is worried about you and Kate."

"Did she say something?"

"She didn't have to say anything. It was all over her face."

Beau clamped his teeth together. Riley was right, but

his relationship with Paige was none of his business. Beau tamped down the words before they spilled out.

"I'll make it up to her."

They hadn't spent much time together lately. Maybe they needed to carve out time for another date. Although their last one hadn't gone so well. Kate again. Was he in denial?

"Have you found out anything else?" Riley asked. "About Kate's past?"

"Nothing substantial. I have Abby on it, but I haven't heard back. I do think she's running from someone. That's why I've been sticking kind of close."

"*I'll* stick close. You worry about Paige."

Something pinched hard. Jealousy? He didn't want to think so. "You're leaving in less than a week."

"And Kate's leaving in three," Riley said pointedly.

Beau balked at the reminder, however true it might be. He couldn't stand the thought of her on her own, someone after them. Who would protect her and Jack? And why was he more concerned about them than about his girlfriend's feelings?

You're a real jerk, Callahan.

"You better not hurt her."

Beau's eyes aligned with Riley's. He met his brother's challenging gaze with a stubborn look of his own. Riley hadn't cornered the market on feelings for Paige. Beau didn't want to hurt anyone, least of all Paige. But pain was a part of life, and sometimes it was unavoidable. He sure hoped this wasn't one of those times.

. . .

Eden slid up in line, holding Micah's hand. Beside them, Riley chatted about boot camp with a middle-aged man who'd served in the army.

They'd spent the day browsing through shops, catching up with neighbors, and admiring the gingerbread houses. The rest of the family had gone home, but Riley had offered to stay and wait until Santa's line went down.

The jolly old man was sitting on a big silver chair in front of a miniature white house with red shutters and a red metal roof. White lights twinkled in the dusk.

As they neared the front of the line, Eden squatted next to Micah. "Do you know what you want to ask Santa for?"

He nodded vigorously. He'd been calm since his nap, and the rest of the day he'd seemed content to explore the festivities and try new foods in junk food alley.

"Do you want to tell me so I can tell Santa?"

He shook his head. They inched forward in line, putting them next. She watched as the toddler ahead of them took one look at the bearded man and let out a screeching wail. Her dad tried to mollify her, but there was no changing her mind about old Saint Nick. A few minutes later the dad scooped her up, with an apologetic look at Santa and the photographer, and carried her off.

"It's our turn," Eden said.

Riley waited by the photographer while Micah dashed up to Santa's chair. The man reached for her son and settled him in his lap.

"His name's Jack," Eden said.

"Ho! Ho! Ho! You're not fixing to cry on me, are you, Jack?"

Jack's eyes were wide as he stared with wonder into Santa's face, shaking his head.

"Good! Santa needs both his eardrums. Now, young man, have you been a good boy this year?"

Micah's eyes swung to her, some of the excitement draining from his face. Did he question that? Did he somehow blame himself for his dad's death? Why hadn't she thought of that till now?

Her heart clenched, and her eyes stung. She swallowed hard. "He's been the best boy I could ask for."

"Well, then! The Mama seal of approval! That means I have to do my very best to make your wishes come true. So tell me, what would you like for Christmas, young Jack?" Santa's rosy cheeks bunched in a smile.

Micah looked at her, questioning. She nodded her encouragement, ready to step in if he needed help expressing himself.

But Micah leaned into Santa and whispered something. Eden's heart took flight at the very basic fact that her son had spoken again. Most of what he said was lost in the clatter around them, but one word reached Eden's ears, making her heart catch.

Home.

Santa's eyes flittered to hers as Jack leaned away, staring up with hope. Saint Nick's smile faltered. He pushed up his glasses and looked directly at Jack. "So," he said, his voice lower now. "You want to go home, eh?"

Jack nodded vigorously.

Eden's heart ached. She'd had no idea he'd been longing for the impossible. Home was the last place they could go.

Santa must have seen the look on her face. "Well, now . . . Santa will do his best, Jack, but sometimes these things are complicated. Is there something else you'd like? A toy, perhaps? A new game? Or how about a nice baseball glove? Come spring, you can play catch with your mom."

Jack shook his head as the photographer asked them to look his way. He snapped the picture, but Eden didn't need to see it to remember the hope that gleamed in her son's eyes. Hope that she'd have to steal from a boy who'd already lost so much.

CHAPTER 19

Beau leaned back in the computer chair, rubbing a hand over his jaw as he considered what he'd just uncovered. His first solid lead.

He'd wanted to watch Jack sit on Santa's lap, but Paige needed to get up early and Riley had offered to stay with him, giving Beau the evil eye as he'd done so.

Aunt Trudy had turned in early, leaving the house too quiet. He couldn't stop thinking about his conversation with Kate in the chapel, and he suddenly remembered she'd been on the computer the night before. Maybe she hadn't been looking for new recipes after all.

His suspicion was confirmed. The Internet history turned up new and surprising developments. Disturbing developments.

He reached for his phone and dialed his cousin, hoping it wasn't too late to call.

Abby picked up on the third ring. "Guess who had a lobster dinner tonight?"

He gave a little smile. "Not you."

"Well, yes, that's true. But Ryan was very grateful."

He heard his friend say something in the background, then Abby giggled. "Ryan says hi."

"Tell him hey."

"Stop it . . ." There was muffled laughter. "Ryan!"

Beau could well imagine what was going on between the lovebirds. He winced. "Am I interrupting?"

"No, no." There was laughter in her voice, then a static sound as she shuffled the phone. The sound of a door closing.

"Okay, I can talk now. Sorry it's taking me so long to get your info. I'm coming up with a lot of Kate Bennets, but nothing in—"

"That's not her name. That's why I called. I asked her directly today, and she didn't answer. Then I just got on the computer. She's trying to buy a fake ID."

"Your gut was right then."

"She also looked up an article about some alleged criminal with ties to the prescription drug market. Apparently his case has gone to trial."

"What's his name?"

"Lucca Fattore. But I'm going to have Sheriff Colton look into that. He has connections. I couldn't find much online."

He remembered the way Kate tensed up every time he suggested outside help and vowed to make sure Colton kept it on the down low.

"Any chance you found her real name?"

"Nope. Just that she was trying to figure out how to get false documents."

"Maybe you can finesse some info from her kid? Did I just say that?" He heard the wince in her voice.

"Believe me, it already crossed my mind. But Jack is mute, or at least he has been for a while. Like I said, the two of them have been through hell and back."

"Sounds like it. Well, if there's anything else I can do, say the word."

"Will do."

Abby put Ryan on the phone, and the two of them caught up before Beau rang off a few minutes later.

His eyes flashed back to the screen. Back to the photo of a man who was somehow connected to Kate. He had cold eyes and deep marionette lines that marched down to his flattened lips. He wasn't a man Beau would want to meet in a dark alley—not unarmed.

He looked to be in his sixties—too old to be a love interest—with weathered olive skin and brown eyes. Her father? Grandfather? He supposed he could see a resemblance to Jack, and Kate also had brown eyes. Perhaps they were related. How else would she have ever gotten connected with a man like Lucca Fattore?

. . .

The next afternoon found Eden and Micah alone at the house, playing Jenga at the kitchen table. She'd gone to church with the Callahans. It had been wonderful to worship with fellow believers again.

Pastor Daniels had preached on the husband's role in marriage. Eden had cringed when she saw the sermon title in the bulletin. But Pastor Daniels had different ideas from Antonio's. The Bible said the husband was supposed to love his wife as Christ loved the church—that he was supposed to be willing to die for her. The pastor went into great detail about that.

Antonio had never mentioned that scripture, and he'd sure never demonstrated it. The sermon gave her a lot of food for thought.

The chapel was smaller and friendlier than her former church, which made it harder to maintain a distance from people. But she had to. It would do no good to get close to anyone and could cause plenty of harm if the wrong words slipped.

Especially to the Callahans. Beau's image came to mind, her heart going soft as she remembered his tender care with Micah yesterday. She had to be more careful. She wasn't here to build relationships. This was only a stopping point. A resting place before they continued on the last leg of their journey to Loon Lake. Sure, they could be just as safe in Summer Harbor with new identities. But she longed for the place she'd yearned to escape to as a child. She longed for true freedom.

The notion seemed almost too good to be true.

The family had invited them to the Roadhouse for the Patriots game, but after hearing Micah's request to Santa, Eden knew she needed to talk to her son. She'd also wanted to call her dad while he was still at church, which she'd done as soon as Beau's truck had pulled away.

The block tower wobbled as Micah drew one from the bottom.

"Uh-oh . . . ," she said.

The tower stilled, and he smiled up at her in victory.

"You're a lucky boy." She reached for a loose block. "Did you have fun yesterday at the festival?"

He nodded, watching her pull the block.

He hadn't said anything since he'd sat on Santa's lap. Eden wished she had a psychology degree. She wasn't sure whether to ignore yesterday's milestone or make a big deal of it. But instinct told her not to rush him.

"I did too. I liked the Needhams." Eden had been skeptical when Beau had told her the traditional Maine sweet contained potatoes. But it tasted much like a Mounds bar.

Micah's eyes narrowed on the block he was pulling. His tongue peeked out as he focused.

"Good job," she said when he'd successfully removed the block. "You're good at this game."

His eyes swung to hers, a glint of amusement there.

"Yes, I know you're still winning our secret game too." She'd failed to respond when someone had called her name at church this morning. "But we were tied until this morning."

He'd done remarkably well with switching identities. The game helped, but he was starting to talk now. What would happen if he let something slip to the wrong person? She'd need to talk to him about that, but first things first.

"Jack . . . I know you miss home. Your friends and the house and your own bed. But you know we can't go back there . . . right?"

His eyes met hers, sobering. She hated that she'd dimmed the light flickering there, but neither could she let him live in a fantasy that would only end in disappointment.

"I'm so sorry you're sad about that. I want more than

anything for things to be different." She set her hand on his. "But when Daddy died, it changed everything. I know you don't understand exactly what's going on, but we had to leave to stay safe. And it's not safe to go back home."

His eyes glossed over, fat tears gathering on his thick, dark lashes. "Oh, baby, come here." She scooped him up and held him on her lap. "We're going to be okay. We'll make a new home. It'll be different, but we'll be safe and happy again, and you'll make new friends."

He pushed his nose into the cradle of her neck and shoulder. "Daddy." His vocal cords rasped with disuse.

She hugged him tighter, her chest tightening at the word. The murder of his father must seem like a horrible nightmare. She swallowed against the knot lodged in her throat.

"I know you miss him. I'm sorry you're hurting, kiddo. It's not fair. But I'm going to make it better. I promise. It'll just take a little time. Okay?"

He didn't respond, vocally or otherwise.

"In the meantime, we'll just try and enjoy our time here. You like the ocean, right? And the Callahans are nice. Miss Trudy's a little gruff, but I think she has a soft spot for you. We've gotten to do some pretty cool things while we've been here. We've even made some friends."

"Beau."

She smiled against the top of his head. "Yes, Beau is our friend."

She wondered if they were both becoming too attached to the people of Summer Harbor and if leaving was only going to bring them more pain.

CHAPTER 20

Eden bolted upright in bed. The mattress springs squeaked beneath her. Her heart thudded, her ears tuned to hear the noise again. Micah's quiet breaths from the air mattress beside her filled the darkness.

A moment passed, then she heard footfalls on the steps. Riley's familiar pattern, heavy and slow, always hitting the creak on the fifth tread. She slowly sank back onto her pillow, adrenaline racing through her veins.

Seconds later the door next to hers clicked shut. She worked to steady her heart, but her body wasn't cooperating. It was remembering the last time she'd been awakened from a dead sleep. The last time she'd let the illusion of safety lull her into complacency.

Eden didn't know what had awakened her that night. But then she hadn't known much of anything for months, ever since they'd arrived. Where they were going . . . how long they'd be there . . . or even what their names would be after Micah testified and they entered the WitSec program. All she knew was they were at a safe house somewhere in Tampa.

She sat up in the double bed, her eyes roaming over Micah's sleeping form. She laid a hand on his back, comforted by the gentle rise and fall of his torso. He was her baby. The only thing that mattered in this world, and she wouldn't let anything happen to him.

A clank sounded in the living room, where Walter tended to fall asleep on the couch. He'd probably knocked over that tin of fake flowers again. For a US Marshal he wasn't especially graceful. But then he was getting up in age, almost ready to retire.

When they'd had nothing else to count on, though, nothing standing between them and danger, he'd been there, rock solid, he and Marshal Brown both. She was glad they had extra help now. Marshal Langley had been sent in anticipation of their departure. He'd arrived yesterday, filling the safe house with the odor of cigarette smoke and the scent of the cloves he sucked on. They would return to Miami soon for the trial, and such a move called for higher security. She was nervous about going back.

Eden shuddered at the thought of Micah facing her husband's murderer in court. But Micah's word would buy their freedom. It would also avenge his father's death, putting behind bars a man who'd long been sought by the DEA for his role in the prescription drug black market.

A market that her husband had been neck-deep in. After his murder, she'd been interrogated until she'd been ready to crack. For weeks they hadn't believed her innocent of her husband's activities. The worst of it had been her separation from Micah when he needed her most.

And now the trial was almost upon them, just a few days away. As much as she dreaded the trial, she looked forward to the end of this ordeal. They were so close to freedom she could almost taste it.

She checked the clock. A little after one.

Another noise, more of a thwack, sounded from the other end of the house, then low voices. Angry voices. Eden sprang upright, slipped soundlessly to the floor, and crept to the doorway. She peeked through the wedge of light.

Her heart stopped at the sight. Langley held Walter in a headlock. Then her eyes fell to the floor where Marshal Brown's body lay in a heap, his blank eyes still open.

"Morris will have your head," Walter squeezed out.

"Who do you think brought me in, you moron?"

Walter was fighting hard, spewing words she couldn't make out.

Langley reached for something in his pocket. "She's already dead," he said quietly. "They both are. She just doesn't know it."

"Never," Walter squeezed out, his elbow jutting back, catching Langley in the gut.

The metal of a blade caught the light. But before Eden could open her mouth, the sharp end sliced across Walter's throat. A trail of blood followed behind.

Her hand covered her mouth, catching the whimper before it was released.

Micah! She had to get him out of here.

She eased the door closed, twisting the lock. She prayed Langley intended to wait until morning to make good on his threats.

Working quietly, she grabbed the emergency book bag that had been packed for weeks. Her legs shook as she collected Micah and Boo Bear, grateful he slept so soundly. She unlocked the window and eased it open. Her heart was like a jackhammer in her ears.

Please, God! Please, please, please.

The bag got hung up on the curtains, wasting precious time. Finally freeing it, she dropped it to the ground.

Was that a noise in the hallway?

Fear propelled her through the window with Micah. She fell as she landed, jostling him so much she couldn't believe he still slept. She grabbed the bag, adjusting his weight, and ran, hooking the bag on her shoulder. Cold sticks and rocks cut into her bare feet as she ran toward the darkened woods behind the house. If she could reach the trees before he discovered they were missing, maybe they'd have a chance.

Help us, God!

A light came on behind her, and her footsteps quickened. Almost to the woods. Almost. A gunshot rang out in the night. Eden yelped, sheltering Micah against her shoulder.

Her son whimpered.

They reached the woods, the darkness, and she darted through the trees. "It's okay, baby."

Please, God!

She went deeper into the woods, thankful that the moon and stars weren't out. She ran into trees, scraped her arm against a bush. If she couldn't see, then neither could Langley.

Langley. Why had she trusted him? When would she

learn? She'd gotten black and red vibes from the very first meeting. But he was a US Marshal, and Walter had trusted him.

Walter. She could still hear the scrape of the blade against his throat. The gurgle that followed. The back of her eyes burned.

Stop it. Don't think about it now.

She headed northwest, knowing the woods went on forever in that direction. A creek meandered down the middle of it. They'd need water eventually.

She stopped a moment, listening. Catching her breath. Nothing. Only a few crickets and the wind, making the trees creak overhead. How long had she been running? Twenty minutes? Thirty? Now that she'd stopped she felt the burn of her calves, the raw pain on the soles of her feet. Her aching arms.

"Micah, kiddo, I need you to walk, okay?"

She let him down, shushing his whimpers, and they continued on, walking quickly now. She had to make a plan. He'd expect her to go to the bus stop, so she couldn't do that. There was a burner phone in the book bag. She thought of Walter's supervisor, Deputy Morris. She should call him.

But then Langley's words flashed in her mind. "Who do you think brought me in?"

If Deputy Morris was dirty, she couldn't trust anyone with the US Marshals Service. They could probably even track her with the phone. After all, they'd purchased it for her.

She pulled it from the bag and banged it against a tree until it shattered into pieces. She was shifting the bag onto her shoulder when a new sound reached her ears. She stilled, listening.

The low, repetitive baying sounds were unmistakable. Dogs!

She grabbed Micah's hand.

"Fast, Micah. Run your fastest!"

She was working on sheer adrenaline now. They weren't far from the creek. They couldn't be.

A few minutes later she heard its trickle. She slid down the slope, dropping the book bag twice before reaching the cold, shallow water. She lifted Micah into her arms and struggled upstream, the water tugging at her yoga pants. Her bare feet slipped on the rocky bottom, and her lungs burned. Her body begged for rest. Still she pressed on.

A soft snore pulled her back to the present. Eden's heart raced as her mind settled in the here and now. It was a memory she wished she could forever erase. The rest of the night had been exhausting. They must have lost the dogs at the creek because by the time morning broke they'd safely reached a highway.

Using the money and the hats and wig in the bag, she'd caught a taxi north and switched cabs— and disguises—in Gainesville. She'd taken a bus to Jacksonville, where she'd bought the Buick and started a meandering path north, changing shirts and hats as they went.

She drew in a deep breath and let it out slowly, the now-familiar sounds of the house calming her. At least she had her car back. They could leave at a moment's notice if they needed to. The memory, horrible as it was, was a reminder to trust no one, badge or no. Their very lives depended on it.

CHAPTER 21

Beau grabbed the bundled spruce from one of his teen workers and slung it onto his shoulder. He made conversation with the Parkers, a middle-aged couple who lived just outside of town near the cranberry farm. Mrs. Parker was so fussy she came out in October each year to select her tree. They'd been tagging her trees as long as Beau could remember.

He tied the blue spruce to the roof of their Dodge Durango and tapped the top of the car. With a friendly wave, they pulled from the gravel lot, and Beau went to check on his cashier. She'd been feeling ill at the beginning of her shift.

The small gift shop inside the barn was warm and bustling with customers. There were a few people in line with their jugs of maple syrup and packets of tree preserver. He tidied the boxes of ornaments on the shelves while he waited for the line to die down.

He was rehanging an elf on the Christmas tree display when Sheriff Colton entered the shop.

"Howdy, Beau. Looks like business is good."

"Cranking along. I may be short a cashier in a few minutes, though. Flu's going around."

"That's what I hear." The sheriff palmed his hips, towering over Beau. "How's your aunt's leg healing up?"

"She got her cast off. Just a brace now. She's getting around pretty well."

"Looked like she was enjoying the festivities Saturday."

"Other than being cooped up in that wheelchair. Had to practically force her into the thing."

Sheriff Colton shifted, his red mustache twitching. "She's an independent lady."

"She'll be glad when she's on her own two feet again, that's for sure. We all will." But then it would be time for Kate to leave. The thought left him gloomy.

"Got your message and thought I'd stop by." He scanned the busy shop. "I guess now's not a good time, though."

"I'll make time." He gestured for Colton to follow him down the short hall.

Finding that article about Lucca Fattore had brought a new urgency to Beau's search. And maybe the distraction also helped keep his mind off Riley's pending departure and Beau's confusing feelings for Kate.

He slipped through his office door and closed it behind the sheriff, unzipping his coat as he crossed the small space. It wasn't much of an office, just an eight-by-ten space with a desk and an old metal filing cabinet. But it had been good enough for his dad; it was good enough for him. The desk was mildly cluttered, the only adornments a photo of his family and a plant Paige had given him when he'd taken the farm full-time. He kept forgetting to water it, and now the leaves were brown and curling at the edges.

He sank into his desk chair and gestured toward the only other seat. "I was wondering if you'd ever come across the name Lucca Fattore. He's allegedly connected with the underground prescription drug market."

The sheriff pursed his lips. "Can't say it sounds familiar. Does he have some connection to your housekeeper?"

"Not sure. She did look him up on the computer, though." He started to mention her search for a fake ID, then stopped. Last thing he wanted was to get Kate into more trouble.

"Could be nothing," Beau said. "But it could be something too. I couldn't find much on him on the Internet, other than that he'd been arrested for murder and was standing trial in Miami."

"I'll check with an old friend. He has connections down there."

He remembered the glint of fear in Kate's eyes. "Keep Kate out of it, if you would. I'm worried about her."

The sheriff quirked a brow.

"Her husband was murdered at their house, and her son saw the whole thing. So you know what I'm thinking."

"That Lucca Fattore is her husband's murderer."

"It's a thought."

He ran his hand over his bald head. "If that's the case, she's in way over her head. Her son's an eye-witness. Why isn't she under marshal protection?"

"No idea. I'm not sure of anything except that all this needs to be kept on the down low."

"You got my word. In the meantime, you might want to lock your doors at night."

He'd replaced the locks yesterday on his day off. "Already a step ahead of you. And maybe you could swing by now and then and check on things while I'm working."

The sheriff's lips turned up. "That can be arranged."

Beau had a feeling Aunt Trudy was going to be seeing more than her share of Sheriff Colton.

After the sheriff left, Beau took over for his cashier, and she went home to rest. The night flew by, and his stomach was rumbling by the time he entered the house hours later.

He warmed up by the fire. Kate always had one going when he came home. He loved the smell of burning wood and the soothing crackle of a fire. He just rarely took the time to lay one. The savory smell of pot roast made his mouth water. Kate's cooking had improved considerably.

Riley entered a few minutes later, dusting snow from his shoulders. Paige was on his heels. Beau had invited her for supper, knowing she wanted to spend time with Riley before he left. Zac had come too. Their time together was winding down. Only three days left.

He greeted Paige at the door with a peck on the lips as Riley made a beeline for the kitchen.

"How was your day?" he asked.

"Not bad. You?"

"Busy. I'm starving."

"Something smells good."

They entered the dining room where Kate was setting a basket of rolls on the table. Aunt Trudy hobbled toward the kitchen, but Riley stopped her. "I'll help. You sit down."

She scowled. "I've been sitting all day."

Riley kissed her cheek. "Good. That's what you're supposed to be doing."

Zac pulled out their aunt's chair, making a grand gesture, and she shuffled toward it, mumbling under her breath.

Beau helped Paige into her chair, then went into the kitchen with Zac to grab some drinks. Riley and Kate were working in tandem to get the roast and potatoes onto the serving platter.

She gasped as juices splashed out on Riley's shirt. "Sorry!"

He only chuckled. "It's an old shirt."

"Mistletoe." Zac nodded toward the ceiling above the stove, then turned to the fridge.

Kate and Riley looked up, then Riley's lips kicked up a crooked grin as their eyes mingled. "What's a guy to do?"

Beau braced himself as Riley leaned down and planted his lips on Kate's cheek. The kiss seemed to linger forever.

Every hair on the back of Beau's neck rose. His breath grew shallow.

Kate smiled up at Riley as he drew away.

Riley winked at her as he grabbed the platter. "I just love Christmas."

Zac dropped a few bottled waters in Beau's hands, snagging his attention from Kate's maddening smile.

"Aunt Trudy strikes again," Zac said as he exited the kitchen.

Beau followed, his emotions at war inside, choking him. Aunt Trudy's little game had been a lot more fun when he'd been the lucky winner.

In the dining room he settled by Paige, shaken by the moment in the kitchen, the emotions still roiling in his gut. Aunt Trudy said grace and conversation commenced, but he couldn't get his mind off that kiss. He wanted to deny it was jealousy he'd felt, but he wasn't stupid or stubborn.

He focused on his food, but his every nerve was attuned to Kate, sitting across from him, enjoying her food. Was his brother falling for her?

He'll be gone soon.

Even as the thought soothed him, he chided himself. Was he seriously relieved his brother was joining the marines so he was no threat to Beau's nonexistent relationship with Kate?

You're dating Paige, you idiot.

He suppressed a groan. How had this happened? When did he become such a jerk? His eyes darted off Paige, feeling the familiar pinch of guilt.

He had to tell her what was going on with him. It wasn't right that he was having feelings for Kate, even if she *was* leaving soon. Even though it couldn't possibly go anywhere.

It wasn't fair to Paige. And if he was honest with himself, something was obviously lacking in their relationship if he was developing feelings for another woman. Something had been lacking all along; he just hadn't realized it until Kate had come along with her mysterious eyes and guarded smile.

The timing was terrible, with Riley leaving. Paige was already upset about him joining up, and Beau couldn't stand the thought of adding to her pain. She didn't have family like they did. The Callahans *were* her family.

Besides, he didn't want Riley distracted while he struggled through boot camp. It would be hard enough without the added trauma of knowing Paige was suffering back home.

"Beau . . ." Paige nudged him.

He looked at Paige, realizing she'd already called his name. He felt the eyes of everyone at the table, and his face heated as he realized he'd been staring at Kate.

Paige's lips tightened. "I said, what do you think?"

"Uh . . ." For the life of him he couldn't call up the last conversation. "About what?"

Zac cleared his throat. "Paige wanted to spend some time with Riley before he left. He suggested we go snowmobiling tomorrow afternoon."

They'd had a fresh blanket of snow today, and the farm closed early on Wednesdays. Besides, they hadn't been out yet this winter, and this would be their last chance in who knew how long?

Paige picked at her food. "I think I can get off early, but I have to be back at the shelter by six for a meeting."

Beau nodded. "Sounds like a plan." He'd agree to a night in the county jail if it would erase the sadness lurking in Paige's eyes.

"You should go too, Kate," Aunt Trudy said. "You need to get out more."

Kate offered a smile. "That's okay. I'll keep you company."

Beau wanted to offer to take her place, but with the weight of Paige's watchful stare, he was staying out of this one.

"Nonsense. Jack can keep me company. He can teach me that new game he's been playing on the computer. I'll bet Kate's never even been on a snowmobile."

"Where do you ride?" she asked.

"On the trails," Riley said. "It's a lot of fun. You should come."

There were three sleds and five of them. Math wasn't Beau's best subject, but it didn't take a genius to figure this one out. Paige would ride with Beau. Zac liked to ride alone. That left Kate clinging to Riley. No wonder he wanted her to go.

"Well . . . ," Kate said. "Sure, I guess so. If you're sure you don't mind, Miss Trudy."

His aunt waved the sentiment away, and with that, Beau's fate was sealed.

CHAPTER 22

Riley strapped on a helmet, then turned to Eden. She ducked her head as he put one on her and held still as he adjusted the chin strap.

She was glad she'd borrowed a pair of boots from Paige. The snow was several inches deep, and the wind chilled her to the bone.

Riley was staring over her head to where Beau and Paige were readying for their trip. His brows were pinched together, that vulnerability making an appearance in his green eyes.

"Maybe we can switch partners later," Eden offered.

He scowled. "That's the last thing I need."

Unrequited love was the pits. She glanced over her shoulder where Paige was settling on the snowmobile behind Beau. She wrapped her arms around him, pressing tight to his back as the sled started with a rumble.

Bad enough what Eden was feeling. "Maybe the distance will help."

He gave a rueful smile as he finished her strap. "Here's hoping." He hopped on the sled and fished the keys from the glove box.

A minute later they were flying through an open field on the backside of the neighbor's property. Beau and Paige were behind them, Zac pulling up the rear. The high-pitched whine of the engines filled the stillness of the afternoon, the skis cutting through the soft blanket of snow. The cold air sailed past, making Eden glad for her face mask.

Riley took a sharp turn onto a wide trail that cut through the woods. Eden tightened her grip. The ride was exhilarating. The evergreens rushed by in her peripheral vision, and the wind whooshed past, carrying the faint smell of gasoline.

After several minutes, Riley called over his shoulder. "Ready for the fun stuff?"

"Uh . . . I guess?" She gave a nervous chuckle.

"Hang on!"

It wasn't until they went airborne that she realized how easy he'd been taking it on her. A squeal escaped midair, and she clutched his waist.

Riley whooped.

They landed with a jolt.

"You okay?" he called over the buzz of the engine.

Her heart was pounding, but a smile had broken out on her face. "Yeah!"

He accelerated, and they continued along the trail, going airborne a few more times. Eden had never been an adrenaline junkie, but there was something freeing about sailing through the winter afternoon, the wind in their faces, the world behind them. Time flew by as quickly as the landscape.

She had no idea how much time had passed when

Riley slowed, pulling over, as the others came to a stop alongside them. The low rumble of engines filled the forest.

Paige hopped off the back of Beau's sled, unsnapping her helmet. "Thank goodness. I gotta use the little ladies' room." She rushed into the woods, her boots kicking up fresh snow.

Eden was glad she didn't have to go, since the "little ladies' room" seemed to consist of a snowy floor and evergreen walls.

"What the heck was that?" Beau asked Riley as soon as Paige was out of earshot.

"What?" Riley asked.

"You were driving recklessly. She's a first-timer. She could've fallen off and broken her neck."

Riley's torso lengthened. "I am not reckless. She was fine."

"You want to risk your own life, great. But do it on your own time."

"Guys . . . ," Zac said.

"Slow it down," Beau said firmly.

Riley gave a humorless laugh, shaking his head.

Eden's stomach twisted at Beau's knotty jaw and Riley's defensive posture. "It's okay," she assured Beau. "I'm fine. Really."

Riley's eyes flashed. "You're as transparent as glass, bro."

"What's that supposed to mean?"

"What do you think it means?"

Zac got between the two sleds. "Come on, guys. Knock it off."

A shuffle alerted them to Paige's approach. Beau shot Riley a warning look, and Riley glared right back.

Eden felt helpless to mediate as Paige reached the trail.

"Whew! I feel much better. My turn, buddy," she said to Beau.

He slid back on the machine, letting her take the driver's seat.

When they were all suited up again, Riley accelerated. He darted ahead of the group, his speed a dead giveaway that he wasn't going to heed Beau's warning.

Eden got little pleasure from the thrill of the ride as they zoomed along the snowy path, knowing Beau was behind them, likely seething. She told herself Beau would have spoken up no matter who was on Riley's sled. That he didn't have special feelings for her. He was protective of everyone. It was his nature.

But it might be more. Maybe she hadn't imagined the lingering glances. The casual brushes. As the idea incubated, something inside her went warm and soft.

He's with Paige, Eden. You're leaving in a matter of weeks. You can't stay here, and he's not going with you. You don't need another man. You need your freedom. Haven't you learned yet that love only shackles?

With her dad she'd learned that even shackles employed with love still chafed. Then along came Antonio. She'd thought his love would set her free. But it had only bound her more tightly. And while his death should have granted her the ultimate freedom, it only placed her in a different kind of prison.

I will be free. We will be free. As soon as we reach Loon Lake.

Karen had taken her daughter to the magical cabin in northern Maine every summer. They always invited her along, but her father never let her go. Eden was green with envy every August when they returned with beautiful pictures and enchanting stories.

But would they really be free there? How could she be free when she was always looking over her shoulder? Waiting for Fattore's men to catch up with them? Waiting for them to take her son from her?

The thought jolted her.

She shook it away, her pulse skittering. No. She wouldn't have to live that way. They'd be safe. Fattore would be found guilty soon, even without Micah's testimony. The prosecution had DNA evidence. She and Micah would finally be free.

The cold wind cut into the slice of skin bared between her coat sleeve and glove. For a moment she let the biting pain distract her from the path of her thoughts. Then, seeing there were no turns ahead, she reached over with her other hand to tug the coat sleeve into place.

The sled hit a bump, and they went airborne. She tilted sideways. Her knees tightened around Riley, and she reached for him. But she was slipping, falling . . .

Flying through the air. Her arms flailed helplessly, connecting with something. She hit the ground with a thud. The air evacuated her lungs.

She groaned. Had she thought the snow soft?

She blinked up at the darkening sky, mentally assessing her body parts. It took a moment for the pain in her backside to register. She moved her legs, her arms. Nothing broken. Just got the wind knocked out of her.

Riley hit the ground beside her. "Kate. You okay?"

She was sitting up as Beau and Paige reached them, Beau's worried eyes trained on her. "You all right?"

"I'm fine. Really."

Beau squatted, taking her wrist. "You're bleeding."

The exposed skin had caught a branch or something. Only now did she feel the sting. "It's just a scrape."

"Everything okay?" Zac called as he pulled his sled closer.

"Yeah, I'm fine."

Riley helped her up, and she brushed off the snow. The movement hurt, but she wasn't about to mention it.

Beau sent Riley a withering glance. "You happy now?"

"It was my fault," Eden said. "I let go to fix my sleeve just as we went airborne. Bad timing."

"Let's stop at the Roadhouse and get her cleaned up," Zac said.

Riley tore his gaze away from Beau's challenging stare. "It's getting dark anyway."

"Perfect," Paige said. "I can walk to the shelter from there."

. . .

At the Roadhouse Beau parted ways with Paige. The rest of them followed Zac to his office, their ski pants swishing.

It was a slow weeknight at the restaurant with only a few customers scattered throughout the dining room. Someone in the back room broke the pool balls with a loud crack, and a hearty round of boos followed.

In his office, Zac pulled a first-aid kit from the depths of a drawer.

Riley and Beau both reached for it.

Beau gave Riley a dark look, snapping up the kit. "I think you've done enough for one day."

"You can use my restroom," Zac said. "I need to go check on things in the kitchen. Riley, why don't you go save us a pool table?"

Riley aimed a scowl at Beau before leaving the room.

"It's really just a scratch." Kate headed toward the bathroom attached to Zac's office, pulling up her sleeve. "I can handle it."

She already had her wrist under the water when Beau caught up to her. He set the kit on the counter beside her. The space was tight, and the citrus smell he'd come to associate with her filled his lungs.

When she was finished washing the scrape, she patted it dry with a paper towel.

"Let me see." Beau took her hand, his mouth tightening at the raw flesh. He could throttle Riley. What was his problem anyway?

"That's got to smart." He ripped open the alcohol pad. "This is going to sting."

He ran the pad over the scrape as gently as he could, and she didn't react to the pain. He held her hand, his thumb pressed into her palm as he cleaned the wound.

"It wasn't his fault, you know."

"Don't make excuses for him."

"I was having fun."

"Until you hit the ground?"

Her lips twitched. "Something like that."

She had nice lips, plush and pink. Beau dragged his eyes away. "He knows better." He blew on the wet skin.

Gooseflesh popped up on her arm, and a muscle in her forearm twitched.

His eyes flashed to hers, lingering there, perceiving a subtle shift in her honey-brown eyes. Had her breaths just grown shallow?

She broke eye contact. "He's leaving in two days. I wouldn't want you parting badly over something so silly."

Beau reached into the kit and grabbed a bandage. "You don't have to worry about us."

He unwrapped the bandage and applied it, rubbing over the adhesive once or twice more than necessary. To make sure it stayed put, he told himself.

Riley appeared in the restroom doorway. "Table's reserved."

Beau met his brother's eyes in the mirror, noting Riley's tight-lipped smile.

Kate pulled her hand from Beau's. "I think I'll order some wings. You guys want some?"

"Sure." Beau gathered the trash and threw it into the wastebasket as she left. He snapped the lid on the kit and turned to leave, but Riley leaned against the doorframe and crossed his arms.

Fine. He wanted to talk, they'd talk. "You're lucky she's not hurt worse. What the heck was that anyway?"

"Me? What about you? Making cow eyes at Kate while Paige is practically glued to your back."

Guilt moved in, setting up camp. Again. He didn't want to talk about this with Riley.

He moved to pass.

Riley blocked his path.

Beau glared down at him, enjoying his height advantage.

"Admit it—you've got feelings for Kate."

"I'm not talking to you about this."

"You don't have to talk to me, but you should be talking to Paige."

Beau sighed hard, remembering Kate's words. It was one of their last nights together. He didn't want to send Riley off like this.

"Why don't we go shoot some pool, have a few wings, and relax? I think maybe we're both a little stressed out."

"When are you going to talk to Paige?"

"That's none of your business, Riley."

His brother came up off the wall. "Paige *is* my business, whether you like it or not. You obviously have feelings for Kate, and you owe it to Paige to be honest about it."

"You sure you're not the one having feelings?"

Riley stiffened, something flashing in his green eyes. "What are you talking about?"

"I've seen your little private conversations. Your little mistletoe kiss . . ."

His lips parted. Closed. "You think I have feelings for Kate?"

Beau said nothing, just waited him out.

"And you're jealous. I don't have feelings for Kate, you moron, and I'm leaving in two days. It's beyond obvious what's going on here. Paige doesn't deserve this." Riley gave a laugh, shaking his head. "This isn't like you, man. What about doing the honorable thing?"

His brother knew how to push all the right buttons. Beau's face tingled with shame. He hadn't felt that particular emotion in a while, and he hadn't missed it. He ran his hand over the back of his neck. Riley was right. "I'll talk to her. I promise."

Riley regarded him for a long moment. "Are you going to break up with her?"

Beau shoved his hands into his pockets, making a quick decision. The right one, he believed now. "Yes."

Riley blinked at him, silent for a long beat. "I can't believe this." He gave another wry laugh as he walked into Zac's office, scrubbing his hand over his face. "*Now* you do it," he muttered.

Or at least that's what Beau thought he said. "What?" Beau followed his brother into the office.

Riley paced in front of the desk. "You need to do it now."

"I was waiting till you left."

Riley stopped, his eyes narrowing. "Coward."

Beau straightened. "I didn't want this to be a distraction for you at boot camp."

"Well, it's too late for that."

"Paige is already reeling because you're leaving. I didn't want to dump this on her too."

"And you think stringing her along is the answer?"

"I'm not stringing her along."

"No, you're just waiting until her best friend is twelve hundred miles away before you break her heart. Until she has no one to fall back on, no one to talk to—" Riley paced in front of the desk.

"I didn't think of it like that."

"Well, maybe you should."

Beau blew out a noisy breath. Any way he went here, it wouldn't be good. But Riley knew Paige better than anyone. Besides, the thought of her suffering alone was like a kick in the gut. Maybe Riley was right. He wasn't gone yet. She'd still have someone. For a couple days. And he wouldn't have to pretend anymore.

He frowned, the thought of hurting Paige hitting him like a sucker punch. When had he become a Class A jerk?

CHAPTER 23

Beau waited in the parking lot of Perfect Paws for Paige's meeting to end. He'd ridden the sled home and driven his truck back. After a while the front door opened and a few people trickled out. Five minutes later Paige appeared, turning to lock up the building.

Her eyebrows shot up when she spotted his truck, but her expression shifted as she walked over and got in. "I didn't expect to see you again tonight."

"How was your meeting?"

"Long and boring. You been waiting awhile?"

"Not really."

Her house was a short drive away, but it seemed like an eternity with the overwhelming silence. Beau's mind turned with words and explanations. Dread bloomed inside as he pulled into her drive. He wished he could fast-forward time a couple hours.

Once inside, Paige turned on the lights and hung her coat on the hook. Dasher appeared, wrapping around Paige's legs until she picked him up.

A guarded look he hadn't seen before shadowed her

eyes. "I'd ask if you want something to drink, but I have a feeling you won't be here long."

He guessed his feelings hadn't been as inconspicuous as he'd hoped. His smile felt stiff and unnatural. "Let's sit down."

"I'd rather stand if it's all the same to you."

"Paige . . ."

"You didn't come back to drive me two blocks, Beau. Just say it."

He'd spent the time in his truck figuring out how to do exactly that. But for the life of him, he couldn't recall all those words that were supposed to make this easier on her. Maybe there weren't any.

She cocked a brow, her elfin chin lifting a notch.

"You know I care about you, Paige. I always have, and I always will."

Her face was set in stone. No emotions flickered in her pretty blue eyes. "But . . . ," she prompted.

He hated that she was way over there, that he couldn't hold her hand or somehow soften this.

"Can we just sit down?"

"Go ahead."

He sighed. He was beginning to realize it didn't matter whether they stood or sat or what words he used. This was going to sting.

"Paige, I don't—I don't think this is going to work. You and me. Things haven't felt right for a while now. I don't know if you've noticed . . ."

Her lips tightened.

Tension tightened between them like a line pulled taut. A long, awkward pause tweaked at the line.

"I think maybe it's time to part ways. I'm sorry if this seems sudden. The last thing I want is to hurt you, and I don't want to lose you as a friend, Paige. I mean that. You're like part of the family."

"Is it because of Kate?"

She wasn't pulling any punches. He had to be honest. He owed her that much.

"Yes and no. Nothing's happened, if that's what you're asking. There's no chance of a future there. This is a pit stop for her. But I'm having some feelings I shouldn't be having if things were . . ." He shrugged away the last few words.

"If you loved me." Her eyes turned glassy, and she shifted her gaze to the floor.

Crap. He hated this. "I'm really sorry, Paige. I didn't mean for this to happen."

Her chin quivered, and she bit her lip.

Aw, jeez. He stepped forward, arms out. "Can I give you a hug?"

She stepped away, one palm up. "No, Beau. I just—I need you to go."

"I don't want to leave you like this. Let's just sit down and—"

"I want you to *go*." Her eyes flashed. Her shoulders were stiff, her jaw set. "*Please.*"

He looked at her for one long, helpless minute, then he grabbed his coat off the hook. He turned at the door to find her studying the floor, arms curled tight around Dasher.

"I'm really sorry, Paige."

• • •

Eden closed *Goodnight Moon* and tucked the blanket around Micah. She gave him a kiss on the cheek. "Night-night, kiddo."

"Night."

The simple word pulled at the corners of her lips. He'd said it the past few nights. He'd even said "Mommy" when she'd gotten home tonight. It was the sweetest word she'd ever heard. Finally he was speaking again. One day soon he'd laugh, and his eyes would sparkle.

He must have worn out Miss Trudy because she'd turned in soon after they'd returned with the sleds. Beau had left again in his truck, and Eden had played a few rounds of Go Fish with Micah before his bath.

She flipped the light switch and headed downstairs, stopping in the kitchen for a glass of water. Her muscles ached from the fall, and the scrape on her wrist burned a bit. It could have been a lot worse, though.

She found Riley in the dark living room, the flickering light of the TV his only company. He stared at the screen, but she suspected he wasn't even seeing the football highlights. He didn't notice her appearance until she settled on the opposite end of the sofa.

"Hey. How's your wrist?"

She held it up. "Hardly hurts."

"I'm sorry if I was going too fast."

"You weren't. I had fun. I learned my lesson about letting go."

"Have you ever gone four-wheeling? It's less cold but a lot dirtier."

"I've never done anything like that before." He'd let her drive on the way home. She'd gone a lot slower than he had, but it was fun to have control of the rumbling machine.

"My dad was super protective. I wasn't even allowed to ride roller coasters."

"Seriously?"

She shrugged. She wondered what her dad was doing right now. She hoped he was okay. That he wasn't worried sick for her. She hated that she couldn't put his mind at ease.

Please, God. Keep him safe, and let him know we're all right.

Riley held out the remote. "Change the channel?"

A reporter was interviewing a football player, the volume barely audible. "No thanks. You getting excited about boot camp?"

He sighed. "Sure."

"You don't sound excited."

The light flickered as the program went to a commercial. He set the remote on the table. "The timing couldn't be worse."

She wasn't sure what he meant but didn't want to pry. If he wanted to explain, he would.

They watched a commercial, then another in silence. She wondered where Beau had gone. It had been a few hours since he'd left. She hoped his disappearance didn't have anything to do with the tension between him and Riley.

Riley's phone buzzed on the end table, and he checked the screen and answered the phone. "Hey." There was silence for a few seconds. "I'm sorry, honey." She'd never heard those tender notes in his voice.

He ran his hand over his face as he listened for a minute or so. "Sure. No, of course not. I'll be right there."

He was already on his feet by the time he hung up.

His countenance shifted once he'd pocketed his phone. He stabbed his hands into his coat and jerked his boots on, his eyes tight and flinty.

"Everything okay?"

Riley snatched his keys off the table. "When my brother gets back, tell him he's a real jerk." A moment later the door slammed shut.

. . .

They spent the last evening before Riley's departure at the Roadhouse. Riley convinced Eden to come along, and since it was his last night, she agreed.

The place had grown on her. It had a friendly, casual vibe. The wall of windows provided a beautiful view of the rugged coastline, and the wooden walls and comfy booths made it feel homey. The back wall, lined with old license plates from virtually every state in the Union, gave the Roadhouse an eclectic feel. She imagined the big deck overlooking the ocean was pretty popular in the summer.

Miss Trudy had elected to stay home, insisting she could take care of herself for a few hours, and Paige's absence was notable. Eden wasn't about to ask where she was. The tension between Beau and Riley was palpable.

Laughter sounded from the poolroom where Micah grappled with a pool stick twice his size.

Eden pushed her plate away and sat back in the

booth. She'd eaten her share of wings and curly fries. Conversation had petered out. It had been mostly her and Zac keeping it going, but he'd gone to the kitchen a few minutes ago. An awkward pause had settled over the table.

She was relieved when Beau excused himself. She watched him walk toward the poolroom with that fluid stride of his. Micah was lining up a shot, and when he pulled his pool stick back, Beau grabbed it. Her son turned and smiled. Beau ruffled his hair.

"You know you've got him all twisted up inside."

Her eyes darted to Riley. "What?"

"You can't be surprised. You have to notice the way he looks at you."

Her pulse fluttered even as she called herself all kinds of stupid. She licked her lips. "He's with Paige."

"Not anymore."

She blinked, her mind reviewing the past twenty-four hours. Beau's disappearance last night, the phone call to Riley, Paige's absence tonight.

She couldn't be the reason for the breakup . . . could she? As attracted as she was to Beau, there was no chance of a relationship, and she wasn't into casual flings. She was sure he wasn't either.

Across from her, Riley shifted. He had a napkin knotted in his hand, and he was aiming a dark look at Beau's back. She suddenly realized what all this meant. Riley had enlisted to escape the torture of his brother's relationship with Paige. Now, on the eve of his departure, that relationship was over.

"Oh, Riley. I'm so sorry."

He shot a wry smile her way. "Yeah, great timing, huh?"

She thought of Paige, and guilt pricked hard. "Is Paige okay?"

He lifted a muscular shoulder. "Her heart's broken, you know? She knew something wasn't right, but she thought it would pass."

It would pass . . . or it would leave town? Paige was no dummy. If Riley had picked up on Beau's interest in her, surely Paige had too.

"I feel like this is all my fault."

Riley's face softened. "Beau knows nothing can come of his feelings for you."

"Feelings?"

He lifted a brow. "What did you think was behind those pathetic looks?"

She guessed she hadn't thought that far. Hadn't dug that deep. A panicked feeling swept over her, making her breaths go shallow. She couldn't let anything come of this. Even if she weren't leaving, she didn't want a man. Love was for the birds.

"I'm really sorry all this has happened. I feel responsible."

"I only wish you'd come along a few months ago. How's that for selfish?" He glowered at Beau. "It's not your fault, though."

She took in the vulnerability in Riley's green eyes, and her heart squeezed. Not only was the woman he loved heartbroken over his brother, but he was also leaving, unable to be there for her. "What are you going to do about Paige?"

His eyes swung to hers. "What can I do?"

He was leaving tomorrow, and he'd be gone for a long time. She wondered if Paige would be married to someone else by the time he'd served his stint.

Fate could be cruel. Eden knew that all too well.

CHAPTER 24

The family piled out of Aunt Trudy's Ford Explorer. Zac helped their aunt while Beau lifted the hatchback and reached for Riley's duffel bag.

"I got it," Riley said.

The tension between them had eased only a little since their argument. Riley had spent a lot of time with Paige. She'd elected to say her good-byes last night rather than coming with them today. Beau still felt awful, like he'd let them both down. It wasn't a feeling he wanted to get used to.

The Bangor airport was busy, the short-term parking lot nearly filled. They made their way to the door along the short walkway, Beau beside his aunt, ready to steady her. People bustled by in their L.L.Bean coats and boots, their luggage rolling behind them, the wheels crunching over the salted pavement.

They waited while Riley checked in. Security was a short walk from there.

Riley faced his family, wearing a thin smile. "Guess this is it."

Zac was the first to embrace Riley. "Keep your chin up, bro."

"Always."

"We're proud of you."

Aunt Trudy came next. She hugged with one arm, balanced on her crutches. Riley patted her back.

When her blue eyes turned glassy, it was about Beau's undoing. It was only boot camp. Riley wasn't being shipped out to the Middle East.

Yet.

Beau's eyes stung at the thought. A huge knot had hardened in his throat. He couldn't believe his baby brother was headed to the military. He was torn between pride and dismay.

You'll keep him safe, right, God? 'Cause I'm trusting him to You. What other choice did he have? He wasn't used to letting go, and he didn't like it one bit.

"You'd better write," Aunt Trudy said from Riley's arms.

"I will."

"And call."

"It's only a few months, guys. Then I'll be back for ten days. Long enough for you to see my shaved head and feed me some good home-cooked food before I leave again."

Aunt Trudy stepped away, inconspicuously dabbing at the corner of her eyes as Beau moved forward.

A shadow flickered over Riley's jaw as he met Beau's eyes.

Beau wished this week had gone differently. Wished there wasn't this ugly thing between them. He reached out a hand and his brother clasped it, pulling him in for a hug.

Beau slapped his back a couple times. "Take care of yourself, little bro."

"I will."

"I'll be praying for you."

Riley drew back, wearing a crooked grin. "I'll need it. Don't forget you promised to run Lola when it warms up." Riley lived on his motorcycle in the summer.

"I won't."

The smile fell from Riley's mouth as he looked at Beau for a long moment.

There was so much Beau wanted to say, but the words jammed in his throat.

"You're my brother," Riley said. "You always will be, and I love you, man."

Beau swallowed against the knot in his throat. "I love you too. I'm sorry about—"

Riley waved him off. "We're cool." With a final smile he grabbed his duffel bag, his gaze swinging over their family. "Take care, you guys."

As he made his way toward the security officer, he gave a final wave. A few moments later they watched him advance down the cordoned lane.

Beau put his arm around Aunt Trudy, blinking against the tears. "He'll be all right," he said, but he wasn't sure which one of them he was reassuring.

CHAPTER 25

Eden joined Miss Trudy in the living room. A cartoon flickered on the TV, and her son had fallen asleep in the recliner, his head tilted at an awkward angle. His black lashes fanned across his beautiful olive skin. She wished he could always be at peace like this.

"Looks like someone ran out of steam." Miss Trudy's knitting needles clacked together. She was making something red and fuzzy.

"I guess we'll save his bath for the morning." It would make things rushed getting ready for church, but Eden didn't have the heart to wake him.

"It's too quiet without Riley."

"I know you'll miss him."

The family had seen him off to the airport this morning. Beau had gone straight to work afterward and hadn't come home until after supper. He'd gone upstairs for a shower awhile ago. Probably trying to warm up. It had turned brittle cold today, and another dusting of snow had already begun.

Miss Trudy nodded toward the TV. "I was thinking of watching *It's a Wonderful Life*. You want to watch it with me? The DVD's on the bookshelf."

"Sure. I haven't seen it in years. Let me just get Jack to bed, and I'll put it on." She leaned down to pick up Micah, feeling every ache from the fall.

"I'll get him," Beau said as he came down the steps.

"That's all right."

He nudged her out of the way. "You're still hurting from your fall."

He scooped up her son, shifting him in his arms as he headed up the stairs, Eden following. The yummy smell of Beau's cologne wafted behind him, and she pulled in a deep breath.

She couldn't help but admire his physique. He didn't need to exercise at a health club as Antonio had. His work kept him active and strong. It was obvious in the broad line of his shoulders, in the way they tapered down to his lean waist.

"You know you have him all twisted up inside." Riley's words had been heavily on her mind today. Was it true? And what would happen now that Beau had broken up with Paige?

Nothing. Nothing will happen, Eden, because you're leaving soon and because you're not looking for a relationship.

In the bedroom, she pulled down the covers, and Beau eased Micah onto his air mattress. His flexed muscles released, shifting, as he let go of his burden.

Eden moved closer to tuck Micah in. The scene reminded her of a real family. A real mom and dad. She pushed the image from her mind. They'd never had that, not even with Antonio. She'd parented Micah, and he'd done the same—none of it together.

She pulled the covers over her son, and he turned toward the wall, heaving a soft sigh. She planted a kiss on his cheek and turned out the light as they left the room.

Downstairs, Miss Trudy had already found the DVD and put it in the player. She was hobbling back to her chair as they entered the room.

"Come sit, Beau. We're watching *It's a Wonderful Life*."

"Don't mind if I do."

Miss Trudy started the movie and flipped off the lamp as Beau and Eden settled on opposite ends of the sofa. The white lights twinkled on the mantel garland and on the tree, giving the room a soft glow. The fire Eden had set earlier still wavered in the fireplace, crackling and popping softly.

The black-and-white movie began slowly, but soon Eden was caught up in George Bailey's financial problems. When the movie was well under way, she noticed that Miss Trudy's chair was empty, her knitting basket tucked nearby.

"Where'd she go?"

"To bed, I guess."

The rest of the movie was just as she remembered. At the end Eden gave a sigh as the credits rolled and the music played. Sometimes it was nice to believe in happy endings, just for a little while.

Beau flipped off the DVD and switched to a local TV channel where the news was playing. A seafood shack in Folly Shoals was closing after almost fifty years in business. There was a two-vehicle accident on Pond Road due to the slick road conditions. The Schoodic Baptist Choir would be performing their annual Christmas cantata tomorrow at 6:00 p.m.

The news broke for a commercial. She should go to bed, but for some reason she wasn't tired yet.

"I like what you've done with the house." Beau's voice was a low rumble that she felt deep inside.

"The Christmas decorations growing on you?"

He gave her a little smile. "It's not just that. It feels . . . homier? Can I say that without sounding like a girl?"

"It must be my superb cooking skills."

His smile was a traffic stopper. "You've come a long way, no doubt about that."

She chuckled. "I had nowhere to go but up."

. . .

Beau knew better than to respond to that comment. "How's my aunt's therapy coming along?"

"It's painful, but she's fighting through it. She's a strong woman. The doctor said she'd get her brace off next week. Maybe before Christmas."

It was only a week away, and they hadn't really talked about when Kate would leave. "You're welcome to stay beyond that if you'd like. I could use some help getting the farm cleaned up after it closes. You could make a little extra money."

"Thanks. I'll . . . have to see how it goes."

A silence settled over the room. She was watching the TV as it flickered to a local commercial for used cars.

The thought of her leaving soon put a pit in his gut. He'd gotten used to having her around. She was a good listener and a caring woman. Her love for her son was a sight to behold. When it came to protecting him, she was tenacious and strong. But he sensed an underlying vulnerability that made the man in him want to take care of her. He wasn't sure she'd appreciate that sentiment.

"I'm sorry about Paige," she said.

Their gazes connected, and he read the questions there. "How'd you know?"

"You're home on a Saturday night."

He hiked a brow.

She gave a sheepish look. "And Riley may have said something."

He gave a tight smile. "I'm sure he did."

"It's been pretty tense around here. I hope you were able to make up before he left."

Beau nodded slowly. "We're brothers, above all else. It's not the first argument we've had, believe me."

Beau had checked in with Paige this morning via text. She'd answered short and sweet. He'd let her know she was still welcome to spend Christmas with them. He was worried she'd have no place else to go.

"I wonder if Riley's there yet," she said.

Beau perused her face, looking for signs of interest. "He was supposed to land at five, so I'm sure he is. It'll be a grueling few months."

"He's up for it, I think. He's a tough guy."

A worm of jealousy niggled through him, and he didn't like it. He didn't want her thinking about Riley.

What was going on? How had he developed feelings

for this woman so quickly? It was as if she'd cast a spell over him. He wanted her thinking about him, he wanted her dreaming of him, he wanted her in his arms.

Come on, Callahan.

He'd just broken up with Paige, and hello . . . Kate was leaving soon. She was in some unspoken danger, and he had more questions about her than answers. The last time he'd come near her she'd pushed him off like he was Satan's spawn.

He angled his body toward her, only a throw pillow between them. He studied her in the faint light. Who had hurt her? Was it Lucca Fattore or someone else? Her father? Her husband? He had a million questions, but she was a closed book.

She caught him staring. "What?"

"Just wondering about you."

"Wondering what?"

"Everything. What were you like as a child?"

"I don't know. I guess I was quiet. I always had my nose in a book. There wasn't much else to do."

"What about friends?"

She shrugged. "There was April, a girl who lived in the trailer next to us. Her mom, Karen, was really nice and kind of took me under her wing. I would've lived over there if I could've."

"Didn't you like your house?"

"I told you about my mom passing. Things were good until then. But my dad had agoraphobia—he was afraid of going out in public. He was also afraid of being alone. So after my mom died, I wasn't allowed out of the trailer much. He sent me to the grocery because he was too afraid to go himself and sometimes to the library. He liked to read."

"What about school?"

"Dad homeschooled me after Mom died."

He tried to imagine being trapped in a trailer with a fearful father. It must have been very lonely.

"If he was afraid to leave the house, how did he make a living?"

"He mowed lawns. He could handle being outside okay. That's how I was able to spend time with April and her mom. I kind of lived vicariously through them."

A dreamy look washed over her face. "They'd take this trip every summer to their cabin and come back with pictures and stories. I used to dream about that little cabin. I'd get books at the library and read about where they went and pretend I went too.

"Karen would tell us Bible stories—she knew them all. She helped my faith grow. She was loving and patient and always inviting me to go places with them, even though I always had to say no.

"When I was fifteen they got a new computer, and she gave me her old one. I spent a lot of time on that thing. I'd always loved art in school, so I developed an interest in designing websites. Karen let me design one for her business—she made snow globes, all different kinds. I loved the ones with angels especially. She loved Christmas, and their trailer had snow globes everywhere all year round. I know it sounds kind of strange, but I thought it was wonderful. We used to wind them all up and dance ourselves silly."

Beau pictured a young Kate shaking those globes,

watching the snow fall. Dreaming of being someplace else. Spinning until she was dizzy. He was glad she'd had a place to go. A place where she felt loved and cared for. It sounded like she'd been the one doing the caring in her own home.

He remembered the way she'd pushed him off her in the barn. She'd been afraid of him. Where had that come from? Not a father with agoraphobia.

"Can I ask you something?"

She looked away. "You can ask."

"Who hurt you?"

She turned back, giving him a long look.

"The way you reacted in the barn a few weeks ago . . . that's the reaction of an abused woman."

She turned away, staring at the TV for a long, quiet minute. "I wasn't abused. Not really."

"That's an ambiguous statement."

She kept watching the TV as the news came back on. Her breathing had accelerated, and her hands fidgeted in her lap. He waited her out.

"My husband didn't hit me, if that's what you're thinking," she said finally.

"Then what did he do?"

She curled her arms around her body protectively.

Had anyone protected her ever? She seemed so independent, so capable. But if things were as bad as he thought, she had to be scared. He wanted to take her in his arms, tell her he'd be the one. He'd keep her safe. But she wouldn't welcome that.

"My husband and I—we didn't have a normal marriage, except maybe in the beginning."

"What happened?"

She shook her head. "I was young and stupid and desperate to get out of the house. I met him when he came to town for some kind of ER training."

"He was a doctor?"

She nodded. "He wore a suit, and he was kind, and every time he smiled at me my pulse would race. One day he asked me to have dinner with him, and I did. I sneaked out of the house after my dad was asleep. I started sneaking out a lot.

"I felt so free those nights. We eloped a few months later—I knew my dad would never approve. After we were married we moved to Antonio's hometown. Dad was devastated. I felt terrible for leaving him, but I just needed to be free of that trailer so badly. But as the months went on I began to realize I wasn't free at all. I'd fallen for a man who just wanted someone to control."

"Why didn't you leave him?"

She gave a short laugh. "I tried. But by then we'd had Jack. He threatened to take my son away."

"You have rights."

"Not in that county. He was very rich and had a lot of clout with all the right people. He could've made it happen, and I couldn't stand the thought of losing my son. I was trapped."

"Right back where you started."

"In so many ways."

"That still doesn't answer my question."

She looked at him, as if not remembering what it was.

"How did he hurt you?"

Even the darkness couldn't hide the shame that

washed over her face. She lowered her head, sank deeper into the couch.

"You can tell me anything. It won't go any further."

"I don't like talking about it." Her voice was a thready whisper.

"Have you *ever* talked about it?"

She met his eyes, shaking her head.

He let the silence play out a minute before he spoke. "Kate . . . whatever he did to you—you didn't deserve it. You're a wonderful person, a terrific mom. You're special, and you deserve to be treated that way. I hope you know that."

In the background the news moved on to weather, but Beau couldn't take his eyes from Kate and the emotions washing over her face, the glimmer of tears in her eyes.

"I thought he was the answer to all my prayers—my knight in shining armor. At first I noticed he was a little controlling and obsessive about certain things like our schedule and where things should be put away. But then we started arguing. He insisted on a maid, and I preferred to take care of my own home. He didn't want me to work, and I was bored. I thought having a child might help, and he agreed. But as soon as Jack was born, he wanted me to hire a nanny." She shook her head. "I wouldn't give in. No one else was going to raise my son. I wanted to be with him every moment."

He remembered the soulful way Jack had called for his daddy after the car had backfired. "What kind of father was he?"

"Better than you'd think. He was busy with work, but he made time for . . . Jack. As Jack got older I started doing some work from home—designing websites for small, local businesses. I didn't tell my husband, and when he found out, he was furious. He demanded I give it up. That was the last straw for me. I threatened to leave."

She shuddered. Her hand fell to the pillow between them. "He made it very clear that if I left I'd never see my son again. And I believed him. I'd seen him at work, all the hospital politics. He was ruthless. After that things were tense. There was no relationship, no tenderness or kindness."

"What about friends? Wasn't there anyone you could count on?"

She gave a rueful smile. "My old friends were long gone. He didn't like them. And my new friends—it was hard keeping up a front that everything at home was okay. If someone befriended me, asked me to go to lunch, I'd just make excuses. It was easier that way. Eventually they gave up."

"Sounds lonely."

"It was. I walked on eggshells all the time, worrying about upsetting him. If anything went wrong it was my fault—at least, that's what he said. And when someone says that enough, you believe it. You don't feel capable of making good decisions or even thinking straight. I lost a little piece of myself each day. He used to remind me all the time of the Proverbs 31 wife. He let me know how short I fell."

"What about him? What about a husband loving his wife the way Christ loved the church?"

"He never talked about that."

"I'll bet he didn't."

Her fist tightened on the pillow. Her breaths came more rapidly. "He also insisted that—that I owed him for all he did for me. I wasn't working, after all, and I was living in his gorgeous house. I was wearing designer clothes he paid for and having dinner at the country club on a membership he'd bought, and I was traveling to Europe on his dime. But all I wanted was my son and my freedom.

"He had ways of threatening me to get what he wanted. And even though we no longer had a real relationship, he wanted . . . other things to stay the same. He called it my 'wifely duty.'"

Beau's gut twisted hard. Anger welled up inside, burning hot toward a cruel man who was dead and deserved to be. He took a deep breath, forcing it down.

He set his hand on hers. "Kate . . . I'm sorry."

She turned to him, tears and shame shimmering in her eyes. "And so I did it," she whispered. "Every Saturday like clockwork. For month after month after month, I did exactly what he wanted, when he wanted, how he wanted."

He drilled her with a look. "It's not your fault, Kate. That's called rape."

"He was my husband."

"That doesn't give him the right to force you."

"He didn't hold a gun to my head."

"Didn't he? If he'd followed through on those threats it would've killed you."

"The week before he died, I found out he'd been cheating on me with a nurse at the hospital."

Heat flushed through Beau as he worked hard to hold back a few choice words. He wished the guy were still alive so he could beat him to a pulp.

Her fist tightened under his hand. She lifted her chin and laughed, but there was no humor in it. "No man will ever touch me like that again." Her firm voice wobbled as she blinked back the tears.

"No man should ever touch you against your will."

Her body was stiff, the line of her shoulders taut, her arm flexed. She was a bottle of soda, capped and shaken, ready to explode. He wanted to ease off the lid and let out the pressure. But how?

"You don't have to be so strong all the time," he said.

Her chin wobbled as she fought for control.

"A lot has happened to you. Things you didn't deserve. It's okay to just let go."

She shook her head. "If I do that I'll never stop."

"It only feels that way. You're still blaming yourself for what happened, aren't you?"

Her lip trembled, and she caught it between her teeth.

"It wasn't your fault. You're a good mom. You did what you had to do to keep your son. Your husband was the only one at fault."

A tear got loose, tumbling down her cheek. Another followed. Her face started to crumble. She covered it with both hands, and a sob broke free.

His heart cracked in two. He wished he knew what to say. Wished he could fix it. He touched her arm, and when she didn't flinch away, he gently tugged her. "Come here, Kate."

She resisted only a few seconds before giving in. She fell limply toward him until her head hit the pillow on his thigh, her hands still covering her face. Sobs wracked her body.

An ache opened up inside him, yawning wide. He couldn't imagine how hard her life must have been. How broken her spirit must have become. She was drowning in guilt and shame, and he wanted to take off her shackles and set her free. But that wasn't his job.

God, release her.

He ran his fingers through her hair. So soft. She trembled against him.

"That's it, Kate. Just let it all go."

Her grief was so real and big. What kind of man treated a woman that way? As if she were a possession to take at will. It disgusted him. It made him want to put his fist through a wall. But that wouldn't help Kate. He wasn't sure even this was helping. It was breaking his heart. That was for sure.

"You're going to be okay," he whispered. "You'll see."

He continued to run his fingers through her hair, whispering whatever came to mind. When he wasn't talking, he was praying for her. When her sobs settled into a soft cry, he let his head fall against the back of the couch and closed his eyes.

CHAPTER 26

Something tugged Eden from a sound sleep. She kept her eyes closed, fighting the pull of morning. She was warm and toasty and . . . lighter somehow. Her breaths lengthened as oblivion drew her deeper into its embrace.

A creaking noise sounded above her. Why was there creaking over her head? She was on the top floor.

Her eyes cracked open, blinking against the morning light. They fell on the fireplace, the coffee table. A jean-clad knee.

The night before came rushing back, and her breath froze in her lungs. She'd fallen asleep. On Beau's lap. Why hadn't he awakened her?

She heard only faint, steady breathing. Overhead another creak sounded. Micah must be up and moving about.

She had to get up. Preferably without waking Beau. The mortification of last night's confession and her subsequent breakdown came crashing down on her. Why had she told him all that—her deepest shame laid out bare. But she couldn't process last night. She had to deal with now.

She assessed the situation. A blanket was draped over her, the knitted afghan that always rested on the sofa back. One of her hands was tucked beneath her cheek, the other under Beau's thigh. They'd shifted in the night, and one of his legs was stretched out alongside her. He'd fallen asleep against the arm of the sofa, and she was wedged between his leg and the sofa back. The weight of his hand rested on her shoulder.

She turned her head slowly . . . and met Beau's sleepy brown eyes.

"Morning." His voice was morning gruff.

She pulled her hand from his thigh and bolted upright, drawing the afghan to her chest as if she weren't fully dressed in yesterday's clothing.

"You fell asleep," he said.

"You should've woken me," she croaked.

His lips tilted in a sideways smile. "I would've except I fell asleep too."

"You probably have a terrible crick in your neck."

"I slept great, actually. You?" Had his voice always been so deep and yummy?

She remembered the way she'd wept all over him. He probably had a lifetime of snot and tears all over his jeans. Her face heated. What had gotten into her? She never did that. Never just let loose like that. She had to hold it together. If she didn't, who would?

Though she had to admit, she'd slept like a baby.

The floor creaked overhead. She tossed the afghan aside and leapt to her feet. "Jack's up. I'd better get him ready for church."

She ran up the steps before he could reply.

. . .

Sheriff Colton joined Beau and Aunt Trudy in the foyer after church. "Afternoon, Beau. Trudy."

Beau clasped his hand. "Colton. Good to see you."

Aunt Trudy lifted her chin. "Sheriff." She looked out the window where yesterday's snow swirled in a glittering spiral.

"You should join us for dinner," Beau said. "Aunt Trudy's got a roast in the Crock-Pot."

The sheriff's eyes glanced off Aunt Trudy. "Ah, wish I could. I do love your cooking, ma'am. But I'm on duty in a few minutes. My deputy had a family emergency."

"I'd better go see what's keeping Kate," Aunt Trudy said, excusing herself.

Sheriff Colton watched her go, a wistful look on his face. His cheeks were flushed from the brief encounter.

"You should just ask her out, Colton."

The pink stain darkened, clashing with his red mustache. "Why would I do that? I was just trying to catch you before you left. I did a little checking with my friend like I told you I would."

After a quick glance around, Beau led him to a quiet corner of the vestibule. "What'd you find out?"

"He's a bad character, that Lucca Fattore. He's wanted in the prescription drug market, but no one's been able to nail him. He's on trial for the murder of Antonio Martelli, who I'm guessing was Kate's husband. If that's the case, her name is Eden—Eden Martelli."

Eden. The name suited her.

"The feds suspect that Martelli was in deep with

Fattore. They think he was undercutting him." He gave Beau a pointed look. "Martelli was either stupid or as arrogant as all get out. You don't cheat a man like Fattore. He likes to get his own revenge, which is why he was the one pulling the trigger, not some hired hand."

"So they'll put him away for the murder?"

The sheriff gave a tight-lipped smile. "They've got lots of circumstantial evidence, but probably not enough to put him away. They had DNA evidence, but it came up missing. Martelli's kid saw him get shot, and they had him and his mom at a safe house. But the marshals turned up dead—slit throats. The Martelli woman and her kid disappeared. That's all my contact knew, and you said keep it on the down low, so I didn't press him."

"No, that's fine. Thanks for your discretion."

"We should probably contact the DEA, Beau. It sounds like—"

"No. We don't even know for sure if Martelli was Kate's husband. This could be something else altogether."

It wasn't. Everything Kate told him lined up. But Colton didn't know all those details. Maybe he could get Kate to tell him the truth. Persuade her to go to the authorities and get this creep locked away for good.

"Fattore must've found the safe house and killed the marshals," Beau said. It was a wonder Kate and Jack had escaped.

"That's what I'm thinking. That's one man that needs to be locked away."

Colton was right. He'd talk to Kate about going back, he decided, as he drove them home a little later.

It would be hard for her to subject Jack to additional trauma, but his word could put away an evil man. Then she could settle down and stop running, stop looking over her shoulder. His experience told him it wouldn't be that simple. Not with a network like Fattore's. But he'd help. He'd keep them both safe if it were the last thing he did.

CHAPTER 27

After lunch Eden headed to the Roadhouse with Micah and Beau to watch the Patriots game. Aunt Trudy stayed home, claiming to need peace and quiet. It was a good thing because the game was close, and the crowd was rowdy.

Eden always liked the Roadhouse's atmosphere, but it was even better during a football game. The place was packed, the TVs blared, and every play was met with unanimous support for the Pats. She loved watching her son during the games. He'd become an ardent fan, cheering at all the right times, receiving high fives from Beau and Zac.

She couldn't help but notice the way the Callahan brothers turned heads as they mingled with their friends, but neither of them seemed to notice the feminine appreciation. Paige had been right about their being the town's most eligible bachelors.

At half time Zac asked Beau to run out for ground ginger. The Shop 'n' Save was closed, but the Kitchen Crate in town carried spices. He invited Eden to come along. Micah didn't want to leave, and Zac told her to go on. She acquiesced, knowing Zac would take good care of him.

"I thought everything was closed on Sundays," she said as they walked out to the parking lot.

"Not with Christmas in less than a week."

As they approached his truck, Beau tossed her the keys.

She caught them in her cold hands. "What?"

"You drive. Aunt Trudy said you need practice driving on the snow."

She gave him a scowl as she slid into the driver's seat. Beau's truck rumbled as she started it. She pulled slowly from the lot and onto the street. The pavement was covered with packed snow, but it wasn't very slippery.

"Turn left on Main," he said when they reached town. "The store's on the right, just past the coffee shop."

The street was lined with cars, parallel parked against knee-high snowbanks. People strolled the shoveled sidewalks in their buttoned-up parkas and winter boots, carrying handled bags. The red, white, and blue Open flags hanging outside the stores waved in the wind. Christmas lights twinkled in storefront windows even though the sun hadn't set yet.

"There's a spot." He pointed to a space in front of the yarn shop.

She pulled alongside an old black GMC and put the truck in reverse, looking behind her. She couldn't remember the last time she'd parallel parked. But it was like riding a bike, right?

Holding her breath, she turned into the curb and waited for the right time to cut the wheel back. But she waited too long, and the truck's tires bumped the curb.

She let out her breath and started forward again,

turning the wheel. *Let's try this again.* Back, back . . . The truck plowed into the snowbank with a scraping sound.

Her shoulders tensed as her gaze flickered off his eyes. "Sorry."

"You're kind of bad at this." She heard the smile in his voice and looked to see his eyes twinkling.

She exhaled softly, relieved he wasn't upset about the truck. "I'm just out of practice."

"That snowbank begs to differ." One side of his lips turned up in the kind of smile that should be illegal in all fifty states. Maybe worldwide. It would be a service to women everywhere.

"I just need to line it up."

She pulled forward, but there wasn't much room. Inches. She reversed and bumped the curb again. Forward again. Backward. Forward. Back. She didn't seem to be getting anywhere. She tensed, waiting for him to snap.

"I was wrong." There was laughter in his voice. "You're *really* bad at this."

Her spirits lifted at his playful tone, and all the tension drained away. Her shoulders fell, her arms relaxed, her fingers loosened on the wheel. "Shhh. I need to focus."

"You need a hybrid and a parking space the size of a runway."

A laugh slipped out as her gaze flickered over him. "That is not nice."

"Did you just snort?"

"No." She bit her lip, backing up again. Slowly this time, cutting the wheel.

"Yes, you did. You totally snorted."

"I do not snort." She hit the curb. A laugh escaped, finishing with a snort.

"Oh my gosh. You're drawing a crowd."

"I am not!" She laughed, looking around, hoping it wasn't true. It wasn't except for a teenaged kid who stood outside the coffee shop with a steaming cup and his phone, probably tweeting about bad women drivers.

"The *Harbor Tides* is going to show up any minute."

"Stop it."

"Man dies of old age while waiting for woman to parallel park."

"Stop it!"

It had been forever since she'd bantered with a man. It felt good. Like a big, warm hug at the end of a long week.

She pulled forward, turning the wheel, then backed up. And there was that snowbank again. *Crunch.* They jolted forward against their seat belts. She bit her lip.

"We're going to miss the entire second half. Switch me seats."

"This parking space is too small."

"Sure it is. Switch me seats."

"Fine, but it's the space, not my parking skills." She put the truck in park then unbuckled her belt. As she reached for the handle, he scooted next to her.

Okay, they'd do it his way.

She twisted to crawl over him, putting her left hand on the seat back beside his shoulder. But he was sitting on her other hand, and she lost her balance as she tugged it free. She put her left foot down, shifting her weight, almost falling on him.

Then realized her foot was grinding into his.

She looked at him, eye to eye, practically on top of him. "Sorry!"

Her foot felt for purchase and landed on her purse. She tipped.

He chuckled, his dark eyes glimmering. "You are a hot mess, girl."

His deep laugh loosened something pleasant inside, stirring up things she hadn't felt in far too long. And the look in his eyes wasn't hurting either.

She hiked her second leg over him, laughing at her own clumsiness. Finally she twisted over, falling into the passenger seat.

Beau's eyes connected with hers, the warmth in them making her heart roll over and beg for mercy.

"Lucky for you," he said, "you have a great laugh."

. . .

Beau knew he had to talk to Kate about her past. It was the whole reason he'd invited her on the errand. But seeing the pretty smile on her lips, the tinge of pink on her cheeks, he couldn't bring himself to do it just now.

Man, she was beautiful. And that laugh of hers. Like a melody that said more than lyrics possibly could. It was the first time he'd heard her really laugh, he realized. It had only made him want to hear it again and again. She deserved to have a little laughter in her life, and he wanted to be the one making it happen.

Tearing his eyes from hers, he pulled the truck forward, and a couple of corrections later, the truck was parallel to the curb.

"Show-off," she tossed over her shoulder as she exited the truck.

She was relaxed enough to tease him now after being a tense wreck only minutes ago, and it made him feel like Superman.

Eden. Just the sound of her real name made him think of lush gardens and natural beauty. He had to be careful not to say it, though—it would only scare her away. Maybe when he talked to her tonight she'd open up enough to tell him herself. He wanted all the barriers between them gone.

They found the ginger in the store, chatting and playing as they made the purchase. By the time they made it back to the Roadhouse, the second half was well under way.

Zac took the bag as they entered the noisy restaurant. "What took so long?"

"Kate had an interview with the *Tides*," Beau said with a straight face.

An elbow landed in his gut. He grunted.

"Oo-kaay, then." Zac headed toward the kitchen.

Beau made a big deal of rubbing his stomach. "Harsh, Kate. Really harsh."

Between the Roadhouse noise and the tight game—with the Pats coming out on top—Beau didn't have a chance to talk to her.

Later that night he wondered if he was ever going to. She'd gone upstairs to tuck in Jack ten minutes ago.

Remembering the intimacy of the night before, he wondered if she'd even come back down.

Aunt Trudy was knitting away in her recliner, watching a reality show set on an island in the Caribbean somewhere.

Awhile later Kate's footsteps sounded on the creaky steps. The tap kicked on in the kitchen, and she entered the living room a moment later, taking the opposite end of the sofa.

"Working on Riley's sweater?" she asked Aunt Trudy.

"I'd hoped to finish it before he left. I don't think he's allowed to receive packages."

"Well, shoot," Beau said. "I thought that was for me. You know red's my best color."

"You'll be lucky if I make you anything." She frowned at Beau. "Don't think I haven't noticed Sheriff Colton's coming by more often."

He shot a look at Kate, but she was watching the contestant on the reality show attempt to make a shelter with palm fronds.

"What makes you think I had anything to do with that?" Beau asked.

"You can just tell the sheriff that he can keep his doughnuts and his pies to himself. I'm not interested."

"Oh, no. I'm not getting in the middle of this."

She pursed her lips, her needles clacking louder.

"I don't see what's so bad about him anyway. He's a nice guy. Make some woman a fine husband, if you ask me."

Aunt Trudy grabbed her basket, tossing her project

inside. "Well, I didn't ask you, did I?" She grabbed her crutches, stood, and hobbled from the room.

A few moments later her door clicked shut.

· · ·

Eden turned to Beau after Miss Trudy left the room. "Poor Sheriff Colton. He doesn't stand a chance."

"You never know. She might be stubborn, but he's way more patient than I ever gave him credit for."

She watched the woman on the reality show attempt to make a fire with two pieces of driftwood. "That's never going to work. Where do they find these people?"

The TV light flickered in the darkness. Her mind wandered from the banal TV show to Beau, sitting at the other end of the couch. She couldn't help but remember last night's conversation. She couldn't believe she'd opened up like that. Couldn't believe she'd wept in his lap.

But then she remembered their errand today, and her soul relaxed. She enjoyed his company. He was so unlike Antonio. If things were different—very different—he might ask her on a date. She might say yes, and they'd tease and banter all night and end up at her front door where he might kiss her good night.

But her chances for that had ended before they'd even begun. And as much as she might like the idea of a romantic relationship, she'd taken off her rosy glasses a long time ago.

The TV program broke for a commercial.

"Kate . . . I need to talk to you about something."

Beau was leaning back against the sofa, his ankle over his knee, hands resting on his thighs. His gaze flickered off her.

A worm of apprehension wiggled through her. "It's too close to Christmas to fire me. That would just be mean."

He didn't even smile at her attempt at levity. "It's about your husband, your past."

She pulled the pillow into her lap. "About what I said last night?"

"Not exactly." He looked at her and continued, his voice a low hum in the dim room. "Awhile back I checked the history on the computer and saw you'd done a search for a man named Lucca Fattore."

Her heart sped and her fingers clutched at the pillow.

"I couldn't find much on him, so I asked Sheriff Colton to look into it for me."

Her whole body tensed. "What?"

"You wouldn't answer my questions, Kate, and I needed—"

"You had no right!"

"You're living in my house, with my—"

She jumped to her feet. "Then I'll leave!"

He sprang to his feet and moved to block her way. "Kate . . . settle down."

She was shaking, her pulse skittering haphazardly, her breath catching in her throat. If the law knew where she was, so did Fattore's men. Maybe they were already on their way.

Her throat tightened, her eyes burned. She shoved the heel of her hand into Beau's chest. "I trusted you."

He grasped her arms. "I was worried, Kate, and

rightly so. If what Colton told me is true, you're in way over your head."

"Now they'll find us." She tried to shake him off, but his grip was secure. "Let me go. We have to leave."

"Don't be crazy. You're safer here than you are on your own."

"Don't you see? If Sheriff Colton's been poking around, they'll find out. They'll trace him right here to Summer Harbor. They'll hunt us down and kill us in our beds. *All* of us!"

"No. He was discreet. He only checked with a buddy of his. Someone he trusts. He didn't bring you into it."

"You don't know what you're talking about. You have no idea who these people are and how far their reach extends."

"Then tell me."

She looked away, catching her breath. Her eyes burned and her throat ached. She needed to calm down. Think. The TV light flickered blue across the room. The Christmas lights twinkled on the mantel. What was she going to do now?

"Tell me what you know," she said when she could think past the panic.

"Fattore is wanted for dealings in the prescription drug market. Your husband worked for him. It's speculated that he double-crossed Fattore in some way. Fattore killed him, and Jack was the only witness. Both of you were taken into protective custody, and sometime later the marshals overseeing your case turned up dead. You and Jack went missing, and the feds are searching for you. That's all I know."

A heavy breath escaped Eden. He loosened his grip on her as she forked her fingers through her short hair.

"There are dirty cops involved. That's why I needed you to stay out of this. Why I can't have Sheriff Colton bumbling around in—"

"He was discreet. I trust him."

Her eyes cut to him. "Like I trusted you?"

"You *can* trust me, Kate. I only want to help."

"There is no help for this, Beau. I just need to get to—away. Someplace safe. Fattore will be found guilty, and then it'll all be over." She and Jack would finally be free.

"He won't be found guilty. Not without Jack's testimony."

"Yes, he will. They have DNA evidence."

Beau's eyes pierced hers for a long moment.

The look on his face made a knot tighten in her stomach. "What?"

He looked at the TV, then back to her, his eyes softening. "The evidence went missing."

Her breath escaped. No. She shook her head. Now they had nothing. He'd never be found guilty.

"We can get you back safely. Jack can testify, Fattore will be put away, and all this will be over."

"No. We tried that route. I watched a marshal—the one the *feds* sent to keep us safe—slit the throats of two good men. We were supposed to be next. I can't trust any of them. I'm not taking my son back there! I'm not."

"Okay, okay. Tell me what happened. Tell me everything. We'll figure this out."

Heaving a sigh, she told the story starting with

Marshal Walter, whom they'd become so close with. She told him about Marshal Langley and the vicious murders and her terrifying escape. "I heard him tell Walter that their boss was in on it too. I can't trust any of them."

"Tell me how you ended up here. How you covered your trail."

"There was money in the emergency bag Walter packed for us. Disguises too." She explained how they changed hats and shirts and cabs and bought a car with cash in Jacksonville before making their way farther north. "I switched plates with another car in Jacksonville, a tourist from Georgia. And I cut and dyed my hair there too."

He nodded slowly. "You did a good job, Kate."

His approval felt good. She wished she didn't care, but she couldn't deny that she did. Even if he had broken her trust.

"I'll do anything to keep my son safe. And right now, I think that means leaving."

"Where are you going that they can't find you? You're safer here with me. With us. We'll take extra precautions."

In her mind she saw the line of blood on Walter's neck. Marshal Brown's blank-eyed stare. They'd do the same thing to her son without a second thought.

She closed her eyes against the image. "These people are ruthless, Beau."

He palmed her face, and she opened her eyes. The steadiness in his dark eyes calmed her. Her scattered thoughts began settling into place, and her racing pulse slowed.

"I won't let anything happen to you, Kate."

"You can't be here 24/7."

"The heck I can't. I'll get Zac to cover my hours. We're only open four more days, then it's Christmas Eve. I'll have the sheriff keep an eye out. Nobody knows you're here, right? You haven't contacted anyone? Family? Friends?"

"No." The calls she'd made to her dad didn't count. "There's only my dad, and I haven't talked to him since before we were taken into protection." She squirmed at the half-truth.

"Good. I think everything's going to be okay."

His thumb moved along her jaw, making every cell leap to life. It was only because she was scared. So scared.

"What will you tell Zac and Miss Trudy?"

"I'll fill them in on the basics. They need to know there's a possibility of danger."

She thought of Miss Trudy, helpless on a pair of crutches, and big, lovable Zac. These people had come to mean a lot to her. She didn't want to put them in harm's way.

"I'll keep you safe, Kate. Both of you. I promise."

She balked at the words. She knew he meant to reassure her. And she needed to do whatever was in Micah's best interest. But they were so familiar, like the ones her dad used to say to keep her home. *"You can't go. That's not safe, honey. I don't care if all the other kids are going."*

Safe. Safe. Safe. Was there really such a thing? It didn't come in the arms of any man. That she knew.

But running off on her own with little money and

no plan wasn't the smart thing to do. She already kept a bag packed just in case. She was ready to leave at a moment's notice. She'd do whatever was necessary to keep her son safe. And right now, that meant trusting Beau.

"Kate . . ." His thumb moved across her jaw, drawing her eyes to his. They were coal black in the shadows, glittering with something she was afraid to define.

"Tell me your name," he said, his voice low and smoky. "Your real one."

He already knew too much. More than she'd ever wanted him to. And now he was asking for more.

"Why don't you just look it up?"

"I want *you* to tell me."

The magnetic pull of his eyes, his voice, was a warning flare. Her name was such a small thing. Just a little piece of her. But she wasn't giving it up. She'd already given up too many pieces of herself.

She stepped away, letting his hands fall to his sides. "Good night, Beau," she said. And she turned toward the stairs.

CHAPTER 28

I need your help," Beau said into his phone. He pulled the final window shade down and began pacing the living room.

"What's wrong?" Zac answered.

"I just had a talk with Kate. She's in trouble—more than we thought. I need to stick close to the house this week. I know you have the Roadhouse but—"

"Consider it done. Shelley just got back from Boston. I'll see if she can cover."

Shelley was a former manager who stayed home with her toddler but filled in now and again.

Beau sighed. "Thanks." Just knowing he could stay close to home made him feel better.

He filled Zac in on Kate's situation, the weight of it feeling heavier with each passing word.

"Holy moley," Zac said when Beau was finished. "She's in deep."

"'Fraid so. I'll need you to keep your eyes open while you're working. I'm sure Sheriff Colton was discreet, and Kate did a great job covering her tracks, but like I said, we don't know who's involved. While you're working the farm, pay attention to who comes down the drive."

"What's Sheriff Colton doing about all this?"

"I haven't filled him in on the latest. But I will. I'll need his help."

"Won't he be duty-bound to turn Kate over to the feds?"

"She'd be as good as dead if he did. Kate and Jack both. I can't risk that."

"*You* can't risk it? Sounds like you're getting pretty invested in her, Beau."

"You say that like it's a bad thing."

Silence hummed across the line. "She's in the middle of a pretty big mess."

"Through no fault of her own. She's the victim here, Zac."

"I know, I know. But that doesn't change the circumstances. What'll happen if this Fattore guy is found guilty? Will she be off the hook?"

"It's not likely he'll be convicted. But either way, she's got a price on her head. Kate witnessed the murder of two marshals. They'll want her for that alone, not to mention the fact that she can finger two moles at the fed level."

"So basically she'll be looking over her shoulder the rest of her life."

"Not if I have anything to say about it."

Kate wouldn't be happy about his interference, but her feelings on the matter were secondary to her safety.

"Kate isn't the only one you'd better be guarding, my friend."

Minutes after Beau hung up he pulled a box from under his bed. He keyed in the code and opened the case, breathing in the metallic smell of his .40 caliber pistol. He hadn't handled it since he'd quit his job. It felt good in his hands. Weighty and familiar.

He'd called Colton and filled him in on everything he'd learned. He shoved a magazine into the receiver, and it snapped into place. If someone showed up intending to hurt Kate or Jack, they'd come face-to-face with his Glock 23.

CHAPTER 29

Eden's nerves were fraying. She felt like a sitting duck. Beau hung close to the house, barely stepping outside long enough to chop wood. Having him around was a comfort even if needing him did chafe at her pride. But she had to let that go and do what was best for Micah. The danger was real, and even though Beau was certain Sheriff Colton's source was trustworthy, she didn't buy in so easily.

Aunt Trudy was cranky, having had enough of being dependent on someone else to get her out of the house. Eden stayed busy, making the house sparkle, trying new recipes, and helping Miss Trudy wrap presents. She'd even helped Micah write a letter to Riley, who would need news from home to keep his spirits up. If he knew the danger she'd exposed his family to, he'd probably be on the next plane back to Maine.

After their initial discussion about her past, she and Beau avoided the topic. They fell into the habit of watching a Christmas movie each night. She sensed Beau wanted to put her at ease, and the routine helped. But she wasn't oblivious to the drawn shades and the locked doors or the way his ears perked each time a car came down the drive.

He went to bed after her each night, and in the morning when she plodded down the stairs, she found him sipping coffee at the kitchen table with Miss Trudy. She was beginning to wonder if he slept at all.

On the night before Christmas Eve she tucked Micah into bed, pulling the soft quilt to his chin. He smelled like Ivory soap and damp hair. She'd tried to hide her stress from him the past couple days. The little boy was finally coming out of his quiet shell, and she didn't want to set him back.

He obviously liked having Beau around all day. They played Go Fish and Jenga, and Beau let him help with minor household repairs. Micah was particularly enamored with the electric screwdriver and had sought out every loose screw in the house. The thing was as big as he was, but Beau helped him steady it.

"Presents tomorrow?" he asked. The sound of his little-boy voice still made her heart sing. He'd been stringing together words more and more.

"One present tomorrow *night*. The rest on Christmas Day."

His big brown eyes pleaded as he clutched the cover. "Two?"

"One." She kissed him on the cheek. "But nice try."

After turning out the lights and saying good night, she padded down the stairs. *A Christmas Carol* was on tap for tonight, though Eden could see from the closed bedroom door that Miss Trudy had already turned in for the night. Looked like it was just her and Beau.

Her pulse skittered at the thought, and she reminded her heart that nothing was going to happen. She was going to get her nightly glass of water, settle on the opposite end of the sofa, watch the movie, then offer a polite good night. Just as she had last night and the night before that.

When she entered the kitchen she spotted Beau at the sink. Her heart leapt at the sight of him, not quite buying into her pep talk. He wore a black thermal shirt that showed off his muscular frame and a pair of jeans that hugged him in all the right places.

"All tucked in?"

Her eyes jerked to his, her cheeks warming at her thoughts.

She approached the sink and tugged the mug from his hand, nudging him aside. "Stop doing my job, mister."

"It's just a few odds and ends."

That voice, deep and throaty. And the faint whiff of his spicy cologne wasn't doing much to distract her from the fact that they were alone in the quiet kitchen.

"I already feel bad enough that you're missing work. And poor Zac, trying to run the farm and a restaurant."

There you go, Eden. Bring his brother into the room with you.

"We got it covered. And hey, I'm getting stuff done around here I've been putting off for years."

"Jack really likes working with you."

And by all means, bring your son into the picture too.

"Thanks for letting him help. I know he slows you down."

"He's pretty handy with the tools for a little guy." He took the mug from her and dried it with the dish towel as she pulled another cup from the suds.

"He probably stripped every screw in the house."

Beau's lips turned up. "Nah, he did really well."

She ran the washcloth over the mug, then rinsed it, the warm water rushing over her fingers. She turned off the faucet, and Beau took the mug from her.

The refrigerator cycled on, purring quietly. She checked for more dirty dishes and found nothing, so she pulled the plug. The water gurgled down the drain.

Beau handed her the towel and put the mug in the cabinet beside him. She glanced at him as she dried her hands. He sported a five o'clock shadow on his square jaw, a look she'd always loved, but never so much as now. She wondered if it would feel bristly or soft against her palm.

"Mistletoe," he said softly.

"Hmm?" She followed his gaze to the hook above the sink. The familiar sprig of greenery had found its way back to the sink.

Her eyes fell to him, and she gave a nervous laugh. "Your aunt is downright relentless."

The corner of his lip kicked up.

Nice lips. Slightly full on the bottom, nicely curved on top. Perfect for kissing.

Stop it, Eden.

"She is," he said. "Relentless *and* ornery." He shifted closer until they were almost touching. Until his manly smell enveloped her. "But she's not the one who moved it."

Not the one who—? Her eyes searched his face. Something flared in his dark mocha eyes. Her heart flopped over. Oh.

Oh.

She *hadn't* been imagining things. Wasn't imagining the softening in his eyes just now or the way the air seemed to hum around them.

He cupped her chin, coming closer, their bodies a breath apart.

Step away, her brain screamed. But her body was having none of that. His warmth surrounded her, seeping into her skin. Her breath caught in her throat, and her lungs failed at the very basic task of emptying.

"There's something here." His voice was like liquid honey. "We've been dancing around it for weeks." His thumb moved across her jaw, stirring every cell to life. His eyes pierced hers, holding her captive. "I've been trying to ignore it, but . . ."

"We should," she croaked. "We should just ignore it." Her heart went to war with her mind. She'd never been so torn between want and need.

"That's one way to go. But it hasn't worked so far. Not for me. I don't think it's working for you either."

Yes it is. The lie caught in her throat, jamming up anything else she might say.

"Am I wrong?"

She watched his lips move. They looked so soft. The beautiful shade, a light dusky pink, was her new favorite color. If she designed a website for her feelings right now, that's the color she'd make it.

He tucked her hair behind her ear, the motion sending

a shiver down her spine. "Maybe we should just . . . get it out of our systems."

Not a bad idea, her heart said.

Ridiculous, her brain replied.

His eyes were filled with wanting, those lighter flecks like tiny sparks of passion. They ignited something inside her she hadn't felt in years. She'd forgotten how this could feel, wasn't sure she'd ever felt it quite so strongly. Impossible to resist.

"It might work," he whispered. He lowered his head, slowly, coming closer. His breath fell on her like a tantalizing prelude.

Then his lips touched hers, soft and supple. Barely a brush. So slow and careful, as if he wanted to make it last. She strained toward him, and he rewarded her with another brush of his lips.

A curl of warmth unfurled in her chest. Heat rippled through her, down each limb, all the way to the tips of her fingers and toes.

His hand slid along her jaw and into her hair, making every hair follicle tingle with awareness. Her heart rolled over and played dead.

This man. This kiss . . .

The pressure lightened, and he drew back a fraction of an inch. A whimper caught in her throat.

"I think it's working," he whispered. His breath fluttered her lips, teasing.

"Definitely." She leaned toward him until their lips met again.

He kissed her more hungrily this time, and she opened her mouth to him. Her insides clenched pleasantly, a hug from the inside out. His mouth was magic, making everything outside them cease to exist.

Her hands found his shoulders, firm and solid under her palms. Greedy, they skimmed upward and sank into the softness of his hair.

He pulled her closer, and her heart took flight. He was right. She'd been fighting this for weeks. She never would have made it this long had she known how it would feel. How *he* would feel. She could happily stay here for the rest of her life.

The rest of your life?

She shut down the voice. She couldn't stop now. It felt so good. So right. Beau was a good man. He was strong, capable, reliable, and, *let's be honest*, so deliciously attractive. She deserved this, didn't she? She'd been through so much, and it was just one little kiss.

One little kiss?

Okay, maybe there were feelings too. Maybe he'd gotten under her skin just a bit. Maybe she wished this never had to end.

Whoa. You're leaving, Eden. Remember?

She wasn't sure who'd given her brain permission to speak, but it was too late now. It was making some good points. Points even her swooning heart couldn't ignore. She lowered her hands, slowly, reluctantly, to his shoulders.

"Beau . . . wait."

His mouth moved over hers one last time, and she wrung every last drop of satisfaction from his lips before pulling away.

"Wait." Her eyes opened, sweeping over his face.

His breath was ragged, and those eyes . . . dark and lidded. His lips . . . damp and swollen.

Was it too late to say, *Never mind*?

She closed her eyes against the visual assault. *Think. With your brain. Repeat after me: "This can't happen."*

. . .

"What's wrong?"

Beau's unsteady breath mingled with Kate's. Her eyes were closed, and a tiny frown huddled between her eyebrows. Her lips were pink and lush, and he couldn't stop his thumb from sweeping across them.

She trembled as a shiver passed through her, and her fingers tightened on his arms.

"I can't do this." She opened her eyes. "I can't do this, Beau."

"Why not?"

"This can't . . . go anywhere. I'll be leaving soon and—"

"So don't. Don't go."

She pushed away, and his arms fell. "I have to. It won't be safe here forever."

He wanted to tell her he was going to change that. But she'd freak out if she knew Sheriff Colton was reporting to the feds all that Eden had told him.

"Where you going to go, Kate?"

"There's a place—it's best if you don't know where. We'll be safe there."

"Safer than here? Are you trained with a gun? Is

there a family there to look out for you? A community that has your back?"

She took a step back. "I'm endangering all of you just by being here."

"I'm trained for danger. I won't let anything happen."

Something flickered in her eyes, something he didn't like. Then she blinked and the look was gone.

She was feeling guilty. Maybe thinking of running. And if she ran in the middle of the night, she'd be lost to him for good and in more danger than ever.

"Promise me you won't leave without telling me."

"I'm not planning on it."

That wasn't the answer he needed. His eyes pierced hers. "Promise me."

The furrows between her brows deepened as she took a step back. "I can't do that. I don't know what's going to happen. I'll do whatever's best for Jack and me. That's the only promise I can make."

She lifted her chin, and he knew that was the best he was going to get. Looked like he'd be sleeping on the sofa for a while.

She took another step back. "I think I'll turn in early."

"Kate . . ."

She met his gaze, and he melted at the tragic look in her eyes. He wanted to take her in his arms, just to hold her. But he knew his touch wouldn't be welcome.

"We have to be more careful," she said. "I don't have the time or energy for a broken heart."

He felt a squeeze in his chest. "I wasn't planning to break your heart, Kate."

Her eyes fell to the floor before rising back to his. "Nobody ever does."

A fist tightened in his gut as he watched her retreat. He stood there for a long time, her words hitting hard, sinking deep. She'd been let down by a lot of people, and his name wasn't going to be added to the list.

CHAPTER 30

The next night they enjoyed Christmas Eve dinner together. Eden felt privileged to be included in the poignant moment as the family paid tribute to Mary Callahan. Today was the twelfth anniversary of her death. There were tears and laughter around the table as Zac and Beau shared stories, remembering both their mother and their father.

Miss Trudy had done most of the cooking, and the food was delicious. Her leg was healing quickly. Early next week she'd get her brace off, and then what?

The candlelight Christmas Eve service came next. Beau was like glue at her side. He followed her into the pew, taking the aisle, his body alert, his eyes scanning the crowd.

The sanctuary was beautiful tonight, aglow in white twinkling lights, red tapers flickering on the altar. A manger scene was front and center on the stage, the hay rustling under the lazy whir of the ceiling fans.

The building burgeoned with friends and neighbors, and their pew was tight with family. Beau's arm pressed into her shoulder, his thigh whisper close. She'd relived

last night's kiss until it was engrained in her mind. Every
brush, every touch, every heartbeat. She'd lain awake for
hours remembering, savoring.

This morning she'd met his eyes across the table and
had seen a reflection of her every thought. But just as
quickly, she shut down the moment. The feelings were
there, yes. But she had to push them down, for both
their sakes. He made her forget that she was on the
run. And even if she weren't, the freedom she sought
wouldn't be found under the umbrella of any man. Not
even Beau Callahan.

The pastor took the platform, and the crowd became
reverently quiet as he gave an invocation.

Beside her, Micah took her hand, and she squeezed
his tight. She drew in a breath and released it silently in
a long exhale. *Just a night of peace, God. A quiet time to
reflect on this holy night. To be thankful for our blessings
and Your continued guidance.*

When the prayer ended they sang songs—Christmas
carols so familiar no one needed a hymnal. One song
fed into the next, the organ resounding boldly, voices
joined in sweet harmony.

She looked around the crowd at the faces, many
of them now familiar. Sheriff Colton on the aisle
two rows up, a head taller than everyone else. Marty
Bennington, the horseman, Margaret Lefebvre who
ran the Primrose Inn. And there was Frumpy Joe and
his wife, Charlotte. Noticeably absent was Paige. She'd
driven down to visit friends in Portland for the holiday.

When the music faded, the crowd was seated, and
Pastor Daniels began reading the story of Jesus' birth

in a clear, strong voice. She liked that he didn't stop to teach or embellish. When he reached the end, he closed his Bible and let the scripture speak for itself. The organist played through the gentle chords of "Silent Night," the congregation joining in. When the last strains had drifted away, they trickled from their pews, an awe-filled silence leading the way.

Eden kept Micah close, and Beau's hand settled on the small of her back. Even through her coat, his warmth seeped into her skin. In the quiet reverence of the magical night, she couldn't help but wish . . .

No.

She wasn't a child wishing for the impossible. She was a grown woman with responsibilities and needs. A need that beckoned her miles from here to a place she could call her own. A place where she could find quiet and peace. A place she could put down roots, become self-sufficient, and make her own decisions.

The crowd tightened as they funneled out the door. She was jostled into Beau, and her elbow connected with something hard at his side. As he raised his hand to hold the door for her, his coat rode up, revealing a holstered gun.

The weapon, gleaming and metallic, shattered her peace. A gun had started this whole mess. A gun had stolen Micah's father from him. She could still see the bright splatter of blood on Micah's cheek, on his favorite Superman T-shirt. His father's blood.

Beau tugged down the jacket as she met his sharpened gaze.

At the house, Micah darted for the porch, eager to

open a present, while Zac helped Miss Trudy from the car. Eden huddled deeper into her coat as Beau walked beside her toward the house.

Her eyes cut to him as they climbed the porch steps. She stopped in front of the door, taking his arm.

He paused, twin pools of black coffee staring back.

"I don't like guns, Beau," she said.

He gave her a long, searching look. "I don't like being unprepared."

"You said the sheriff's contact was trustworthy."

"And I believe that." His voice rumbled quietly in the cold night air, his breath vaporizing between them. "But there are still people out there who want you and Jack dead. I won't live in denial. If they come, I'll be prepared. I won't stand by while people I care about are hurt. I wouldn't be able to live with myself if anything happened to you."

His words were firm and sure, his posture confident and ready. He was in full deputy mode, and she realized with surety that he'd been a fine officer of the law.

"All right?" he asked.

If she was going to trust him to help keep them safe, she couldn't take away his tools—as much as those tools might frighten her.

"All right."

. . .

It was after midnight by the time she got Micah bathed. His eyes were sleepy, but his body was restless. She tickled him and wrestled with him as he scrambled into his pajamas. He wore a mile-wide smile by the time she dropped him into bed with a bounce.

She was ready for bed herself. Beau had promised to set the presents under the tree for Micah to find in the morning. She'd bought a little something for everyone. She was so grateful to the Callahans. Despite the circumstances it was turning out to be a wonderful Christmas.

She flipped off the light and crawled into her own bed, easing over to the edge as she listened to Micah's brief prayer.

"Dear God, thank You for my new art set. I know it's from Santa, but I love it so, so much. Thank You for Mommy and Beau, and Miss Trudy, and Zac. And Riley too. Amen."

"Amen." She squeezed his hand. "Now you better go to sleep or Santa won't bring you the rest of your presents."

"Did you set out the cookies?"

"Of course."

"And the milk?"

"It's on the mantel."

"Mommy?"

"Hmm?"

"I'm worried about tomorrow."

She thought of the stress she'd been under since Beau and the sheriff had discovered their secrets. Maybe she hadn't been so good at hiding it. Or maybe she wasn't the only one who had seen Beau's gun.

"About what, honey?"

"'Member when I sat on Santa's lap?"

"Yeah . . ."

The ticking of the clock filled the silence. She made herself wait for him, giving him time to form his thoughts, his words. It took a little longer now.

"I don't want to go home anymore," he said.

She opened her eyes, remembering his wish. Even after their talk, she'd worried he wouldn't understand.

Hope buoyed her spirits. "You don't?"

He shifted on the air mattress. "I want to stay here. I like it here. With Beau and Miss Trudy. I could help on the farm. Beau said they make maple syrup in the spring. I can put it on my pancakes."

"Oh, sweetie . . ."

"In the summer he mows and cuts the trees with sharp knives. I can't help with that, but I can clean up his mess. Beau said he helped his dad when he was my age."

"Baby . . . we can't stay."

"But I want to," he whined.

"I know but—"

"Don't you like Beau and Miss Trudy?"

"Of course I do. But, kiddo, this isn't our house. We don't—" *Belong here*, she started to stay. But that wasn't true. She did feel as if they belonged here.

No. They belonged in Loon Lake where the perfect little cabin, nestled in the woods, awaited.

"Can we stay? Please?"

"Honey . . . it's late. And you'll want to be up early to see what Santa brought. Let's get some sleep. We'll talk about this later."

She thought he might argue, but the long day must

have finally taken its toll. He lay still, and soon his breathing was deep and even. Long after that, Eden stared at the darkened ceiling, wondering what their future held.

CHAPTER 31

"S anta came!"

Beau bolted upright on the couch at the sound of Jack's voice, his heart thudding like a jackhammer.

The boy scampered down the steps in his Superman pajamas in the predawn light. He jumped the last two steps, ran to the tree, and skidded to a stop.

"Look, Beau!"

Beau rubbed the sleep from his eyes, dredging up a smile. "I see, bud. Looks like you've been a good boy this year."

"They're not all for me, silly." Jack got down on his hands and knees and began snooping.

"I reckon not. I've been good, too, you know. Is your mom awake?"

"No, but she said I can come down when it's light out. I waited and waited, and it's light out now."

Beau's lips ticked up. Jack had a generous definition of "light."

Jack was back on his feet, climbing up on the hearth. He pulled the plate off the mantel, his brown eyes going wide. "He ate my cookies!"

"Of course he did." And they were tasty. "Let's get

you a bowl of cereal, then I'll call Zac. We can't open presents until the whole family's here."

Jack's face fell.

Beau chuckled, ruffling the boy's sleep-mussed hair. "It won't take long. You'll see."

Forty-five minutes later, his family was gathered in the living room. On the floor Jack tore off paper as fast as his hands could fly. Christmas carols played on the radio, and a fire crackled and popped in the background.

It had been years since they'd had a Christmas like this. It was long overdue, he realized. For a moment he pictured his dad in the corner recliner, his feet kicked up, watching the chaos of Christmas morning. He remembered the way his dark eyes sparkled a moment before his lips turned up. Remembered the deep chuckle that followed. From across the room, he could almost see his dad giving his famous two-finger salute.

"This one's to Jack, from Santa." Zac pushed the gift toward Jack.

Beau watched as the boy opened the gift he'd gotten him.

As the last of the paper fell away, a smile lit his face. "A tool kit!"

"Wow, that's awesome." Kate helped him open the box. "Someone must've told Santa what you wanted." She shared a smile with Beau.

She looked as fresh as a spring morning in her yoga pants and faded pink T-shirt. Her face was freshly scrubbed, her silky blonde hair flittering around her pretty face. Where was the mistletoe when he needed it?

Jack pulled out the working plastic screwdriver, sized for a small boy. The tool whirred into action.

Zac had gotten Jack a Patriots jersey, and Aunt Trudy had made him a Superman cape. It was already tied around the kid's neck. Aunt Trudy oohed and aahed over the leather Bible cover Kate had bought her and seemed pleased with the Knitting Nook gift certificate from Beau.

Zac opened a black sweater from Aunt Trudy and a wallet Riley had left for him. He'd gotten Beau a quality pair of work boots he'd eyed in L.L.Bean weeks ago when they'd made a trip into Ellsworth.

Beau waited patiently for Zac to reach the bright red box near the tree stand. When he finally did, he read the tag and handed it to Kate.

"This one's for you, Kate. From Beau."

Across the room, Kate read the tag. Her gaze bounced off his, a little smile tilting her lips as she peeled off the paper. The room seemed to shrink to only the two of them, the carols and chaos fading away. Her fingers worked the tape until the paper was gone, then she unfolded the flap of the white box. She lifted the gift from its nest.

Aunt Trudy was exclaiming over a gift she'd just unwrapped, but Kate's eyes were fixed on the snow globe, her lips parting just before they tilted upward in a nostalgic smile. She tipped the globe upside down, gave the wind-up key a couple of twists, then turned the globe upright, watching the snow fall past the golden angel inside. Her smile widened.

Beau could barely hear the plinking notes of "Let It Snow," but Kate's smile was all that mattered.

Her eyes cut to Beau. He sensed the movement all around them, but he saw no one but Kate. Her beautiful honey-brown eyes, her sweet spirit, her quiet strength.

"Thank you," she mouthed as she pulled the globe to her chest, her eyes filling.

The moment lingered, and his chest seemed to open, yawning wide. His lungs constricted until his next breath seemed impossible. This woman made him come undone. He was more than attracted to her. She'd found a way into his heart. He knew in that moment, with a surety that shook him to his core, that he loved her.

The thought slammed into him with the force of a snowplow. How could it be? Love didn't happen this fast. Did it? In a matter of weeks?

Kate tilted her head, something shifting in her eyes as she searched his face.

He fixed a smile on his lips and let out his breath when she broke eye contact.

She tucked the globe carefully into the box and dropped the wrapping paper into the waiting bag.

When they were finished with the presents, Aunt Trudy pushed to her feet, hobbling. She held out a trash bag. "All right, let's clean this mess up."

Bright shreds of paper and cockeyed boxes littered the room. They went into action, the carols keeping things festive. Beau picked up a silver bow near Kate and stuck it on her head.

"Thank you," she said, beaming.

He held out a bag while Jack stuffed it with wads of wrapping paper. He could smell the yeasty aroma of the cinnamon rolls Kate had slid into the oven awhile ago, and his stomach gave a deep grumble. Across the room, Kate dumped an armload of paper into a bag Zac held.

He was so aware of her. Even when he wasn't looking at her, his sensors followed her like a beacon.

"Mistletoe." Aunt Trudy pointed at the ceiling above Kate and Zac. "Lay one on her, Zac."

Beau's heart gave a hard squeeze as his brother made a big deal of sweeping Kate into his arms, dipping her backward, and laying a loud smooch on her cheek.

He heard Aunt Trudy applauding and Jack giggling, but he couldn't tear his eyes off of Zac and Kate. He wanted to rip his brother's hands off of her. He reminded himself that it meant nothing. That Zac was still in love with Lucy.

Kate's laughter was still ringing out when Zac brought her upright, embracing her in those gorilla arms of his.

Beau gave him a shove. "All right, that's enough," he said in a tone that didn't quite reach playful.

Zac cuffed him on the back of the head, his eyes twinkling.

After they'd stuffed themselves on cinnamon rolls, Aunt Trudy shooed them outdoors. They rode the snowmobiles for a couple hours, laying new tracks in the freshly fallen snow. They took it slow, Kate driving Riley's sled and Jack riding behind Beau, wearing his old helmet. He thought about Kate a lot as the machine cut through the pine forest, its high-pitched whine echoing off the hills.

He thought of their kiss—had it really been two days ago? The image of Zac's kiss barreled into his mind. When everyone had filtered into the dining room for cinnamon rolls, Beau had confiscated the mistletoe. If anyone was getting another kiss from Kate, it was going to be him.

After sledding they hung out around the house, talking and laughing. Zac did his imitation of the Christmas tree shaker, and Eden laughed so hard she had to wipe tears from her eyes. The sheriff stopped by later in the evening, much to Aunt Trudy's dismay.

Beau followed him out to his patrol car when he left, stuffing his hands in his jeans pockets to keep them warm. Their boots crunched on the shoveled walk as they left the golden puddle of the porch light. The sun had gone behind the hills, and the western sky was swathed in deep purple hues.

"Got any news for me?" Beau asked when they'd cleared the house.

Sheriff Colton turned at his car, popping a mint into his mouth and offering one to Beau.

"My contact, Oakley, wanted to meet with Kate. I told him no, and he wasn't happy. She's wanted for questioning in the murder of Marshals Walter and Brown. Needless to say, Marshal Langley told a different story from Kate's—Eden's."

"She's not going anywhere. It would be suicide, and you know it. They'd no sooner have her in their custody than the moles would find a way to—"

Colton held up a palm. "It's what I told him. He agreed to speak to Chief Deputy Chambers about putting surveillance in place for Marshal Langley and Deputy Morris. Needless to say, Chambers is going to be resistant. These are his men, and he trusts them."

"Well, two of his marshals turned up with slits in their throats. Does he really think his witness is the culprit? An innocent young mother who's been traumatized?"

"I know, I know. Good news is Chambers trusts Oakley. They go way back, so don't lose hope."

Beau palmed the back of his neck. "I wish I could do something." He'd gladly speak to Chief Deputy Chambers on Kate's behalf, but doing so would only lead them right to Summer Harbor.

"When's Oakley talking to the chief?"

"Tomorrow. Say your prayers."

"I'll do that."

He was distracted when he entered the house a few minutes later, his mind full of worry and dread. He bypassed the noisy dining room where a game of Uno was under way and went upstairs. He needed a few minutes to regroup.

The light was on in Kate's room, and he paused at her doorway watching as Kate set a suitcase on the bed.

"What are you doing?"

She jumped, then wilted, palming her chest. "You scared me."

"Sorry. What's with the suitcase?"

The latch clicked as her fingers sprung it free. "It's almost time for us to go."

"Aunt Trudy's still on crutches."

"Only for a couple more days. Besides, you're here all day now. You don't need me around."

"I'm only here to keep you safe."

"Exactly. The sooner I go, the sooner you can get back to work, and the sooner everything will return to the way it was."

He covered the distance between them in two steps. "Nothing will ever be the way it was, Kate."

She turned to grab a stack of T-shirts from a laundry basket. "Of course it will be," she said calmly.

But her hands were shaking, and she tucked her hair behind her ear in that nervous gesture of hers.

He grabbed her hand. She was a breath away, her eyes on the floor between them, her hair falling forward again. The sweet citrusy scent of her had become as familiar as the tangy scent of the ocean. He pushed her hair behind her ear, the silky softness teasing the pads of his fingers.

"I don't want you to go, Kate."

"You know I can't stay."

He nudged her chin upward until her eyes met his. Those eyes, filled with tragedy and strength. She thought she had to do this all alone. He loved her enough to see it through. He'd lay down his life for her—he knew that with every cell in his body.

But he knew her too. He knew his declaration wouldn't be welcome, just as his kiss had not been. And still, he needed her to stay long enough for the feds to do some surveillance. Long enough for them to uncover the moles. Everything would be different then. She wouldn't have to fear for their lives, wouldn't have to look over her shoulder, wouldn't have to run off to some cabin in the woods.

"Just for a little while," he said. "If Oakley had tipped off the moles, they'd have been here by now. I'd feel a lot better if you stayed till the trial's over."

A couple weeks, maybe. Not nearly enough time.

"We won't be safe even then. I know who they are. They're not going to let that go. Not ever."

"Till New Year's then."

He saw the refusal in her eyes and pulled the mom card. "Stay here where it's warm and safe. Jack likes it here, and he's doing so well. He'll love our New Year's celebration. We have a countdown in the town square, and we drop a lobster. After midnight we light fireworks off a barge in the harbor. It's a lot of fun. You don't want to miss it."

. . .

The clock ticked on the nightstand behind her, marking time. Beau's thumb swept over her jaw. He was so persuasive. Not his words so much as his touch, his presence. All reasons she should shove their belongings in the suitcase and head out the door.

And yet . . .

"I don't know . . ." She couldn't think when he caressed her face so gently. All her rational thoughts scattered like flurries on the wind.

"Next week we can go snowmobiling again. You know Jack loved it. And we'll take him sledding on Mulligan's Hill—that's where we sledded as kids. We'll just hang out, have fun. He deserves a little fun. You both do. Come on, what do you say?"

She remembered Jack's words in bed the night before. He loved it here. It had become a temporary home, these people his temporary family. He needed security right now, normalcy. And the Callahans had provided it in spades. Would a few more days really hurt? The cabin wasn't going anywhere.

"I'm not ready for you to go." His voice was thick and smoky.

She fell headlong into his onyx eyes, and her heart wavered at the wistful look there. Her heart, her mind, her body. His nearness made her insides hum, made her breath catch in her throat. His spicy scent filled her nostrils, and she drew in a deep breath of him.

He cupped her face, his eyes mingling with hers. "Stay," he whispered. "Please."

She could deny him nothing when he looked at her that way. When he spoke to her that way. They'd stay for a week. Just one more week. What would it hurt?

"Just till New Year's."

His lips turned up a fraction of an inch. She'd missed those lips. Had it been only two days? It seemed forever since she'd been in his arms. She leaned closer. She shouldn't, she knew that. But her body, her heart, knew something different.

His lips brushed hers, softly. Slowly. Just once. Not nearly enough. Her heart pounded against her ribs as he drew away.

His thumb stroked over her lip, a poor substitute. His restraint showed on his face. He was being smart.

Not pushing his luck. After all, she'd said this was a bad idea, and now she was kissing him again. But she couldn't seem to get her head and heart on the same page.

Would it be so awful to enjoy this while it lasted? How attached could she get in a mere seven days? It would be a good memory to take with her, something to keep her warm during the lonely winter nights.

CHAPTER 32

They slipped into a comfortable routine over the next few days. Aunt Trudy got her brace off on Monday, and they celebrated at the Roadhouse over a seafood platter.

Micah stayed busy with his new art set and tools. In the afternoons they took out the snowmobiles. Eden wasn't jumping hills or doing fancy tricks, but she was getting pretty adept at handling the machine.

Beau showed Micah all the places where he and his brothers had played in the woods—a spot where they'd once had a tree house, a cave they used to play in. It was on the side of a hill, beneath a rock ledge, the opening so small only Micah could squeeze through. Inside he found an old Hot Wheels car that had once belonged to one of the brothers.

Eden checked the computer regularly for updates on the trial, but it seemed to be on hold for the holidays. She waited, praying Fattore would soon be behind bars.

The end of the day had become her favorite time. They had a fire each night, and after Micah and Miss Trudy turned in, she and Beau continued their classic Christmas movie routine. Even though the holiday was over, it still felt like Christmas with the twinkle lights and the scent of pine in the air. She was reluctant to let go of the season.

Beau claimed the middle of the sofa, his thigh pressing against hers, his warmth seeping through her jeans. With the lights out and the house quiet, the rest of the world seemed to melt away.

He held her hand sometimes or put his arm around her, and every now and then, he'd lean close and brush her lips with his. Her heart would lurch in her chest, and her palm would find the scruff of his jaw. It was always over too quickly. He seemed to be practicing restraint, and Eden knew that was only wise. Already her heart was aching over the thought of leaving him. Of leaving the Callahans and Summer Harbor.

But late at night when she lay in bed, she'd remember how it felt to be trapped in her marriage to Antonio, trapped by her own uncertainty and fear, the walls closing in under the tight fist of his control. She remembered how it felt to walk on eggshells, every decision based on what he'd think and what he'd do. She remembered how it felt to question her own thinking, her own sanity.

And she remembered Karen's cabin that waited up north. She'd seen the place in her mind's eye a thousand times. She imagined herself and Micah, finally free and independent and able to move and breathe. Her soul gave a deep sigh at the image.

In the winters they'd have a crackling fire each night. They'd curl up in a homemade quilt while they sipped hot cocoa and talked about his school day.

The warm months would beckon them outside to

bask in the warm sunlight. They'd take the canoe onto the lake, breathe in the fresh air as the water rippled quietly past.

She could almost hear the high-pitched call of the kittiwake and see the broad, scalloped wings of an osprey soaring on a backdrop of blue. She could see the colorful tulips in Karen's garden, ushering in spring, their long, elegant stems pushing from the ground, their velvety petals unfurling.

She'd go to the grocery whenever she liked, to the library, or take a walk just because she wanted to. She'd buy clothes in every shade of the rainbow and read whatever she liked. She'd make her own money and spend it however she darn well pleased. She'd make her own choices, her own decisions, and no one would tell her what to do or when to do it.

Leaving Beau would be hard. But she would never give her soul to another man again, not even him.

New Year's Eve seemed to sneak up on her. A little before ten that night Eden, Beau, and Micah bundled up in their winter gear and piled into Beau's truck. Miss Trudy's friends had picked her up earlier. They found a parking space at the library and walked to the town square. Darkness had long since fallen, but the town was still lit with Christmas lights and the quaint streetlamps Eden had come to love.

The square was filled with booths selling hot cocoa, sugary treats, and New Year's Eve paraphernalia. Eden bought Micah a glow-in-the-dark necklace, skipping the annoying party horns, but it seemed half the kids on the square already had them. A local band played

"American Kids," and people near the stage danced to the jiggy beat.

The crowd was loud and crushing, but Beau had slipped his hand into hers shortly after their arrival and hadn't let go. They met up with Zac just before midnight and stood amid the energized crowd, shoulder to shoulder as the clock moved closer to midnight.

On the outskirts of the square someone let off a series of firecrackers. Micah pressed into her leg, and she slipped her arm around his shoulder. She'd warned him about the noise before coming, but talking about it and experiencing it were two different things.

Beau took a call, holding one ear so he could hear over the cacophony of music and chatter.

A loud pop sounded, and Micah held his arms up to her. His eyes had taken on that anxious look she hadn't seen in weeks. She lifted him up, and he wrapped himself around her. He'd gained weight over the past several weeks, and his little bony body had filled out. He looked healthier, happier. Except for tonight. It was too much too soon. She should've known better.

The crowd bustled closer together as the minutes ticked down. She shifted Micah's weight in her aching arms.

Beau pocketed his phone and held out his hands. "Let me have him."

Micah went to him without complaint, tucking his face into Beau's shoulder. She gave Beau a worried smile. There was no way she was putting him through a fireworks show.

"That was Sheriff Colton," Beau said over the emcee

at the microphone. "He asked me to help with crowd control after the lobster drop."

She started to tell him she needed to take Micah home after the fireworks, but the crowd, spurred by the emcee, began counting down. "10 . . . 9 . . . 8 . . . 7 . . ."

Beau encouraged Micah to watch the giant fake lobster, creeping ever so slowly down a metal pole. The little boy peeked out from the spot between Beau's neck and shoulder.

"3 . . . 2 . . . 1 . . . Happy New Year!" Party horns sounded all around them as a cheer went up.

Zac gave them high fives, including one for Micah.

"Happy New Year, kiddo." Eden caressed Micah's cheek.

A loud crack sounded, followed by a pop. Micah's arms tightened around Beau, and he tucked his face into Beau's shoulder.

Her eyes aligned with Beau's, his warming as he searched her face. Funny how he could make a crowd disappear with just one look.

"Happy New Year," he said.

"Happy New Year."

He leaned forward, a protective hand on Micah's back, and brushed her lips with his. His mouth was surprisingly warm, and her heart gave a sigh as he pulled away.

The crowd had already begun dispersing. "I have to man the walkway out to the harbor. Are you up for the walk?"

"Actually, I think Jack and I need to go home." She gave a pointed look at Micah and mouthed. *Fireworks.*

Beau rubbed his jaw. "Gotcha. I'll call Colton and get out of this."

"Maybe we can get a ride from someone. Or we can take the truck, and you can get a ride after the fireworks."

"I'll take you. You're not going home alone."

She balked at the order, but before she could argue, Zac spoke up.

"I'll take them home. I'm not staying for the fireworks."

"It's settled then," she said. "Thanks, Zac."

Beau was slower to agree. He looked at his brother for a long minute before he looked back to her. "I won't be long."

He handed Micah back to her, and they parted ways. Micah was very quiet on the ride home. She prayed tonight hadn't set him back too much. She put her arm around him, and he leaned into her side.

When they were pulling into the drive, Zac's phone rang. He checked the screen before he answered.

"All right," he said a minute later. "Be down in a few." He hung up the phone. "The alarm's going off at the Roadhouse. Probably just some kids messing around."

They pulled up to the house and Zac turned off the car, reaching for the door handle.

"Go check on the alarm," she said.

He gave Eden a look. "Beau told me to stay with you."

The order set her teeth on edge. She was perfectly capable of being alone for two seconds.

"I'm fine, Zac. He'll be home soon. I'm leaving tomorrow anyway, remember? We'll be completely on our own then."

Zac stared at the darkened house, looking torn.

Eden reached for the door handle. "Really, we'll be fine. Go on."

He sighed, then gave her a pointed look. "Lock the door behind you."

"I will. Thanks for the ride. I hope everything's okay with the alarm."

Once inside she closed the door and twisted the locks, hearing the rumble of Zac's truck as he started down the drive.

Micah was already curled in the recliner by the window, looking too much like the little boy she'd taken on the run a month and a half ago. Leaving the lights off, she lifted him and sank into the chair with him, hoping he might fall asleep in her arms. But outside the distant sounds of the fireworks show began, the deep booms reverberating through the night air. There would be no sleep until the show was over. She wrapped the afghan around him and tucked his head under hers.

A thunderous boom shook the windowpane behind them, and he pressed closer until she felt the thump of his heart against her own.

"It's okay, kiddo," she whispered.

She closed her eyes, the late hour catching up with her. The faded strains of "American Kids" strummed in her mind.

She wasn't sure how many minutes had passed when there was a pause in the fireworks. A quiet hum rose to fill the brief silence. An engine. Had Zac returned? Beau couldn't be back yet. And yet there had been no lights flooding through the curtains on the car's approach. Her body stiffened at the realization.

The humming ceased as the fireworks resumed.

Heart thundering in her chest, she whipped around and edged back the curtain.

A dark SUV huddled in the shadows. Then someone emerged. Someone tall and broad-shouldered. Fear struck the very marrow of her bones as she recognized the man she'd once trusted to protect her.

CHAPTER 33

Beau watched from the boardwalk as red specks of light bloomed across the velvet sky. People were spread on the rocky beach in front of him, bundled in quilts and blankets. Others lined the retaining wall and perched on piers that jutted out into the water. Boats dotted the harbor, their pole lights barely visible in the wispy smoke from the fireworks. A metallic smell hung in the air.

He'd hoped to head home once the crowd was settled, but Sheriff Colton had been right. People were drinking and antsy tonight. Beau broke up a fight between a love triangle and had to call Colton to haul one of them off. Others had just been loud and obnoxious, but he knew how quickly a little "good fun" could turn into a ruckus.

He went to the fireworks every year, on the Fourth of July, too, but he always forgot until they started that they bored him silly. He scanned the crowd, looking for impending trouble. A group of young men on a moored boat was getting rowdy, disturbing the peace. A little girl toddled toward a live sparkler planted in the sand. Before he could move, the girl's mom swept her up.

A few stragglers wandered around, unable to find a place to sit. Mrs. Miller, his picky Christmas tree customer, wheeled her fussy grandson around in a stroller. Merle Franke, who owned the cranberry bog, wandered around with two steaming cups. Beau pointed him toward his wife on the beach.

"Hey, Beau."

He whirled at the familiar voice. Paige came to a stop a few feet away, cradling a steaming cup between her gloved hands. Her eyes and nose peeked out between her blue knit hat and scarf.

"You're back."

"Didn't want to miss the show." She looked up, the firework casting a golden glow on her face.

"They're good this year."

She shot him a look. "You don't even like fireworks."

"True enough. Who are you here with?"

"Sara and Lauren," she said, naming two of her coworkers. "They're . . . out there somewhere. I went for a drink. I'm waiting for their text. You?"

"Just helping the sheriff with crowd control. How was your Christmas?"

"Good. It was fun catching up with Mary Beth. Christmas dinner was a bust, though. She burned the ham, and we ended up at a truck stop. It was the only place open. Riley called, though. That was a nice surprise."

"He called us too. It was good hearing his voice."

"He seems to be doing well."

"Yep." Beau shoved his hands in his pockets. "He sure does."

An awkward moment settled between them as they ran out of small talk, the fireworks punctuating the silence. He hadn't seen her since the night of their breakup. He wondered how she was doing but didn't feel he had the right to ask.

"I am okay, you know."

His gaze cut to her, but she was still watching the sky.

"What?" she said cheekily. "Didn't think I'd ever get over you?"

"Of course not—"

She shot him a smile. "Kidding, Beau. I had a lot of time to think while I was in Portland. And you were right. Things haven't been right lately. Maybe they never really were. We were missing a certain spark, I think. And honestly, part of the appeal of 'us' was your family. I'm already close to Riley, and you guys are . . . well, the closest thing to family I have. I guess I just wanted to be one of you."

His heart softened at her words. "You already are."

She smiled. "Thanks for that."

"You're always welcome at our house, you know that. Sunday suppers, Patriot games . . . you have an open invitation."

"I might take you up on that. How are things working out with Kate?"

His gut twisted at the mention of her. He watched a red oval spread across the sky. "She's leaving tomorrow."

"I'm sorry. That must be hard."

"Mmm." He didn't want to talk about Kate with Paige. It was awkward. If not for her, then for him. It amazed him that she sounded genuinely sad for him.

But then Paige was a special woman. Just not the right one for him.

She pulled her phone from her pocket, then scanned the beach.

Sara and Lauren waved from the middle of the crowd.

"There they are. I'd better go claim my spot."

"Enjoy the show."

"Take care, Beau."

He watched her go, feeling a little melancholy. Not because it was over between them but because she'd brought up Kate, and now he was thinking about her leaving tomorrow. He'd kept hoping that by some miracle the feds would have collected enough evidence by now to put the moles away. Then Jack could be an eyewitness at the trial, Fattore would be put away, and all of this would be over.

"Howdy, Beau." Charlotte Dupree from the diner stepped up to him. Her bright red hair was tucked into a black knit cap with a fuzzy pom-pom, and she wore a pink scarf that clashed with her lipstick.

"Hey, Charlotte. Enjoying the fireworks?"

A thunderous boom shook him from the inside out just before a spray of blue brightened the sky.

"They're pretty good so far."

"Where's Joe?"

"Aw, he's shutting down the café. He doesn't care much for fireworks. What are you doing out here all alone?"

He shrugged. "The rest of the gang went home, and Aunt Trudy's with her friends."

"Hey, did Kate's brother ever find her?"

A knot of dread tightened in his gut. His eyes cut to hers. "Kate's brother?"

"He came into the café earlier with a picture of her, said he was her brother. He's quite a looker, that one, but he doesn't really look like—What's wrong?"

Adrenaline flooded his system. "What did you tell him?"

"Well . . . I told him she was staying with you all, out at the Christmas tree farm—"

He turned and ran.

"I'm sorry if I . . ."

He couldn't hear anything else. Couldn't hear anything beyond the blood rushing in his ears, his heart thumping in his chest. The blocks whizzed by, a blurry backdrop. He pulled his phone from his pocket, slowing only long enough to dial Kate's number.

His feet pounded the sidewalk. He skirted people, his eyes trained on the library parking lot.

Come on, Kate. Pick up.

The phone rang and rang until her voicemail kicked on.

He called Zac and waited for him to pick up. He'd reached his truck when his brother finally answered.

"Is everything okay?" Beau's breath came in gasps. He started the car and peeled from the parking space.

"What's wrong?"

"Kate. Lock the doors. Someone's looking for her. I have a spare gun upstairs in my—"

"Beau, I'm not there. I had to—"

"What you do you mean you're not there?"

"The alarm at the Roadhouse—crap. I'm heading out the door now."

Beau was closer to the farm. "I gotta go." His words were abrupt. He hung up and dialed dispatch. He couldn't believe Zac had left her there alone.

You shouldn't have let her leave. What were you thinking?

He pounded his fist on the steering wheel as he waited for his call to connect, nearly running down pedestrians in front of the fire station. He braked reluctantly.

Come on, come on, he thought as they moseyed across as if they had all night. When they finally cleared his lane, he floored it.

The dispatcher picked up as he passed Wharf Street. He requested backup, reverting automatically to the clipped language of cop lingo, then hung up the phone. He was tempted to call Kate again. But that would only slow him down.

He turned toward the farm, punching the pedal. He flew over the hills, his tires squealing around the curves. The minutes ticked away too fast.

"Come on, God. Let me get there before he does. Please . . ."

He couldn't stand the thought of the alternative. An image flashed into his mind. Kate on his living room rug, a gunshot wound to her chest. Jack lying in a pool of blood nearby.

No. No, he wouldn't think like that. It wasn't too late. It couldn't be.

It took forever to reach the farm. He pulled into the drive and flew down the lane, forcing himself to slow as he neared the house. His heart pounded at the sight of an SUV parked alongside the house.

He killed the lights and crept as close as he dared before he shut off the engine. The porch light was on, but the house was dark.

He exited the car, withdrawing his sidearm, and proceeded quickly and quietly toward the SUV. It was empty, the engine still warm.

Fireworks boomed in the distance, the flares of light brightening the yard. He approached the porch, pressing himself to the wall. He listened, his heart hammering in his chest. A sizzle sounded as fireworks lit the sky. Other than that, nothing. He couldn't wait for the sheriff. He prayed he wasn't too late already.

The door was locked, so he quietly unlocked it. He eased inside, gun ready, then stepped into the corner, scanning the room. Empty. He pivoted into the dining room, his eyes darting. Nothing. The kitchen was next.

A deep boom blasted through the night. His heart pitched sideways.

Fireworks. Just fireworks. He blew out a slow breath.

He moved toward the kitchen, noticing the faint smell of cigarette smoke. In the kitchen a cool breeze drifted over his skin. He approached the open back door and paused beside it, listening.

Between the booms of the fireworks, he heard it. The distant, high-pitched whine of a snowmobile.

It could be anyone. But who'd be sledding this time of night when the whole town was watching the show? He moved out the back door cautiously. When all seemed quiet, he ran for the barn, scanning the darkness.

Please, God.

As he neared the building his eyes swept the side. His gaze fell on the empty space where Riley's snowmobile had been.

Atta girl, Kate.

But next to that, another vacant space.

CHAPTER 34

The cold wind battered Eden's face as she flew down the trail. Langley was behind her somewhere. She'd seen the headlights flashing in the distance as she'd turned onto the trail. If only she'd thought to take the keys. The engine whined as she gunned it. They hit a hill and went airborne.

"Hang on!"

Micah's arms tightened as they hit the ground with a thump. The sled swerved under her novice skills, and her heart pounded as she fought to correct it. Once she had control, she looked over her shoulder. Headlights cut through the darkness, maybe a half mile back.

She just had to make it into town. She couldn't go any faster. But he was too far behind to catch them as long as she kept this pace—and didn't wreck.

Please, God.

She peeled around a corner, sliding. She eased off the throttle until she had control, then sped ahead. Micah was pressed into her back, his knees clutching hers. She wanted to reassure him, but the buzz of the engine was loud, and she had to focus.

A gunshot rang out. A shriek escaped as alarm barreled through her. She curled an arm backward, clutching Micah to her, needing to know he was okay. His arms were so tight they cut off her breath.

Needing both hands, she gripped the handlebar again. A steep hill rose to the left. He'd lose sight of them for a minute. They were almost to the town trail. From there it would only be a few minutes to safety.

The engine sputtered, and Kate looked down, frowning. A moment later it happened again. Her eyes found the lit gas gauge. The tank was empty. Her chest tightened, choking off her breath.

No! This couldn't be happening.

They were losing speed despite her thumb on the throttle. *Come on, come on.*

But it was hopeless. She was barely puttering along. She pulled the sled into the brush and turned off the lights, trying to think past the buzzing in her head.

They'd never make it to town on foot before he reached them. She scanned the darkness, seeking refuge. There weren't even any evergreens to hide them, only skeletal deciduous trees. Aside from the steep hill to the one side, the ground was flat, offering no hiding places. There was no safety there. They'd be out in the open.

Then she remembered the cave—the one Beau and his brothers had played in. Wasn't it nearby?

But, no. He'd follow her footprints, and then they'd be trapped inside. She stood, frozen, her mind spinning in circles.

The whine of the other sled was growing louder.

She grabbed Micah and lifted him off, running as fast as she could toward the hillside. She stumbled in the dark over a root and nearly went down. She continued along the hill, looking for the rock ledge, her eyes still adjusting to the darkness.

Where is it? Where is it? Please!

There! The rock ledge jutted out just ahead. She bumbled toward it, pitching forward at the small dark hole beneath the ledge.

She pushed her son toward the gap in the wall. "Go, Micah! Crawl in. Fast!"

She looked over her shoulder as the boy wiggled through the opening. The beam of Langley's sled shone through the darkness. He was almost around the corner.

She gave Micah a push, then eased onto her stomach, praying she'd fit. She squirmed through the hole, her head, then shoulders. The smell of loamy earth filled her nostrils. She dug her fingers into the cold soil, pulling, dug her feet in, pushing. Finally her hips cleared the opening, and her legs slithered through.

She felt for Micah in the dank darkness and pulled him away from the gap, backing up until she hit a wall.

He curled into her chest, crying, shaking fiercely. "Mommy!"

"Shh, baby." Her chest rose and fell quickly. She forced herself to slow her breaths and listen.

The high-pitched buzz of the engine was nearing.

Pass by. Please pass by.

The whining grew louder, but the throttle had slowed. *No, no, keep going.*

But there was no doubt the sled was slowing. He'd

seen their machine. The engine died, and Micah's sobs were loud in the sudden quiet.

"Shhh. Baby, we have to be very quiet," she whispered.

Her phone was in her purse at the house. Useless. Langley would follow their footprints. They were trapped. He would never fit inside, but his gun would.

Her eyes stung and beads of sweat broke out on her forehead. *God, are You there? Help!*

She pulled Micah tight. His sobs had quieted. She stroked his hair with trembling hands.

All was silent outside except for the distant sound of fireworks and the quiet rumble of the sled. Then the light on the other side grew brighter, washing into the cave.

"Party's over, Eden," Langley's gruff voice called from outside. "Out. Now."

She grabbed Micah, pulling him to the farthest reach of the space. She clutched his quivering body closer.

Her chest tightened till she could barely breathe. What now? *God, can You hear me?*

"Move it! I know you're in there."

Micah's fingers clawed at her shirt. *I'm so sorry, kiddo.* They should've left weeks ago. She thought of Beau and knew he'd blame himself. The thought made her insides twist.

"Have it your way." Langley's hand pushed through the opening. She saw the shadow of the gun an instant before the blast rang out, blisteringly loud. She shrieked. The bullet bit into the ground nearby. Bits of dirt spewed out.

She twisted, huddling over her son, her heart banging against her ribs.

"All right!" she said. "All right. I'm coming out. Don't shoot." An absurd thing to say. Shooting was exactly what he was going to do.

"Stay here," she whispered to Micah. "Don't come out no matter what you hear."

Micah clutched her, and she pried his hands away, her eyes burning. "Micah. You have to stay." He finally let go, huddling against the wall. "Remember, don't come out no matter what." She ran her hand up his arm, to his face. "I love you."

She let loose of him and crawled toward the gap in the wall, her knees scraping against jutting rocks. At the hole she lay down and slithered through the opening. When she was halfway through, Langley jerked her to her feet, one hand clamped around her arm. With the other he pointed the gun straight at her.

She'd forgotten how big he was. Tall and broad, built like a bear. The lights from the sled hit his profile, carving out harsh angles. His eyes were black shadows under his thick brows.

He looked back to the opening, waiting for Micah, no doubt.

"How'd you find me?"

"Where's the kid?"

"I sent him for help."

"Liar. Get him out here." He pointed his gun at the hole. "Or shall I start shooting again?"

"No! You don't need him. Fattore will be found innocent. You have me. That's all you need."

He seemed to weigh that, his eyes taking on an evil glint under the moonlit night. He shifted the gun back to her. A cold shiver of fear ran down her spine. She was going to die. Right here.

And Micah was going to hear it. Again.

No, God. Please.

The fireworks grew louder, popping and sizzling as the grand finale began. The booms shook the ground under her feet.

"I could just shoot you both right now, Eden, but you know what? You made this so difficult, I think I'm going to have a little fun with you first."

He grabbed her arm and pulled her close, the cold barrel of his gun pressing against her neck. Her heart thrashed against her ribs. She pushed against the wall of his chest, but it was futile. He leaned closer. His clove-scented breath turned her stomach.

His beady eyes raked over her. "Yeah. A little fun first."

CHAPTER 35

Beau flew down the trail on his snowmobile, praying he wasn't too late. He'd put in a call to the sheriff, asking him to approach the trail from town, but Beau couldn't wait for backup. He'd taken a shortcut through the Benningtons' property and was closing in. He'd heard a gunshot a minute ago, and now he only saw the light of one sled in the distance.

There'd be no sneaking up on them, and Beau didn't dare waste the time parking half a mile away.

As he got closer, a cold fist tightened in his gut at the sight. Two figures huddled in the shadows of the hillside. Someone was being dragged through the brush, up to the trail. Beau's heart hammered when he caught sight of Kate.

He slowed, reaching for his Glock, but the man got a shot off first. Beau ducked as a gunshot split the air. He stopped the sled, and it skidded sideways. He dropped to the ground behind it as another gunshot sounded, hitting a corner of the sled.

He looked over the machine. He was only about thirty yards away. He aimed his Glock and got the target in his sight just as the man pulled Eden into his body. She fought for release then drove her foot backward, catching him in the knee.

The man clubbed her on the cheek with the butt of the gun. "Be still, or I'll take you out right now!"

"Drop the gun, and get your hands in the air!" Beau shouted.

"One move, and I'll put a bullet in her head." The man was easing them both toward the nearest sled.

The headlight hit her pale face, and he saw the mark on her cheek. Something red and hot clawed at his insides. He ground his teeth together, his finger flexing on the trigger.

"Drop the gun!" Beau shouted again.

The man ignored the order. They were almost to the sled. He kept Kate in front of him as a shield, the yellow-bellied coward.

Beau sighted the man. His trigger finger twitched, but she was too close. He just needed a split second. *Come on, move to the left, Kate.*

A loud crack split the air. But Beau's finger hadn't flexed on the trigger.

The man's hands fell, and he dropped to the ground, lifeless, beside the sled.

Kate jumped back, then stood frozen, her hands on her face.

There was a movement at ten o'clock, and Beau swiveled, ready. But it was only Colton. The sheriff stepped from the shadows.

Beau ran up the trail, his Glock pointed at the still lump on the hard-packed trail. But one look at Kate's shocked face, and he holstered his sidearm, letting Colton take over.

When he reached Kate he grabbed her and pulled her into his arms. She was cold and shaking, breathing hard.

"It's okay, baby. It's okay now."

"Is he dead?"

Colton kicked the body over.

Even in the darkness Beau could see the bullet wound at his temple. He tucked Kate's head into his shoulder. "Yeah, honey, he's dead. It's over."

Colton laid his coat over the perp's upper body and pulled his phone from his pocket. "Everybody okay?"

"Yeah."

The last of the fireworks finale fizzled out, and sudden silence reigned.

"Jack," she whispered, pushing away. She started down the trail at a clip.

Beau followed. "Is he hurt?"

"No. It's okay now, Jack," she called when she reached the mouth of the cave.

"Mommy?"

"You can come out now, baby. Everything's okay." Her voice was thin and reedy.

He wanted nothing more than to pull her back into his arms. But she needed her son right now.

Micah appeared at the gap in the wall. He squirmed through the hole, and Kate helped him through, then caught him up in her arms. "It's okay. Everything's okay."

Micah sobbed into her shoulder, and she clutched him to her, her eyes closing.

Beau couldn't take it another minute. He gathered them both into his arms. They smelled like earth and fear, and he wanted nothing more than to keep them safe forever.

"It's over," he whispered. "You're safe now."

He took off his coat and wrapped it around them. He didn't know how long they stood like that, both of them trembling in his arms.

Sometime later Colton approached, his footsteps crunching in the snow. "EMTs are on the way."

He needed to get Jack out of there. Beau pulled away and ushered them toward the sled. "Let's get you guys home."

Colton looked at Beau. "I'll need them to come in for—"

"Tomorrow."

"Beau, the feds are going to be all over this one when—"

"Morning's soon enough." His voice was firm. He wasn't giving on this. They'd already been through so much. They needed a warm house and a soft bed.

The sheriff took in the sight of the quaking boy and his mama, her wobbling chin up, holding on by a thread.

He gave a firm nod. "All right. Morning'll do."

Beau slid onto the sled, lifting Micah up behind him. Kate squeezed on next, wedging Micah between them.

"Let's go home," Beau said. The word had never sounded so good.

CHAPTER 36

It took Micah hours to fall asleep. But finally his little body lay still in her twin bed, his breaths coming deeply. Eden shifted away, easing onto her back. Her arm was asleep from the weight of his head, and tingles spread as circulation was restored. She shivered, pulling the quilt up to her chin. She hadn't felt warm for hours, and her head was pounding from the blow she'd received.

She glanced at the clock. It was past three in the morning, and she was wide awake. So much had happened. She was still in shock from the ordeal. In shock from being held at gunpoint, from seeing Beau under fire, from seeing Langley shot in the head.

As if the trauma weren't enough, being trapped had brought it all back. The fear, the insecurity, the vast hopelessness. In recent months she'd pushed those feelings deep into the recesses of her mind. But tonight's distress had freed them, and like buoys they'd burst to the surface.

She felt restless and scared and trapped.

No. You're not trapped, Eden. Not anymore. You're free to live your life any way you want.

Her heart beat out a wild tattoo. She wanted to pull

the covers over her head and hide. But there was nothing to hide from anymore. She'd already broken free of the chains. They were hanging open around her wrists, but she was afraid to flee.

She shook the thought away. There were no manacles, not anymore. Tomorrow she'd put her bags in her car and head north. By day's end they'd be settled at Loon Lake. She'd finally be in control of her own destiny.

She thought of Beau, and her heart twisted. She'd miss him. So much. She'd gotten too attached. What had she been thinking? But she'd never turn her free will over to a man again. Never make a man's needs the center of her life. Never go back to feeling worthless and hopeless.

Her head was cranking. She wasn't going to go to sleep like this. She slipped from beneath the covers and tiptoed down the steps. She could swear the smell of cloves and cigarettes hung in the air. Her mind flashed back, and she could feel the cold metal of the barrel pressed to her neck.

She held her breath until she reached the kitchen. Hands shaking, she poured a glass of water, popped a couple of ibuprofen, and took her glass into the living room. She stopped at the sight of a lump on the sofa. The TV light flickered across Beau's face, and her heart began beating again.

Maybe she should just sneak back upstairs. She shifted to go, and the floorboard creaked.

"You're awake," he said.

"Couldn't sleep."

"Come 'ere." He opened the quilt, and she couldn't stop herself going to him.

She settled against his side. She needed comfort right now, wherever she could get it. And he did feel so good, soft Henley stretched over hard muscle. She burrowed into his side and let his body warm her.

He wrapped the quilt around her and rubbed her shoulder. "You're cold. Want me to start a fire?"

"No. This is good." More than good. Pretty perfect, actually.

Step away from the man, Eden.

But the man was stroking the tender underside of her arm, and she needed this like she needed air. Tomorrow. Tomorrow was soon enough.

"Jack's finally asleep. It took a long time."

They sat in silence for a few minutes. His heart beat against her cheek. She closed her eyes and drew in a breath of him. He smelled so good, so familiar. She breathed again, attempting to memorize the smell. She'd access the detail later when Beau was nothing but a distant memory.

"I thought I'd lost you." His voice rumbled in her ear. "When I got home and saw that SUV . . . my chest got so tight I could hardly breathe." His arms tightened around her. "I've never prayed so hard in all my life."

"You and me both. The sled ran out of gas. We were trapped in the cave." She felt the walls closing in now. She closed her eyes. Reminded herself she wasn't trapped anymore. "I thought we were both going to die."

Beau tightened his grip. "I wasn't going to let that happen."

He laid his cheek against her head. Their hearts beat in tandem for a long minute.

"Tell me your name," he whispered into the silence.

He still wanted too much of her. More than she could ever give him. She suddenly realized his expectations about the future might be very different than hers. The nightmare was over, and she was free.

But that meant very different things to each of them.

"Beau . . ." Gathering her courage, she turned her head, meeting his gaze. She faltered when she saw his warm brown eyes gazing so lovingly down at her. The familiar turn of his nose, the scruffy jaw, those perfect lips . . . all of it drew her in, made her want what she couldn't have.

"I–I'm still leaving tomorrow. You know that, right?"

Shadows shifted as he searched her face. "You . . . you mean to go see your dad? He's probably been a worried wreck."

"No, that's not—I'm not going to see my dad. I have things planned out, Beau . . . a future for Jack and me. That hasn't changed."

His eyes pierced hers, something flickering there that put a hollow pit in the center of her stomach. "And that future . . . it doesn't include me?"

His words, the hurt on his face, tore at her heart. It was all too tempting. This house, this family, this town. This man. They all pulled at her like a riptide. But she knew the dangers that lay that way. She could easily drift into a life like that, and before she knew it, she'd be in over her head, flailing, sinking. Trapped.

She wouldn't let herself go that direction again. She'd made a promise to herself. To Micah.

"We were never going to happen, Beau. I've been through too much to go backward."

He gave her a weak smile. Kissed the top of her head. "You're tired. You've had a traumatic night."

"My answer won't change."

His brows creased as he studied her. That knowing gaze seeing far too much. "I'm not him."

"I know. I know that."

But did she really? She knew there were good men. She thought Beau was one of them. But she'd thought Antonio was, too, and how wrong she'd been.

"Then why? Why wouldn't you stay? You like it here. You both do. You could work for the farm, get your website business up and going again. Nothing has to change. You could stay here."

Right under his thumb.

The quilt suddenly felt like a lead cape. His arm like a restraint. Heat prickled the hair at the back of her neck.

She pushed away, letting the quilt fall from her shoulder. "I won't build my life around a man again."

"I'm not asking you to do that."

She stood. "I have to go. It's for the best."

His eyes searched hers. "You don't trust me."

"I know you're not Antonio. I *know* that. But I thought he was a good man too. I was fooled. For so long I thought it was *me*. He had me thinking I was crazy. That I was worthless. That I couldn't do anything right. But the only thing I was guilty of was bad judgment.

"Don't you see, Beau? It's not *you* I don't trust; it's myself. I lost *me*, and I'm only beginning to discover who

I am. I swore I'd never go back to that. And I won't. *I won't*. No matter how much part of me might want to. No matter how much I might wish things were different . . ."

She flung her arms out. "I want to be free. For the first time in my life, I want to be completely free. I have no idea what that even feels like!"

Her breaths came quickly. Her heart pounded, kicking against her ribs as if she were in the fight of her life. She'd spilled her guts. She couldn't say it any clearer. But the look on his face was tearing her in two.

Beau stood slowly, caution in every line of his body. He took a careful step forward. Then another.

She made herself hold her ground. Her heart felt as if it might pop from her chest. Her nails dug into her palms.

He stopped when he was a breath away. "I'm not trying to take your freedom. God knows you deserve it after being married to that monster. I don't want to trap you or hold you back or control you." He gently cupped her face. "I only want to love you, honey."

Her breath hitched. Her chest squeezed, tightening painfully. Why did this have to be so hard? So confusing. She wanted that. So badly.

Those mocha eyes hypnotized her. He leaned down, drawing closer until his lips met hers. The kiss was so soft and tender her heart turned over in her chest. His thumb moved across her face, stirring every cell to life.

She braced herself against the firm wall of his chest. His heart thumped beneath her palm, hard and fast, matching her own.

As he pulled her closer her hands followed the

muscled planes of his shoulders. His lips parted hers, and a mewling sound escaped from someplace deep inside her. She curled her arms around him tighter until his belt buckle dug into her stomach and his thighs pressed against hers.

His fingers sank into her hair, pulling her back until their lips barely touched. "I love you, baby," he whispered, his voice as thick as honey.

She went liquid, just melted into a puddle. She was helpless against the warmth in his eyes, the gentle assault of his lips on hers. He was like a drug. She couldn't get enough. Couldn't quit him.

But she had to.

She had to.

Her heart cried out in protest. He made her feel so good. So right.

So did Antonio, remember? Then everything changed.

She pushed at the thought. Held it under with all her mental strength. But she couldn't hold it all back. Pieces popped to the surface around her.

The thermostat she was forbidden to adjust. The monotonous hues of her clothes, hanging straight in her closet. The library book hurled into the trash can. Her emotions, stifled. Her life, lonely. Her identity, gone.

Fear clawed at her chest. She tore her mouth away, pushed at him. Her breaths became ragged gasps.

He caught her shoulders. "What? What's wrong?"

The words locked tight in her throat. She shook her head, needing time. Space. Lots of space. "I can't do this."

"I'm rushing you. I'm sorry. We can go as slow as you like. Just stay."

She steeled herself against the look in his eyes and shook her head.

"I see the way you look at me," he said. "I feel the way you respond to me. I've never felt this way, not about anyone. You feel it, too, I know you do." He searched her eyes and she felt exposed, her feelings for him spilled wide open.

He shook his head. "You won't throw this away. You won't go."

A chill passed through her at the eerily familiar words. Her mind finished the thought Antonio had voiced so many times: *No one else will want you.* The walls of her chest closed in, squeezing so tight she couldn't breathe.

"You're wrong."

She stepped out of his grasp and turned for the stairs. When he called after her she shut him out, her feet making quick work of the stairs.

CHAPTER 37

They were both right. Kate didn't leave the next day. Beau and Kate were both brought in for questioning by local law enforcement on New Year's Day. Then the feds had their turn. Kate had looked frazzled yesterday, the circles under her eyes growing darker. When she got home from the hours of questioning, he'd wanted to charge into the station and slam someone against a wall. Couldn't they see what she'd already been through?

But the end results were worth everything they'd endured. The feds had finally scored with their surveillance of Deputy Morris, and he'd sung like a canary once he was behind bars. They had enough to put Fattore away for a long time. Kate and Jack were safe. Free to go.

Beau turned up the cartoon on the TV so he couldn't hear the sounds of Kate traipsing overhead, packing up their belongings. He'd tried to talk her into staying for church this morning, but she was determined to get on the road.

Jack sat forlornly on the sofa beside him, his eyes on the screen, Boo Bear cradled to his chest. His teeth worried his lip. The boy had been quiet the past two days. He talked, but not much. And Beau hadn't seen him smile once.

"You want some hot chocolate to take on the road with you?" Beau asked. "I'll put a bunch of whipped cream on top the way you like."

Jack shook his head, barely sparing Beau a glance.

"You know, I'll bet Boo Bear will like where you're going. Your mom said there's lots of trees and a big lake. Bears like that kind of thing."

He watched for some response. Nothing.

Beau reached over and pulled the boy into his side. Jack leaned into him, pulling his skinny knees against Beau's leg. He was going to miss the little guy.

Jack didn't want to leave. Beau didn't want them to leave. He wished for the dozenth time he could get inside Kate's head and see what she was thinking. Then maybe he'd have the right words to make her stay. She wanted freedom, she'd said. Freedom from what? She was no longer captive—couldn't she see that?

The front door opened and Zac entered on a cold wind, flurries in his hair, as Kate descended the stairs with a suitcase and duffel bag.

Beau met her at the base of the steps. He took her duffel bag and slung it over his shoulder. When he took the suitcase, his hand brushed hers. She didn't even look his way.

"Your car's warming up." Zac blew on his hands. "All set?"

"All set. Ready, kiddo?" Her enthusiasm sounded forced.

The boy slinked from the couch, and Kate helped

him with his coat and boots as Beau carried out her things. He barely felt the cold nipping at his skin. Heart heavy, he opened the trunk and stowed the suitcase and bag. By the time he closed it, Jack and Kate were coming down the walk, Zac on their heels.

Aunt Trudy had said good-bye earlier and left to set up for her Sunday school class.

Kate embraced Zac, saying something in his ear that Beau didn't even want to hear.

He picked up Jack and held him tight. "Gonna miss you, bud."

"Me too."

His throat tightened. "Keep practicing with your tools. Maybe your mom'll let you help hang pictures and stuff at your new place."

Jack hung on for a long moment, then Beau set him on his feet. Zac grabbed him up and did an imitation of the tree shaker. The two of them bobbed around until the boy finally smiled.

Kate turned to Beau. The swelling on her cheek had gone down, but the purplish bruise remained. Her honey-brown eyes lifted to his. There were so many emotions flickering there. Warmth. Regret. Resolution. And underneath it all, fear.

His eyes pierced hers. *Stay*, he thought.

Resolution settled over her features before her eyes shuttered. She lifted her chin a fraction of an inch.

A knot tightened in his throat. *Okay, then. Okay.*

He pulled her close. She wrapped her arms around him, and his heart gave a heavy sigh. He held her tight against the ache in his chest, wishing her nearness would make it go away. He wanted to hold her here forever. But by day's end she'd be far away at a location she'd carefully avoided mentioning.

If he was never going to see her again, he was going to say it one more time.

"I love you," he whispered into her ear. "You're a special woman. Don't ever forget that." His throat ached. His eyes burned. His heart was in shreds, as if it had been dragged for miles over a gravel road.

He hoped his words rang in her ears, louder than the other voices he was sure she heard.

Her chest rose and fell against him. He closed his eyes and drew her in, that sweet, citrusy smell he loved.

Then her arms loosened.

He dropped a lingering kiss to the top of her head and stepped away, his heart banging in protest. He tried to catch her eye, but she only blinked and turned to grab Jack's hand.

"Ready, kiddo?"

Zac opened the door for Jack, and Kate rounded the car. Seconds later she put the car in gear and started down the drive. She didn't look his way, just lifted a hand, staring straight ahead.

The ache inside Beau spread as he watched the car retreat. He stared until all he saw was a plume of steam condensing in the cold morning air. He crossed his arms against the hollow spot opening in his chest. It was all he could do to stand here. To not chase after her. He was a man who solved problems. A man who took care of the people he loved. But Kate wanted to solve her own problems. She wasn't his to take care of.

And it was killing him.

"You're really going to just let her go?" Zac asked.

Beau gritted his teeth. "It's what she wants."

"And that's that? Since when did you give up so easily?"

His eyes cut to Zac. "What do you want me to do, tie her up in the cellar?"

Sounded like something her late husband would have done. Who knows, maybe he had. The thought did nothing for his mood.

"Did you even tell her how you feel?"

He glared at Zac. "Yeah, buttinsky, I did. As you can see, it had a marvelous effect."

Zac held his hands up, palms out. "I'm not the enemy here, bro. I just know a little about where you're at right now."

Beau thought of Zac's ex-fiancée and felt a pinch of guilt. He'd been a wreck for weeks. Still wasn't over it.

Zac stuffed his hands in his pockets. "You don't know how many times I wish I'd done things differently. Now she's gone, and it's too late."

Beau softened at the regret on Zac's face. "Kate's been through a lot. She's looking for freedom."

"And she thinks she'll find it in some backwoods cabin?"

Beau looked back down the drive, empty of all traces of Kate's departure. "She's already free. She just doesn't know it."

CHAPTER 38

Eden turned into the long, plowed driveway. It wound and curved among towering pine trees. The car rumbled over an old wooden bridge that spanned a frozen creek.

She'd called her dad after she left Summer Harbor. He begged her to come back to Hattiesburg, and it was hard to say no. But she wasn't ready for that. Wasn't strong enough. If she went back to that trailer, she'd get stuck in his sticky web and never be free.

Eden turned the wheel as she rounded a curve and emerged in front of a cabin she'd only seen in pictures. It looked different all covered in snow, the flower beds barren.

"There it is," she whispered to herself.

It was a simple log cabin with a wide front porch. A thick layer of snow covered the roof, and a stone chimney marched up the side of the house. Later tonight there would be smoke curling from that chimney. The walk leading to the door had been shoveled, and the drapes in the windows were open. Karen must have sent someone to freshen up the place.

She pulled up to the house and shut off the engine. "We're here, kiddo."

Micah opened his eyes, stirred, then stretched.

Eden stepped outside and shivered against the frigid air, huddling deeper into her coat. She scanned the landscape. The trees stretched into an overcast sky, naked and skeletal, and the cold wind bit at her skin. But nothing could deflate her mood. At least there were no other houses in sight. And maybe the lake was buried under ice and snow now, but it would be gorgeous come spring.

Not as gorgeous as Summer Harbor.

She wrestled the thought to the ground before it could drag her under, then handed Micah his duffel, taking the heavier suitcase. The house key was under the empty flowerpot on the porch, just as Karen had said. If all went well with her business, Eden would eventually be in a position to buy the property. Karen had said she was in no hurry. Someday all of this would be Eden's.

The screen door creaked as she opened it, but the heavy wooden door behind it swung easily on its hinges. Bright shafts of sunlight streamed through sparkling windowpanes, and dust motes danced in the air. The fresh scent of Pine-Sol tickled her nose. The stone fireplace took up the far wall of the living room, and beyond it, a sunny yellow kitchen beckoned.

There was the rug Karen had bought at the flea market and the comfy leather recliner her grandmother had left her.

Eden drew in a breath of clean-smelling air and let it flow out her mouth. She was here. They'd made it. She was going to set the thermostat at seventy-two degrees, and later she was going to draw a bath and fill it all the way to the top. She was going to wear her red pajamas, start a cozy fire, then she was going to cuddle up in that chair and finish the Debbie Macomber novel she'd been carrying around for weeks.

And tomorrow . . .

Tomorrow she was going to the library to sign up for a library card. She was going to bring home a whole stack of novels. She was going to go to the grocery, and she was going to buy Twinkies. She was going to search for a church, and she was going to get in touch with her former customers. She'd do whatever was necessary to salvage WhiteBox Designs.

Eden followed the sounds of Micah's footsteps, finding him in the smaller room that used to be her friend April's. It was still decorated with a frilly yellow bedspread and white eyelet curtains.

"What do you think, kiddo? A whole bedroom all to yourself. We'll get you some Superman sheets and curtains. How'd you like that?"

Micah's gaze wandered around the room. His brown eyes looked tired, like he needed more than a nap. His hair was tousled from the wind, his shoulders slumped. He looked so . . . lost. He'd been clingy and fragile the past couple of days. But at least he hadn't retreated into his silent world again.

Eden sank onto the bed and patted the spot beside her. He climbed up. His feet dangled off the side, and his hands curled in his lap.

She wrapped her arm around him and set her head on top of his. "This is our new home. We'll make new friends and have a wonderful life here. I promise."

Beau's image danced into her mind, his mocha eyes twinkling, those perfect lips tilting in a crooked grin. She could see the crescent-shaped dimple on the side of his mouth, the light brown flecks in his eyes.

She blinked the image away, ignoring the way her chest squeezed at the thought of him.

"You'll see," she whispered. "It's going to be everything we ever dreamed."

· · ·

Beau threw himself into work the next several days. He was outside as soon as the sun rose and didn't return until darkness had fallen. He got rid of the unsold wreaths and cut trees left over from Christmas. He stored the machinery and lights. The gift shop had taken awhile to pack up. He could have kept his help on for that, but then he wouldn't have a way to fill the empty hours.

The house was too quiet without Kate and Jack. The lonely clack of Aunt Trudy's knitting needles was about to send him up the wall. He got books from the library on website design. The farm's pathetic site was in dire need of an overhaul. He was going to figure it out if it killed him—and it just might. He knew nothing about HTML and CSS code, but he had time to learn. It kept him busy, thinking about something besides Kate.

He trudged up the porch steps, eyeing the front door like it was the latest in torture devices. Who was he kidding? He found plenty of time to think about her. She was the first thing on his mind before he opened his eyes in the morning. A constant tug at his heart while he worked. The last thought he had before succumbing to sleep.

He opened the door, feeling nothing but dread. The sun set early in January, and the long evening stretched ahead like an endless highway. He greeted Aunt Trudy. She sat in the recliner, her needles waving under her practiced fingers.

The hooks on the coatrack all taken, he moved things around to free up space. One of Kate's hot-pink mittens fell to the floor by his feet.

He glared at it, sighing hard. *Come on, God. Give me a break. I'm trying here.*

He picked it up, holding it an extra moment before hanging it on a hook beside its mate.

"There's a ham in the Crock-Pot if you're hungry," Aunt Trudy said.

"Thanks. Maybe later. How was your day?"

"Good enough. Had lunch with my book club and stopped in at the Knitting Nook. Got this new yarn. Isn't it nice? I'm making a sweater for Lydia Franke's new grandson."

He looked down at the bright blue ball of fuzz. Kate would have loved the color. He hung his coat on the hook, his hand remaining there. He had to shake this funk. But she was everywhere in the house. In the kitchen, in front of the sink. In the dining room chair across from him. On the end of the sofa, looking up at him with those vulnerable eyes.

He lifted the coat off the hook. "I think I'll head to the Roadhouse for a while."

Aunt Trudy studied him over the black rim of her glasses until he looked away. It was Saturday night. The Roadhouse would be busy and loud. Just what he needed.

"You can't run away from your problems, Beau."

"Maybe not." He slipped into his coat. "But I can stay busy enough to forget them awhile."

The Roadhouse was packed, and the TVs blared. Somehow he'd forgotten the Pats played in the divisional round tonight. The game was already under way, the Pats ahead of the Broncos 10–7.

A server scurried past with a tray of appetizers and drinks. The smell of buffalo wings made his stomach rumble. Maybe he could eat after all. See, he was already feeling better.

A cheer rose up as the Pats got the first down, and Beau clapped, scanning the crowd.

Zac waved from across the room, and Beau headed his way. He had the large corner booth with Paige and several others. They greeted Beau, barely glancing away from the screen as he slid in beside his brother.

Across from him Paige had her long blond hair pulled back into a ponytail. She looked young and spunky in her Pats jersey. How was it that he felt nothing but friendship for her when they'd been together for months? He'd only known Kate for six weeks, and losing her felt like a semi crushing his heart.

He ordered wings and a drink and settled in to watch the game, high-fiving everyone at the table when the Pats put up another touchdown. During commercial breaks he fielded questions about the New Year's Eve excitement. Everyone, it seemed, had heard about the showdown. And everyone wanted to talk about it. The feds had arrived in town the day after in a black sedan rental. They'd stood out like giraffes on the beach in their tidy suits and shiny shoes.

He was glad when the game came back on, capturing everyone's attention. Everyone's but his. After the interrogation he couldn't get his mind off Kate. Wondering where she was. What she was doing. If she missed him.

Did she lie awake at night thinking of him? Or had she forgotten him as soon as she arrived at her cabin? Was the place everything she'd dreamed? Was the shock of the past few months beginning to wear off? He wanted to be there for her. His arms ached to hold her. He wanted to replace all of Antonio's insults with truth.

"For the first time in my life, I want to be completely free. I have no idea what that even feels like."

Maybe it was best he didn't know where she'd gone. Everything in him wanted to chase her down and bring her home.

The game broke for half time, and Zac nudged him. "Need to go check on the kitchen."

Beau licked the barbecue sauce from his fingers and let him out. Everyone else emptied from the booth for a quick game of pool, leaving just him and Paige.

He found a wet wipe and rid his fingers of the sticky residue, wondering if things were about to get awkward.

Paige leaned into the table across from him. "I got a letter from Riley yesterday," she said over the din.

"Oh yeah?"

"I've been writing him every week. To keep his spirits up. He's doing really well. He's sleep deprived and worn out, but he seems mentally strong."

"He always has been. It'll come in handy in the marines."

"Sounds like he's made a few good friends."

A cheer went up from the poolroom, followed by heckling and laughter. Three couples gathered around the table. One of the guys pulled his girl into his arms and laid one on her. Beau looked away.

"You doing okay?" Paige asked, her blue eyes studying him. "That was quite a ruckus on New Year's."

He gave her his best fake smile. "All in a day's work."

"Somebody forget to tell you you're not a deputy anymore?"

He shrugged. Someone was in danger, and he wasn't standing around watching. Especially not when it was someone he loved.

Kate.

Man, he missed her. Missed seeing her sleepy eyes first thing in the morning. Missed holding her on the couch while they watched movies. Missed the eager way she responded when he kissed her. That little mewling sound she made . . .

God, will this ever end?

He took a gulp of his drink, trying to wash away the sudden knot that tightened his throat. He couldn't shake the feeling that he should've done something, said something, to make her stay. He tried to live a life free of regret, but it was hard not to regret a painful ending. Especially when it was permanent.

He shifted in his seat.

Something else, Callahan. Think about something else.

He forced a smile to his lips. "How's your week been? Digging out at work?"

"Oh yeah. I'm way behind. But things are slow overall, so I'll catch up soon enough."

He glanced across the room and caught Nick Donahue eyeing the two of them with curiosity. It reminded him of the scuttlebutt going around at the diner earlier in the week.

"Heard your social calendar is filling up," he said lightly.

Paige caught Nick's eye, and her cheeks flushed. "I had a date last night, and I have another next weekend. Two, actually." She gave him a cheeky smile. "Seems all the single men in town were just waiting for me to become available again."

He chuckled, feeling happy for her. "I don't doubt it, Paige. You're a good catch."

"What about you?"

"What about me?"

She cocked her head, giving him a look.

"She's gone, as I'm sure you know." He frowned into his empty glass, the heavy feeling in his stomach returning. "I don't want to talk about it."

She pulled a face, her eyes searching his. "Fine," she said finally. "Let's talk about Zac then."

"What about him?"

"Hello. He's still mourning that ex-fiancée of his. We should do something."

"Since when have you been such a matchmaker?"

Amusement flashed in her eyes. "I've been taking notes from Miss Trudy."

"Well, you're wasting your time. He'll move on when he's ready."

"Two brokenhearted Callahans are more than I can take. I'm fixing him up with Bridgett Gillespie."

He scowled. "Bridgett Gillespie talks a mile a minute. She'll drive him flat crazy."

Paige lifted a shoulder. "Maybe not. Zac's not very talkative. She'll fill the silence."

"And then some."

"Fine. I'll come up with someone else. How about Sara Porter? She's not too talkative, and she's very sweet."

"Doesn't she have like fifty cats?"

Paige rolled her eyes. "Morgan LeBlanc then."

"She only dates rich guys."

"Well, what about Millie Parker? She's down to earth." Paige lifted a brow. "And she only has one cat."

Beau shook his head.

"What's wrong with her?"

"I went out with her last year."

"So?"

"So on our first date she asked me how many kids I'd want."

"That's not so bad."

He gave her a dark look. "She wanted to help me name them."

Paige's lips twitched. "Men. What is it you guys want?"

A honey-eyed woman with a heart as warm as a summer day.

And there it was again. Why did all roads lead to Kate?

Paige looked across the room, her eyes meeting Nick's. Beau watched as the man gave her a shy smile before looking away.

Paige slurped up the last of her soda. "Well. I think I'll go see who's winning."

Beau lifted his glass in a mini-salute as she scooted from the booth. Someone might as well be winning. It sure as heck wasn't him.

CHAPTER 39

January rolled slowly past. Eden had access to her old bank account now that she was able to use her own ID. She had a nice little nest egg to get her business back up and going. She'd made contact with her old clients, explaining that she was back in business. Almost all of them had moved to other companies, but she had three who were eager to come back. It wasn't much, but she'd build it back up in time. She'd already placed some Internet ads and designed new business cards.

She dyed her hair back to her natural chestnut brown. It had grown to her shoulders now, and she splurged on a layered cut. When she looked in the mirror she barely recognized her image. But she was feeling more like her old self. No, not her old self. A new and improved self.

She'd gotten that library card and added a stack of self-help books to the novels. She'd found a warm church with a pastor who spoke to the empty spot inside her. They were kind people who made her and Micah feel welcome. She filled the cabin with praise music and took long evening baths while she reflected on life, and God, and all the events that had led her to this place.

Antonio's words still flashed in her mind at times, but she worked hard to push them away, to replace them with truth.

Sometimes the voice was Beau's. Her soul longed to remember his loving words. But she pushed those away, too, for an entirely different reason.

So much was going right in her life. If the town was farther away than she'd anticipated, so be it. And if her nearest neighbor was a mile down the road, she could live with that. Maybe the cold winter days made her feel a little stir-crazy, but spring would come soon enough.

Eden wiped down the counter, swaying as the gentle strains of "We Believe" crescendoed to its powerful chorus.

"I'm bored," Micah said from his spot on the sofa.

"Why don't you go draw with your art set? I'll color with you when I'm finished cleaning." She actually enjoyed scrubbing the little cabin until it sparkled. It was different when it was your own space. Your own home.

She gave the counter an extra swipe, noticing Micah hadn't budged. "What about your tools? You could tighten up a few screws around here."

He shrugged. Boo Bear was in his lap. Micah hadn't let him get far away since they'd arrived. He'd had a few nightmares, and most nights he climbed into her bed in the middle of the night.

"I miss home."

Eden set down the dishrag and sank down beside him on the sofa. "Honey, you know that house is gone. The bank had to—"

"Not that one. The farmhouse. I miss Beau and Miss Trudy and Zac." His brown eyes looked so sad, her heart gave a tug.

"I miss them too." Every day. So much her chest ached with it sometimes. "But we're making new friends at church. There's Noah and Evan. You like them, right?"

Micah shrugged. "I guess."

"And Mr. Wallace at the library is very nice, isn't he?"

The older man was a wonder at story time on Tuesday mornings. He drew a crowd with his animated and boisterous voice. Eden was conscious of Micah's need for male influence in his life. The Callahans had filled that role nicely.

But they're gone, Eden. You can't go back. You have to keep moving forward.

Micah pulled Boo Bear into his chest and fixed his eyes on the mute TV screen, where SpongeBob was learning to drive. Her son was still so quiet and withdrawn, despite her efforts to draw him out. Maybe it was just going to take time.

A knock sounded.

She stiffened automatically, her head jerking toward the door. Her heart pounded in her chest. She blew out a breath.

Relax, Eden. You're not in danger anymore.

There was no one looking for them. No feds accusing her of murder. No crooked cop out for blood.

"I wonder who's come to see us." She forced the light note into her voice as she stood and turned for the door.

She peeked out the curtain first, blinking at the sight on her front porch. She couldn't believe what she was seeing. *Who* she was seeing.

Her heart gave a cry of joy. Her fingers couldn't unlock the door fast enough. She swung it open and cupped her mouth as tears gathered in her eyes.

His hairline had receded more in the three years since she'd last seen him, and he wore a day's worth of growth on his jaw. But he was such a welcome sight.

His light brown eyes glossed over. "Baby girl."

She was in his arms an instant later, enveloped by his bearlike hug. "Daddy. You're here."

"I had to see for myself you were okay," he said in that familiar, warbly voice. He pulled away, looking her over, his eyes taking her in. "I've been so worried."

"I'm sorry."

He palmed her cheek. "Not your fault."

"How did you . . . ?"

"Let's catch up inside, can we? The heat in my rental didn't work. I'm cold as an ice cube."

Inside he shucked his coat, his eyes landing on her son. "Micah."

"Kiddo," Eden said, hanging on to her dad's arm. "It's been a long time since you've seen him, but this is my dad, your grandpa."

Micah stared at him. "The one who taught you about football?"

"That's right. And the one we went to visit when you were three."

Micah studied her dad, his brown eyes quietly assessing. "You took me fishing."

Her dad's dark brows popped up. "You remember?"

"No, Mom told me. You helped me catch bluegill. I have a picture."

Her dad sent Eden a grateful smile.

She turned down the music and stoked the fire. When she realized her dad had only had pretzels on the plane, she fixed him a sandwich. They caught up while he ate, Micah asking questions about his home. Eden had a lot of questions of her own. But she waited until Micah scooted off to his room to play with his Legos, her dad's belated Christmas gift.

"Are you warmed up?" she asked as they settled on the couch.

"Yeah, the fire's nice."

"How long can you stay?"

"My ticket's open-ended." He stared at her as if he couldn't believe he was seeing her, his eyes welling up again. "I was afraid I'd never see you again."

Her eyes burned. "Me, too, Daddy. I've never been so scared." She didn't want to think about that now. "How is it that you're here? Your phobia . . . How did you get on the plane?"

"I started seeing someone, a therapist, after you went into protective custody. I knew I had to get better if I was going to be any help to you and Micah. I started on some medication, and it's helped. I've slowly been forcing myself out more and more. Getting involved at church. Leaning on God. Learning to trust Him again. The plane was hard—lots of mile-high praying going on—but I had to see you for myself. I had to see that you were really okay."

"Oh, Daddy. I can't believe you're here." She fell into his arms, drawing in the familiar smell of Old Spice and home. "I'm so glad you're better. I've been worried about you too."

"I've been worried about you ever since you took off with that schmuck."

"I should've listened to you."

"You were in love and determined. I didn't have anything concrete, just a gut feeling."

"I thought you just didn't want me to leave you. I thought you were afraid to be alone."

Dad pulled back. "Why would I be afraid of that?"

She stared at him, confused. "Dad, you never let me go anywhere. You didn't want to be left alone because of your phobia."

His brows crunched together. "I never minded being alone. I was just afraid something was going to happen to you like happened to your mom. I couldn't lose you too. Only I did."

Eden couldn't believe what she was hearing. She shook her head, trying to make sense of it. "You mean all that time you kept me home it was because of what happened to Mom?"

"I know it doesn't make sense. But your mom just left for work one day and didn't come home. I was afraid the same thing would happen to you. I let fear rule my life for so many years, and it chased you away. I'm done with that. I won't let fear keep me from living."

Eden smiled. "I'm glad you're doing better. You look good."

"Was it so bad with Antonio? Did he hurt you? Hurt the boy?"

She stared into her dad's haunted eyes. He'd suffered enough. "He was a good dad. Micah misses him very much."

"I don't understand how all this happened. What was he mixed up in?"

She told him the story from the day she went to the safe house to the day Langley came for her. She told him about her job with Miss Trudy, the Callahans, the Christmas tree farm, and Summer Harbor. Her heart ached at the memory of it all.

"Sounds like I owe these Callahans a big thank-you," he said when she was finished.

"They're good people. I miss them a lot." Her throat closed. Especially Beau. Oh, how she missed Beau. Her chest felt hollow and achy when she talked about him.

"Was that Beau someone special to you?"

She got up to stoke the fire again, clearing her throat. "Why do you ask that?"

"You get this soft look on your face when you talk about him. Even your voice changes. And when I asked about him, you got up and walked away. Seems like avoidance to me."

"The fire was dying down."

He gave her a look. "Maybe we've been apart awhile, but I know my girl. And I've been in love myself—I know that look. Seen it in the mirror too many times to count."

The fire cracked and popped as she tossed another log on. She turned to find her dad's eyes searching hers. "All right, fine. Yeah, he was someone special. Really special."

"Why'd you leave then, baby girl?"

She shrugged. Of course he wouldn't understand. He didn't know how bad things had been with Antonio. How hard it was to walk on eggshells 24/7. How impossible getting through each day seemed. How much of herself she'd lost.

"He sounds like a stand-up guy, and you look like a lovesick woman."

She huffed a soft laugh. "I'm not lovesick, Daddy. I only knew him for six weeks."

"I knew I was in love with your mama after only three days. When I took her hand at the fair and she looked up at me with those big blue eyes, I was a goner."

She smiled at the familiar story. "I know, Daddy."

She remembered nothing but love between her parents. But it was different for her. She'd already made one mistake. And it had almost cost both of their lives. She couldn't risk it again.

"So you ditched the man you love for this cabin, huh?" He looked around the room, frowning. "You always talked about the place like it was the Holy Grail. I guess I just don't see it."

"It's nice. It's quiet."

Okay, maybe it was too quiet. Maybe most days she never heard the sound of another voice outside of their own. Maybe she was as isolated here as she'd ever been with Antonio.

"I came out here hoping you and Micah would come home with me," Dad said.

"Oh, Dad. I'd love to live near you, but I just—I can't go back to Mississippi."

"I realize that now."

"This is my fresh start. This is our new home. I need to be on my own for a while. Just be . . . free. I hope you understand."

"I do understand, baby girl." He gave her a long look, his dark eyes softening in the light. "I understand more'n you think."

CHAPTER 40

Eden's dad was still with them two weeks later. He occupied Micah while she worked and pitched in with the chores and errands. She was so relieved to see him living his life again. He looked better, even younger, despite his receding hairline. His face was more open, his mood more expressive. His presence had a buoyant effect on Micah.

He'd gotten a better job back home and had saved up a good deal of cash, and he was hoping to move out of the trailer soon. He'd spent too many years locked up inside that white box.

In early February a storm system blew into the area, dumping a foot of snow. They went a week without leaving the little cabin, and all of them were ready to tramp all the way to town for something to do.

Eden finished fixing her hair and set down her brush, staring at her image. She didn't look well. She looked better as a brunette, and she liked her new layers. But the skin around her eyes looked too tight, and her mouth was shaped in a perpetual frown. She was pale, and her eyes seemed flat and lifeless. What was wrong with her? She finally had the freedom she'd been seeking, and she was still miserable.

You're just feeling cooped up.

She needed to get her mind on something else. She fixed breakfast, and afterward her dad and Micah went to Micah's bedroom to play while she did her devotions.

She read through the chapter, struggling to focus, hearing the laughter coming from the bedroom, the unsettled beating of her own heart.

Her eyes stopped on a verse. *For God has not given us a spirit of fear, but of power and of love and of a sound mind.*

Her eyes stumbled over the word *fear* and came back to it as it resonated deep within her. Her hand trembled as she marked the word with her finger. She knew all about the spirit of fear. She'd lived with it during those long years with Antonio. During those harrowing months after his shooting.

It wasn't Antonio who had her in bondage now. It wasn't Fattore or Langley. It was fear. Her own fear held her captive. She was as frozen in her fear as her father had been in his phobia. Afraid to live . . . afraid to love.

"What's wrong?"

She hadn't heard her dad enter the room. She stared at him blankly. "Nothing, I just . . . realized something."

That she'd become her own worst enemy. That she was the only one holding her back. She closed the Bible, setting it on the end table beside her dad's readers.

He sank into the recliner across from her. "Micah's having a blast in there with his Legos. He's a good kid, Eden. Bright and affectionate. You've done a great job with him."

"Thanks, Dad. He's come through a lot. I'm proud of him."

"You've both come through a lot."

She toyed with the frayed ends of the afghan on the couch. The soft throw made her think of Miss Trudy. She could almost hear the knitting needles clacking in the silence.

"Wanna talk about it?"

She looked into her dad's caring eyes. If anyone understood fear, it was him.

"How'd you do it, Dad? Get rid of all that fear? I thought coming up here to Loon Lake was the answer to all my problems. I thought I'd be free, finally, from . . . everything. And now . . . I just realized I'm still in bondage."

She swallowed hard and said the words. "You were right about Beau. I love him. And I left because I'm afraid. I'm afraid to love again. The last time was . . . a mistake. I'll never go back to that. Beau's nothing like Antonio, but I'm afraid to trust him. Or maybe I'm afraid to trust myself. I don't know."

"That's just how I felt after your mom was killed. I didn't protect her. How could I trust myself to protect you? And look how badly I failed."

"Oh, Dad, you did your best. I know that. And look at you now. I'm so proud of you. And a little jealous," she admitted.

"When you can't trust others, and you can't trust yourself, you can always trust God. He'll carry you through whatever comes your way."

"Is it as simple as that?"

"Simple . . . yes." His lips tilted sideways. "Easy . . . no."

"Grandpa, come look!" Micah called. "I made a ship."

"Duty calls." Dad pushed to his feet, giving her a tender smile. "You'll figure it out, baby girl."

She watched him go, distracted by her thoughts. She couldn't spend her day ruminating on her issues. She had work to do, and she may as well do it while she had a built-in babysitter.

She wasn't sure how many hours had passed when she heard the sound of a truck rumbling past on the road. She stopped tapping on her keyboard. Turning, she peeked out the curtains. Her heart gave a happy sigh at the sight of the snowplow. Thank God they'd be able to get out soon.

"Look what we found." Micah ran into the room.

Her heart sank at the sight of the object in his hands.

He held the snow globe out to her. She'd purposely left it in one of the suitcase compartments when she'd unpacked. She hadn't been able to bring herself to look at it again. To remember.

She took the globe and cradled the heavy base in her hands. "What were you doing in my suitcase?"

"It's our spaceship. We're going to Venus!"

"It's very hot there," she muttered as he ran from the room.

"Good!"

She looked at the joyful angel inside the globe. The fake snow wafted on the floor, covering the angel from the ankles down. She turned it upside down, gave the wind-up key a twist before she could stop herself. The tinkling notes of "Let it Snow" floated in the air as she turned the globe upright.

Snow drifted downward past the peaceful angel,

settling at her slippered feet. The sweet notes of the song took her right back to the Callahan house. Right back to Beau's embrace. She could almost feel his sturdy arms around her, feel the gentle brush of those perfect lips against hers. Hear him whisper in her ear.

"I love you. You're a special woman. Don't ever forget that."

Those were not the words of a man who was out to control her. They were the words of a good man. A caring man.

"I don't want to trap you or hold you back or control you. I only want to love you."

Her eyes stung, and her throat swelled with tears. She stared into the glass globe, the walls of her chest closing in. She had fallen for Beau. Fallen like those snowflakes, one tiny piece of her at a time.

She missed him. She wanted him in her life. In Micah's life. She pulled the globe into her chest and closed her eyes, listening to the tinkling notes, hearing the words of the song in her head.

". . . the fire is slowly dying and, my dear, we're still good-bye-ing, but as long as you love me so—"

The music stopped, leaving her hanging. Her hands tightened on the smooth glass as vines of fear stretched upward, curling around her, strangling, until she could hardly breathe.

No. She wouldn't give in to it. Not this time.

"I trust You," she whispered aloud.

Even if things go wrong. Even if I can't trust myself or anyone around me. Help me trust You to be there no matter what comes my way.

A note tinkled out, then two, the final notes finishing out the song. *"Let it snow, let it snow, let it snow."*

She gave a little huff of laughter. Her heart was thumping in her chest. She loved Beau. And he loved her. And she was the only one standing in the way of that. She suddenly knew exactly what she needed to do.

"Dad," she called as she sprang to her feet. "I need a favor."

CHAPTER 41

Beau entered the outbuilding and pulled the string hanging from the overhead bulb. Scant light filtered through the musty space. His breath fogged in front of him.

He looked around at the junk that had gathered over the past fifty years. Other than a few pieces of farm equipment, that's exactly what it was: junk. Boxes of old literature, rusty saws, broken tree carts that no one had gotten around to fixing. There was an old cash register circa 1970 on top of an old hot chocolate machine. He had his work cut out for him.

But he was glad for the job. It would keep him busy, and it was something he could do at night. He remembered Aunt Trudy's scowl as he'd headed back out after supper, and felt a pinch of guilt. She was probably lonely. No doubt she missed Kate too.

Kate.

His eyes swept to the spot where he'd first seen her. Over by the back wall. She'd only been a dark huddle in the shadows.

Nothing like assaulting a woman on first sight.

He frowned, looking back on the moment with fresh eyes. She must have been so scared. After what her late husband had put her through, knowing there were men trying to take her life . . . She must have thought they'd caught up with her. A fist tightened in his gut at the thought of the extra trauma he'd caused.

Way to go, Callahan.

He wondered if she and Micah were settled in their little cabin. If she was as happy as she'd hoped to be. If she missed him.

Because, my gosh, he missed her. So much. *The Callahan men love once and they love deeply.* He'd been hearing it since he was a small boy. He could only hope to God it wasn't true. He dragged a gloved hand across his face. When he pulled it away his gaze fell to the ground. He'd never noticed the bed of hay over in the corner. She must have pulled it from one of the old, moldy bales stacked against the wall and used it to keep them warm.

Daggonit, I'm not going there tonight.

He fished his earbuds from his coat pocket, plugged into his cell, and started his favorite country playlist. He jacked up the volume, then grabbed the first box. Seeing it was just a bunch of old brochures, he carried it out the back door to the burn pile. The metal stuff he'd set aside to deal with later. His breath fogged in front of his face, and the cold air nipped at his nose.

The outbuilding would be the perfect place to store the maple products he was planning to sell online—if he ever figured out how to set up the site. It was just the right size and already had built-in shelving. The door needed a better lock, though, and he still hadn't replaced the windowpane Kate had broken that night, though she'd insisted on paying for it.

His eyes swung to the broken pane as he entered the building again, his thoughts lingering there. On Kate. Everywhere he looked, reminders.

His boots crunched in the fresh snow as he carried another box out back. He dumped it in the burn pile and set his hands on his hips, tipping his head back. The clouds had parted overhead, and the stars were pin-pricks of light spread across a black canvas. Hundreds of them. Flurries fell, wetting his forehead, his cheeks. Still he stared up into the heavens, his throat tightening.

"What do you want from me?"

His words were barely audible over the mournful tune blaring from his cell. Some country singer croon-ing about heartbreak. He knew the feeling all too well.

He continued gazing up at the stars.

Maybe he *should* go after her. Maybe he hadn't tried hard enough. Maybe she was missing him as much as he missed her. Finding her would be a challenge, but that had never stopped him before. Surely she'd left a forwarding address with the post office.

But no. That's what her psycho, controlling late hus-band would have done: hunt her down. She needed to be free to make her own choice. And she had.

"For the first time in my life, I want to be completely free. I have no idea what that even feels like."

The words tore at his heart every time. He mentally cursed Antonio for all the damage he'd done. All the hurt he'd caused. Beau exhaled hard, his breath evapo-rating into the sky.

Every night. Every night he did this. He'd been so sure he was doing the right thing, giving her space. But the longer she was gone, the more he questioned himself. He was weary of the battle. He wanted a sign. A burning bush would be nice.

"What am I supposed to do?" he asked the heavens.

A flash drew his eyes, and he caught the tail end of a shooting star as it faded into the darkness. He closed his eyes and made a wish. But when he opened them again, nothing had changed. The music played on, the outbuilding waited behind him in dire need of purging, and he was still alone.

. . .

Kate spotted the sign for the Christmas tree farm and slowed her car. Her heart was like a bass drum in her chest, pounding, reverberating through her whole body. She turned into the drive and wiped her sweaty palms down her legs.

She'd gone over the words dozens of times on her trip here. What she'd say, how she'd say it. But now that the moment was near she feared they weren't enough.

She checked the clock and saw it was after seven. She should've called. It was a Friday night. What if he wasn't even here?

What if he's out with another woman?

After all, she'd been gone six weeks, and she had no hold on him. She'd left of her own free will. Maybe she was too late. Maybe his feelings had faded as quickly as her car's exhaust had evaporated behind her.

The thought made her insides twist painfully. What if she was in this all alone? What if twenty minutes from now she'd be headed back up north with dashed hopes and a broken heart?

No, she refused to believe that.

She rounded the curve and climbed the hill, her heart finding a new speed.

It had started snowing as she'd entered town, big, fluffy flakes that splashed onto her windshield. Remembering the snow globe, she'd taken the flurries as a positive sign. Now the symbol seemed as flimsy as a sheer curtain.

She crested the hill and coasted down the incline. At the bottom the fringe of her lights caught on something red off to the side. Beau's truck was parked in front of the outbuilding. A dim light shone through the window, illuminating the windowpane she'd broken. The front door was cracked open a sliver.

Surely he wasn't working this late. He never worked after supper, not even during the busy season. She slowed and pulled in beside the truck.

A moment later she got out of the car and approached the building, her boots crunching in the fresh snow. She stopped at the door to catch her breath, quaking in her boots. Her heart beat violently against her ribs, her breaths came quick and shallow, and her mouth felt as if it were stuffed with cotton. She drew a deep breath.

God, help me.

The door creaked quietly on its hinges as she pushed it open. Flurries blew in, swirling wildly around her. She scanned the dank space and found it empty. Her gaze caught on the open back door. She was about to move forward when he appeared in the doorway.

He stopped in his tracks, his eyes falling on her, then widening. His mouth slackened. He pulled earbuds from his ears, his gaze raking over her.

She wondered if he liked her as a brunette, and her hand went straight to her hair.

He was a welcome sight in his sturdy work coat and jeans. His hair was a bit longer, tousled from the wind. His jaw sported a five o'clock shadow, and his eyes looked fathomless in the dim light.

Everything she'd rehearsed flew out the window at the sight of him, standing there looking so beautifully rugged. Suddenly she wanted him to know her. All of her. She could trust him with all the pieces.

"Eden," she blurted.

He blinked as if he wasn't sure what he was seeing, hearing.

"My name . . ." Her voice wobbled, and her heart felt as if it would burst from her chest. "It's Eden."

He stared at her for a long, agonizing moment. Her chest felt like it might collapse on her. Her lungs constricted, obstructing her breath.

"Why are you here?"

She gave a nervous laugh. "I was in the neighborhood?"

His lips didn't even twitch. His eyes had lost that shell-shocked look, leaving nothing but inscrutable shadows.

She shifted. Her legs felt like jelly, and her stomach had tightened into a hard knot. She swallowed hard, licked her dry lips.

"Okay, I was—obviously that's not true." An empty

feeling expanded in the pit of her stomach. She tucked her hair behind her ears. "I had all this planned out, and now I don't remember any of it. But I had to see you. Talk to you.

"I thought leaving would give me my freedom, Beau. And in some ways it has. I can put the cans away with the labels facing backwards, and I can let clothes sit in the dryer for two days if I want. I can read novels and buy junk food and go over the speed limit. I can fill the tub all the way to the top and run to the store without worrying what my mileage will show and turn the thermostat up to seventy-five if I feel like it."

Beau's eyebrows lowered, and he cocked his head to the side. "So what's the problem?"

The tender notes in his deep voice heartened her. "The problem is . . . I'm free from everything but my own fear."

He frowned. "You don't need to be afraid anymore. They're locked up. You're safe."

"I'm not afraid of *them*." She gave a wry smile. "I'm afraid of *you*."

His eyes flashed. "I would never hurt you."

"I know that. That's not what I—" She shook her head. "I'm not saying this right."

Think, Eden. Where to start? At the beginning?

"When I first came here, it was hard to trust anyone. It was especially hard to trust men. But the more I saw you, the more I realized you were one of the good guys. You were always gentle and caring and giving. It was new to me. I guess part of me was falling for you even then. But I was safe, because you were taken. But then you broke up with her, and you kissed me . . . and nothing was the same after that."

"For me either." His voice rumbled deep and low, and his dark eyes softened.

"I didn't realize until I was in that cabin that I'd never have true freedom if I continued to let fear hold me captive."

"What are you afraid of?"

"I held back with you because I couldn't trust a man again. I was afraid of ending up right back where I'd been. But somehow, even knowing that, I couldn't stop it from happening. Even though I tried so hard. Even though I left . . . it happened anyway."

He took a step, then another. He didn't stop until he was a touch away.

Her heart raced, and her breaths grew shallow. So close. She wanted to grab him and kiss those perfect lips.

"What happened, honey?"

She melted at the endearment, at the look in his eyes. "I fell in love with you." Her words left her mouth on a rush of air.

Something flared in his eyes. He pulled off his gloves, his eyes never leaving her, and cradled her face. His hands were warm and rough against her cold cheeks.

"Eden . . . ," he whispered. "I love you too."

Her heart rolled over in her chest at the sound of her name on his lips.

He leaned down and kissed her. This was no soft, barely there brush. He took her mouth as if he was desperate for it. As if he'd thought he'd never taste her again. He pulled her against him, into his warmth.

She melted into his chest. Her fingers found the soft strands of his hair at his nape and lingered there. Her lips parted on a breath, and he took full advantage. She gave back, move for move.

She couldn't believe she was here, back in his arms. She'd missed him so much. Missed this. The way he made her feel. Wanted. Loved. Cherished.

He pulled back a moment later, and she whimpered in protest. But he didn't go far. He rested his forehead on hers, his eyes closed. Their breaths came raggedly, the space between them heating up fast.

She was home. His arms were home. She felt it all the way down to the warm marrow of her bones. She cupped his scruffy jaw, delighting in the rough scrape against her palm. She pulled in a breath of him, savoring it.

"If I'm dreaming, don't wake me." His voice was as thick as honey.

"You're not dreaming." She traced the shape of those lips. They were damp and plush and too far away. "You have really nice lips. I missed them."

One side of them kicked up, his eyes opening. "Is that all you missed?"

She couldn't count on both hands everything she'd missed about Beau. About the Callahans, about Summer Harbor. It was a special community. She felt at home here, and it would be a great place to raise Micah. She wanted that for him.

"I'm coming back to Summer Harbor."

Beau pulled her closer on a sigh. "I am dreaming."

He probably imagined her falling right back into the Callahan household as though nothing had changed. But she wasn't ready for that. She needed time to stand on her own two feet without the threat of danger hanging over her head. She needed to get to know herself, remember who she was.

She pulled back and looked him in the eye. "Beau . . . I need to get my own place. I've started my website business back up, and I want to make it viable. I need to work on this fear issue I'm having. It's not going away overnight. This is still . . . scary for me."

He cupped her face, his eyes piercing hers. "Take all the time you need, honey. I'm not going anywhere."

A smile tilted the corners of her lips just before he brushed it away with his own. She couldn't think anymore with his mouth on hers. With the tingly heat moving up her limbs and settling down deep inside. She was suddenly seeing a whole new side to all this freedom, and she liked it. She liked it a lot.

EPILOGUE

"Hurry up." Beau gave her rear end a pat as she got in the passenger side of his truck. "We're going to be late."

"Late for what? Nothing's even open."

With a furtive smile, he closed the door and walked around the truck.

She buckled her seat belt, rubbed her sleepy eyes, and slumped against the seat. Micah had spent the night with her dad, who'd moved to Summer Harbor last month. He'd found a good job at the elementary school, doing custodial work.

When Beau opened his door the dome light came on, bright against the predawn sky. He turned the engine over and spared her a smile as he set his arm across the seat to back from her drive.

"Are you going to tell me why you're dragging me out of bed at the crack of dawn?"

He winked. "Patience, my love."

They rode through the darkened town, quiet and empty on the summer morning. There was a little life at the harbor as lobstermen got an early start on their days.

Just past the harbor, across from the rocky beach, he slowed and parallel parked across from the boardwalk. Zip, zip, and he was tucked into the space between a car and a delivery truck.

"Show-off," she muttered.

"You can't be good at everything."

He opened her door, grabbed a quilt from the back of the truck, and pulled her toward the beach. When he found a spot covered with thick sand, he stopped and spread out the blanket.

"It's a little early for sunbathing," she said.

"I don't remember you being so grumpy in the morning," he teased.

"I didn't have time for coffee."

He lowered himself to the blanket and pulled her down in front of him. She settled against his chest, his warmth driving away the chill in the air.

"Madam . . ." He handed her a thermos she hadn't noticed before.

"Oh, bless you." She poured the hot brew into the lid, took a sip, and shared with him. Much better.

The smell of the brew mingled with the tangy scent of sea air. The cool breeze fanned her skin, pushing her hair from her face, and the water lapped the pebbled shore. The clouds on the horizon were beginning to brighten, the black fading to dark hues of blue.

A couple months ago she'd mentioned that she'd never watched a sunrise. He seemed intent on being there for all her firsts. The first time she rented a house. The first time she opened her own bank account. The first time she swam in the ocean. She embraced her freedom, and Beau was there, supporting her however he could.

The past four months had been the best of her life. She'd worked hard to grow her business, and she now had enough to sustain her without dipping into her savings too much. Things were going well for the farm too. She'd designed a website—snowy blue with white and silver. It had turned out great, and Beau's online business was up and running.

Riley had returned home for his ten-day leave after boot camp in March. The time had gone by too fast, and before they knew it he was on his way to Camp Geiger in North Carolina for School of Infantry. He finished that in late May and was now stationed in Afghanistan. They'd heard from him twice so far. The family worried, but he seemed to be thriving as a marine.

Micah was also flourishing. He'd made friends in their neighborhood and was due to start kindergarten in the fall at the school where her dad worked. Her son had started seeing a counselor, and Eden was beginning to see more of the old, carefree Micah once again.

She was experiencing a little of that herself. Beau had been a big part of it. He listened to her when she needed to talk, played with her when she needed to laugh. He called her just to say he missed her and did crazy things like waking her during the predawn hours to watch the sunrise together.

She still struggled with some issues. When he was moody she sometimes felt anxious, and when he got into his caretaker mode, it made her feel smothered. But they talked it out and worked to resolve the issues.

Beau was good at solving problems. He had patience. It was her new favorite trait.

He tightened his arms around her, and she snuggled in closer. His breath warmed her temple, sending a shiver down her arms.

He rubbed the gooseflesh away. "Cold?"

"Nope." She replaced the empty thermos lid and curled her arms around his, perfectly content in his embrace.

Shades of periwinkle appeared in the sky now, swathed in purple. Pink and yellow began washing over the sky. It seemed to grow brighter by the second, the pink glowing so brilliantly it almost hurt her eyes. The colors were reflected in the harbor, turning the water a radiant shade of purple. The light silhouetted the boats moored there, their masts pointing like skinny fingers toward the sky.

Just when she thought the view couldn't be any more impressive, a sliver of pink slipped over the horizon.

"Beautiful," she whispered, not wanting to break the spell.

He pressed a kiss to her temple. "New beginnings usually are."

They watched in silence as the sliver turned into a semicircle, and the semicircle became a glowing pink globe, balanced on the horizon. She was in awe of the beauty. Of the very idea that this happened every morning behind the scenes while she slept.

Beau shifted, his hand leaving her stomach, and she missed it. But it returned a moment later, holding something small and square.

He opened the box, and her eyes widened. She sucked in a breath.

A solitaire diamond winked back, reflecting the pink rays of dawn. She turned and met his eyes, those beautiful brown eyes, focused solely on her.

"I love you, Eden Martelli," he said in that low, smoky voice. "I love your beautiful smile and the way your laugh brightens the whole room. I love your warm heart and your quiet strength. I love how tender you are with Micah."

She placed her palm over her aching heart, catching her breath as he continued.

"I want nothing more than to spend the rest of my life with you. I want to cherish you every day. I want to laugh together and celebrate every new beginning together. I want to be Micah's daddy—and maybe give him a brother or sister or two . . ." His lips kicked up at the corners.

They went flat again as a somber look washed over his eyes. "You're the love of my life, Eden. Will you marry me?"

"Oh, Beau . . ." He took her breath away. He made her believe in new beginnings and happily-ever-afters.

"I don't want to rush you. We can be engaged for as long as you want, but you're it for me. You're the one. There'll never be another."

"Yes," she breathed. "I want all of that, and I want it with you."

The smile that curled his mouth was priceless. Love shone in his eyes as he lowered his lips to hers, brushing them ever so tenderly. His kiss was a soft exploration, a confident proclamation, a gentle promise. She absorbed it all, welcomed it, gave it right back.

When his arms tightened around hers she forgot all about the ring. All about the sunrise and the birds awakening nearby. She forgot about everything but the man holding her—the one who'd shown her what love could be. What love was supposed to be.

Another beautiful day had begun. It was the beginning of many more, and she could hardly wait to see what each one held.

DISCUSSION QUESTIONS

1. Who was your favorite character? Why? Who did you most relate to?
2. What was your favorite scene in the book? Why?
3. Riley's way of dealing with Beau and Paige's relationship was to join the military. Have you ever run from a problem? How did that work out?
4. After Beau's mom died, the Callahans let Christmas traditions fall by the wayside. Have you ever faced painful reminders of the past? How did you deal with them?
5. It took Eden awhile to trust again after her experience with Antonio. Discuss how trust is built and lost.
6. Eden had been married to a man who controlled her every move. Discuss his methods of control and why you think Eden may have been susceptible to them.
7. Antonio used scripture to justify his abuse. Does this happen in the church today? What would you do if you were in Eden's marriage?
8. Discuss the role of the husband according to scripture.

9. If you discovered a friend was suffering under a controlling husband, what advice would you give? How would you help her?

10. Eden thought she'd be free at Loon Lake but discovered fear was holding her captive. Discuss a time when fear held you captive. How did you overcome it?

ACKNOWLEDGMENTS

Writing a book is a team effort, and I'm so grateful for the fabulous team at HarperCollins Christian Fiction, led by publisher Daisy Hutton: Ansley Boatman, Katie Bond, Amanda Bostic, Karli Jackson, Kristen Golden, Elizabeth Hudson, Jodi Hughes, Ami McConnell, Becky Monds, Becky Philpott, Kerri Potts, and Kristen Ingebretson.

Thanks especially to my editor, Ami McConnell: friend, advocate, and editor extraordinaire. I'm constantly astounded by your gift of insight. Thanks also to editor LB Norton, who has saved me from countless errors and makes me look so much better than I am.

Author Colleen Coble is my first reader. Thank you, friend! Writing wouldn't be nearly as much fun without you!

I'm grateful to my agent, Karen Solem, who's able to somehow make sense of the legal garble of contracts and, even more amazing, help me understand it.

Thank you to Mainer Susan Faloon, who kindly agreed to read this manuscript to make sure I'd gotten the setting details right. Any errors that made it into print are mine alone.

Kevin, my husband of twenty-six years, has been a wonderful support. Thank you, honey! To my sons,

Justin, Chad, and Trevor: you make life an adventure! It's so fun watching you step so boldly into adulthood. Love you all!

Lastly, thank you, friend, for letting me share this story with you. I wouldn't be doing this without you! I enjoy connecting with friends on my Facebook page, www.facebook.com/authordenisehunter. Please pop over and say hello. Visit my website at the link www.DeniseHunterBooks.com or just drop me a note at Denise@DeniseHunterBooks.com. I'd love to hear from you!

ABOUT THE AUTHOR

Bestselling novelist Denise Hunter has received the Holt Medallion Award, Reader's Choice Award, Foreword Book of the Year Award, and is a RITA finalist. She lives in Indiana with her husband and their three sons.

. . .

Visit her website at www.denisehunterbooks.com
Twitter: @deniseahunter
Facebook: authordenisehunter